# CARD GAME

A NOVEL BY DAVID BULITT

*Card Game*

Published by Wheatmark®
1760 East River Road, Suite 145
Tucson, Arizona 85718 USA
www.wheatmark.com

ISBN: 978-1-62787-255-3 (paperback)
ISBN: 978-1-62787-256-0 (ebook)
LCCN: 2015931485

rev012015

# ACKNOWLEDGMENTS

It's been a long time coming. From sometime in college, I wanted to write a novel. Between law school and mortgages and kids and jobs, it took me almost thirty years to get here. There are many people who helped along the way, and I am unspeakably grateful and proud to be able to thank a few of them now.

Thanks to New Orleans writer Nancy Lehman, a friend of a friend, who offered to read the first draft, and a few weeks later, wrote me in an email: "my verdict is—it's great." That's one I will never delete.

Thanks to Sarah Neilson, who gave me a Seattle girl's perspective and edited an early version of the book.

Thanks to fellow gym rat, John Robbins, who shared some great stories for me to poach between rambunctious reviews of *Game of Thrones* and *Boardwalk Empire* episodes.

Thanks to Garry "Doc" Ruben, who, knowing my childlike

weakness when it comes to anything of a medical nature, helped me with a vital piece of the story in such a way that I was able to stay prone.

Thanks to my earliest reviewers, "Downtown" Johnny Baldwin, Jim Rosenberg, and Chip Mitchell, for being honest.

Thanks to my parents, who have always been proud of me. That's still a good thing, even at fifty-four.

Thanks to my grandfather, Ben Weller, who I still miss every day. This is for you, King Benny.

To my good friend Cheryl Baldwin of Sweet Boo Design, thanks for reading my mind and creating the *Card Game* jacket cover design.

To the amazingly brilliant and thoughtful Lyric Winik, who took me on as a pet project and read the story again and again, pushing me endlessly in purple to "open it up." Thanks for paying it forward.

Thanks to my daughters Amanda, Zoe, and Josie for believing in me and (almost) never rolling their eyes when I talked about my writing a novel.

Thanks to my daughter Natalie, who is always in my thoughts, and I hope that somehow this book will help her find herself.

Thanks to Bruce Springsteen and Southside Johnny Lyon, whose music has pumped me up during good times and propped me up through the bad.

Thanks to my real-life card-game buddies, who have supplied me with endless laughs and a lifetime of friendship—you know who you are.

Thanks to my wife, Julie, both my biggest fan and sharpest critic, who is brimming with boundless creativity, patience, and support.

And, finally, to all of you folks who listened politely but looked at me like I was nuts, maybe you're right. But here you go. I did it.

# ACKNOWLEDGMENTS

It's been a long time coming. From sometime in college, I wanted to write a novel. Between law school and mortgages and kids and jobs, it took me almost thirty years to get here. There are many people who helped along the way, and I am unspeakably grateful and proud to be able to thank a few of them now.

Thanks to New Orleans writer Nancy Lehman, a friend of a friend, who offered to read the first draft, and a few weeks later, wrote me in an email: "my verdict is—it's great." That's one I will never delete.

Thanks to Sarah Neilson, who gave me a Seattle girl's perspective and edited an early version of the book.

Thanks to fellow gym rat, John Robbins, who shared some great stories for me to poach between rambunctious reviews of *Game of Thrones* and *Boardwalk Empire* episodes.

Thanks to Garry "Doc" Ruben, who, knowing my childlike

weakness when it comes to anything of a medical nature, helped me with a vital piece of the story in such a way that I was able to stay prone.

Thanks to my earliest reviewers, "Downtown" Johnny Baldwin, Jim Rosenberg, and Chip Mitchell, for being honest.

Thanks to my parents, who have always been proud of me. That's still a good thing, even at fifty-four.

Thanks to my grandfather, Ben Weller, who I still miss every day. This is for you, King Benny.

To my good friend Cheryl Baldwin of Sweet Boo Design, thanks for reading my mind and creating the *Card Game* jacket cover design.

To the amazingly brilliant and thoughtful Lyric Winik, who took me on as a pet project and read the story again and again, pushing me endlessly in purple to "open it up." Thanks for paying it forward.

Thanks to my daughters Amanda, Zoe, and Josie for believing in me and (almost) never rolling their eyes when I talked about my writing a novel.

Thanks to my daughter Natalie, who is always in my thoughts, and I hope that somehow this book will help her find herself.

Thanks to Bruce Springsteen and Southside Johnny Lyon, whose music has pumped me up during good times and propped me up through the bad.

Thanks to my real-life card-game buddies, who have supplied me with endless laughs and a lifetime of friendship—you know who you are.

Thanks to my wife, Julie, both my biggest fan and sharpest critic, who is brimming with boundless creativity, patience, and support.

And, finally, to all of you folks who listened politely but looked at me like I was nuts, maybe you're right. But here you go. I did it.

# 2013

It's the first game since Tom dropped out. That's what we're calling it. He dropped out. Dropped dead really, but none of us wants to see it that way.

It was already my turn to host. So here we are, six thoroughly middle-aged men, our bellies in varying degrees of softness, our hair—or what is left of it—slowly sinking into gray, filling up my kitchen table at a little after eight on a Monday night. Except for Tom. It was my idea to keep his chair out, a memorial to the guy who lost more money in this game than the rest of us combined. Don't get me wrong. None of us is the greatest card player in the world. Tom was just impressively bad, that's all.

Otherwise, it looks like any other poker night. MKat, a.k.a. Mike Katzman, who remains a perennial charmer, got here first.

1

Last to arrive, Don, the classic nice guy, and Baldwin, both best friends since third grade. Then there is Gregg, known as Wocky, MKat's permanent foil, and Mark, the most successful of our crew. Financially, anyway. "Got rid of the toy car. I've already made my contribution to the environment," Mark announced at a game a few months ago after trading in his Prius for a ninety-five-thousand-dollar, fully loaded BMW. None of us will wait for Vinnie, who texted me that he is on his way. He's often a no show and when he does make it, rarely arrives until after the first hand is played.

But however much things seem the same, I'm antsy, hopping from my seat to the kitchen counter, darting outside to check the grill. Because last time, without Vinnie, we were seven. And numbers are always the first way things change. We couple up, we break apart. It isn't just poker that's a numbers game.

The guys are nervous too. You can feel it in the room. It sits there like the heavy weight before a summer thunderstorm. Even as we all try to act like nothing has happened, we are checking the backs of our hands for the first splatters of rain.

Two things I can count on—we still have our same high school nicknames and our long-ago assigned seats. In that there is no deviation. After filling a plate, Don, whose real name is Eric, has squeezed his way between MKat and Wocky. MKat smiles for a second and pats Don's ever-expanding belly, but his eyes never leave Wocky's face as he gets to his fifth reason why Randy Edsall, the University of Maryland football coach, needs to be fired. Wocky answers back, and my ears close. Regardless of the topic, MKat and Wocky have had a running "friendly fire" kind of conflict for years. In his permanent spot between them, Don fills the role of mediator, our own card-game version of Switzerland.

Tired of MKat's dissection of Maryland football, Wocky makes a rustling noise in his throwback M. C. Hammer-'80s-style parachute pants, turns, and asks me, "Where's the beer, Bro? Don snagged the last one." Except for most of the lawyers and a few self-impressed judges I work with day in and day out, most everyone calls me by my initials, "JB." With this group, however, I am forever "Bro." In tenth grade, I started calling everyone "bro," so it became their nickname for me. Pretty much every group of guys in this hemisphere has stolen it since then.

"Beer vault in the garage," I tell him. I keep a knee-high, dorm-room-size fridge in the garage, always stocked with ice-cold Rolling Rock, the same beer my grandfather liked to drink until the company sold out to the giant Anheuser-Busch. After that, he refused to twist even one more top off a little pony bottle of the stuff, likening the sale of its Latrobe, Pennsylvania, brewery to a communist invasion. "I'd rather see a Chinese flag flying outside the White House," I heard him say more than a few times. But the beer is still cold and wet and that is good enough for me.

"Anything but Rock in there?" Wocky asks.

"What do you think?"

Wocky walks out to the garage, grabs a beer from the vault, and sits back down. "You need to get into some other beers, man. IPAs, maybe some Guinness. At least a Corona with a lime."

"Anyone who puts a lime in his beer doesn't get dinner. Not in this house." I feign a punch-drunk boxer's stance, and Wocky nods, snaps the top off, and takes a long, admiring swig. "For a mass-market product, it is pretty fucking good, I have to admit," he says while standing a shade too close to MKat.

"You want to sit down there, Wock?" MKat asks, his head at Wocky's waist. "Any closer and I would think you're hoping I'll give you a quick blowee."

Realizing the uncomfortable proximity between his midsection and MKat's head, Wocky answers, "Uh, no thanks. I didn't bring enough quarters," backs away, and sits down. Baldwin snickers, and I blow out my breath, maybe for the first time.

MKat is now chattering away about a girl from high school he ran into at the grocery store a few days ago. Back in third grade when a few of these guys became friends and long before I glommed onto the group, someone decided that "Mike Katzman" just didn't fit. Probably quick-witted from the day he was born, he was nicknamed "MKat," like the med-school entrance exam. I've only really known the guy as MKat; I think it was two or three years after we started hanging out that it hit me that I still didn't know his real name. Recently divorced, MKat walks and talks with the same cocky fearlessness he had thirty years ago. Unlike Wocky, he still has most of his hair and retains an uncanny ability to charm the pants off a girl when he sets his mind to it. Of course, the girls are now closer to fifty than to twenty, but the legend persists and that is really all that matters.

Mark, the "least tall one" of the group, has taken his seat on the other side of the table, sipping some higher-shelf bourbon I brought back from Kentucky a few months ago. His high school "Jew 'fro" having long since receded, Mark now keeps his hair "high and tight." I guess he wears it that way partly in an effort to camouflage the steady spread of gray. In high school, you couldn't have trusted the guy with your remote control, but a lot has changed since then. Having made gobs of money taking his company public a few years back, he doesn't have too much to worry about. At this particular moment, Mark is zoned into his own world, trying without much success to queue up the ferret scene from *The Big Lebowski* on his iPhone. No can do. "Fucking piece of shit," he grumbles, and tosses the thing across the room like a kid's doll. Maybe you still can't trust him with your remote.

MKat flashes a big smile after Mark's iPhone whooshes over his left shoulder, next to Don's ear, before it finds the floor and shatters.

"Jesus, Mark. That thing's expensive," Don says, looking behind him at the broken phone.

"Like it matters to that guy," Baldwin pops in.

"Still, he shouldn't throw a phone in Bro's kitchen," Don says, sincere as always.

As the guy who volunteers to shuffle the decks between most hands and is always trying his best to keep the game moving despite the array of conversations whirling around, Baldwin sits at the far head of the table across from me. It's about the only time when we all are together that he isn't right beside Don. No matter how many times I see those two, I still think of the old comedy team Laurel and Hardy. Baldwin, "Laurel," is pasty and thin, with a pencil neck supporting his fully shaved head. Like "Hardy," Don is wide and square, with a furry, black moustache. They've been best friends since they were little and, as hard as it is for me to believe, still talk to each other on the phone every day. About what, I am not sure. The idea of two fifty-plus-year-old men having daily phone conversations with each other seems a bit odd to me, but, at the same time, I find myself oddly jealous of their ability to talk with such frequency. As someone who has a kind of do-not-pry-in-other-people's-lives mantra, even in my oldest friends', it's probably me who is odd, not the two of them.

Baldwin absent-mindedly strokes the back of his smooth head and breaks open the two new decks of cards I picked up earlier today at the local Rite Aid. "I love new decks. Like fucking a virgin," he says as he peels off the cellophane and tosses the jokers aside.

There is the usual whoosh of air as the cards crackle, and we all turn our attention to the game. Tom would have been right in the middle, between Mark and me. For more than half my lifetime, these guys around my kitchen table have been my closest friends. We have been young and single, then married, then dads; we've failed, succeeded, divorced. Parents have died, children have disappointed or done well and left home. We know who has been in a financial hole, who is set, who has screwed around on his wife and who has wanted to, and yet none of that ever really matters when we lay our cards down.

What is it that has kept us here on so many Mondays? Kept us giggling like ten-year-old girls, telling and retelling stories about our now, in some cases, ancient sexual escapades, criticizing each other without any conscience, and bickering over nonsensical bullshit? Kept us coming back for more than thirty years to shuffle, deal, draw, and call?

The card game.

# ONE

Tom was the first to go. Actually, it was one of the few bets he ever won. No luck in draw, none in hold 'em, and even less in showdown. The guy was a monthly banker to the rest of us, assuming you consider his donating about fifteen bucks a month to seven other guys a banker.

The only one in the game not born a Jew, Tom was the son of two devout Catholics—Mass on Sundays, confession every week, Lent every year, all that stuff. They were both pretty active at St. Paul's, a hulking, rectangular, white-block-and-stained-glass structure off New Hampshire Avenue in Silver Spring, Maryland, and within walking distance of Tom's childhood home. Tom spent lots of time in that church, helping his mother with bake sales, calling kids' numbers for Bingo games on Sunday afternoons, and assisting with the innumerable fundraisers—fish fries and spaghetti nights.

While his mother, Annie, handled the games and nourishment, Tom's dad, John Porter, built whatever the church needed. He was a natural at carpentry and probably needed no more than an hour to build you a boat out of a couple of two-by-fours. John was a federal government lifer; Uncle Sam was his one and only employer once he got out of high school back in the mid-'50s. The family lived in a small house, and John took the bus downtown to work while Annie drove the same 1975 Buick Skylark. The family didn't seem to have much money, but Tom's dad must have squirreled away every extra dime. He left a tidy sum to his boys after he died.

Building and fixing things around the church made up a good portion of John's non-working hours. His most prized creation was the thirty-foot cross that stood on the front lawn of the church, hovering over the cars as they sped by, like some sort of Catholic bird of prey. Tom was proud of his dad, but like the rest of us, that giant cross scared the shit out of him.

For all his work, Hail Marys, and Catholic devotion, Tom's father died of a heart attack when we first started the card game back in 1978. His mom never fully recovered from the loss. Unfortunately, instead of finding comfort in her faith, she looked for solace in a fellow by the name of Jim Beam. About a year and a couple hundred empty bottles later, Annie Porter passed out one night and never woke up. Like her husband, her heart had just stopped while she slept. Tom spent the rest of his high school years living with his aunt, uncle, and their eight kids. Except for a little minor debasement of the place years later, Tom refused to go back to that church.

With that kind of family history, Tom was sure he would be the first of our group to cash it in.

Tall, lanky, with straw-blond hair and a surfer's face, Tom

stood out in a group of dark-haired, brown-eyed Jewish guys. We all loved sports, but, except for Tom, none of us was good enough to make any of the school teams. Tom could run like no guy I had ever seen and lettered in both cross-country and track at Sherbrook High School. He was born with only one testicle, and we all joked that Tom was able to run faster than most anybody else because he had a smaller "package" to carry around.

After leaving Sherbrook, Tom went to the University of Maryland with the rest of us. But while most of us made it out in four years, it took him about six, including summer school, but he finally got through and got his degree, a bachelor's in business administration. We all swore that Tom was a true inventor, the Ben Franklin of "the gap year." While Tom was at Maryland, the cross-country coach saw him running around campus and asked him to come try out for the team as a walk-on. Tom wasn't interested. He could run for hours; there was no doubt that he could have made it. But after three years of high school locker rooms, Tom couldn't bear the thought of another bunch of guys just waiting to jump out and call him "One Nut" at any given time.

Ironically, the guy who lived to run also loved to eat, and after finally graduating college in 1985, he drifted from one grocery store job to the next. He stacked fruit, cut deli, and carried older folks' groceries to their cars. As long as he was surrounded by food, he was happy.

A couple of years later, when he turned twenty-seven, two things happened to change Tom's life. He married Lianne, his longtime Jewish girlfriend from high school, and he got the trust fund money his parents had left him. On the surface, Lianne seemed pleasant enough, but since our first encounters in high school, there was something about her I never really liked. She was one of those know-it-all types who have an opinion about everything. As the boys and I liked to joke, she wasn't very pretty but at least she had a lousy personality.

One night back in high school sometime in 1977 or '78, depending on whose version you believe, I was out with Tom, Lianne, MKat, and his girl of the week. My date for the night was a particularly psychotic little thing, but, man, was she cute. She went to another school, and, to this day, we argue over what her name was. After some requisite groping at the movies, we stopped at the local Bob's Big Boy for a few Big Boy Combos, hot fudge cakes, and what MKat and I were sure was going to be some under the table pawing of our dates. I wasn't all that hungry, for food anyway, so I ordered a coffee. Lianne looked at me like I was shooting heroin.

"What kind of kid orders coffee?" she shrieked. "Are you forty or something?"

Sorely tempted to tell her to shut the fuck up, I thought the better of it, looked over at my little version of Squeaky Fromme, and tried to ignore Lianne's stares and persistent blathering. She just wouldn't let go. "Seriously, Bro, you're really getting coffee?" she kept saying.

MKat, smiling as usual and knowing how much I wanted to put Lianne's head in a bowling bag right then, turned his head to the side and mimicked her: "Yeah, Bro, are you really getting coffee?" I tried to ignore him, although MKat had a way of making you laugh at just about any time, in any situation. Even in a moment like this, when I felt a little like Ted Bundy, Lianne refused to stop. (Although I never mentioned it again, I've always wondered what went through her mind years later when Starbucks burst on the scene, opening thousands of locations and selling billions of cups of coffee worldwide to a whole lot of kids under forty.)

Tom, thankfully, did what any good friend would do; he leaned in and kissed her, pouring his tongue so far down Lianne's windpipe that I thought she was going to pass out. In the middle of his mining her throat, Lianne pushed him away. Catching her breath, she muttered, "You're gross," and excused herself to the ladies room. Little Squeaky took her hand from my lap and followed Lianne.

We all moved on from our high school girls. Except for Tom. He stayed stuck to Lianne. They had been together longer than a lot of people stay married when Tom decided to marry her. Doing so was no simple feat; her parents had some pretty firm ideas, and those did not include Lianne marrying a Catholic kid. Or maybe, after everything, it was some kind of Jewish penance to which Tom brought his own Catholic guilt. Whatever the reason, Tom shelved his Hail Marys and decided to convert. He took all the Judaism classes, learned how to cook Jewish foods, and even started speaking both Hebrew and Yiddish. It's a little like the people who have to study for the American citizenship test; Tom knew more about the Jewish faith than the rest of us combined.

True to his word, his kids went to Hebrew school and shared a B'not Mitzvah, the family celebrated Hanukkah and Passover, and when his daughters were younger, they all dressed up and went to synagogue on the High Holidays and a few Friday nights during the year. For a kid who grew up Catholic, he was a pretty good Jew.

# TWO

I was the first of the group to get married. Laurie and I met at a fraternity party in my senior year at Maryland, stayed together while I was in law school, and got married in 1986.

One night in early 1988 when Laurie and I were living in our first place, a small condo in Silver Spring where you could almost spit from one outside wall to the other, Tom called and told me he needed a ride to "this guy's house." For a guy who spoke regularly in long sentences without periods or commas, he was brief, curt even.

"I need you to come pick me up. Won't take long," Tom said. "Like in fifteen. Get on over, okay, Bro?" he added, without taking a breath.

I felt like I was walking into Springsteen's "Meeting across the River"—some strange encounter "on the other side."

More than a little concerned, I thought it was fair to ask Tom where he needed to go and why he needed to get there.

"Look, Bro," he said, "just come get me. I need the favor. Not sure if I'll be able to drive home after."

I hung up the phone, nodded my head, and let out a deep and lengthy sigh. Laurie recognized my telltale signal of exasperation.

"Which dummy was it, and what does he want?" Laurie asked.

"Tom. Shit if I know. Has some 'issue.' Wants me to pick him up and take him somewhere. It seemed like a big deal." I clicked off the TV and told her that I would be back later.

"The guy always has some 'issue.' Just don't be too late, *Bro*." Laurie laughed, grabbed her "big-ass glass" of white wine, and went across the apartment to the serenity of her bathtub. I waited a few seconds, just long enough to catch a quick peek of her pulling her tank top over her head.

Laurie caught me gawking and turned her lip up in a sexy-but-sorry-you-can't-stay kind of smirk. "Better go, *Bro*. Your boyfriend is waiting," she said as she dropped her bra onto the floor and closed the bathroom door.

When I got to his place a few minutes later, Tom was already waiting outside, holding a small book in his hand. He hopped into the car and told me the address. The book, it turned out, was a Hebrew prayer book.

"Okay, what the fuck are you doing with that, and what is the problem?" I demanded.

"What's it look like, Jew boy? I'm going to a service. Got to get circumcised actually. It's the only way I can be a Jew, and then Lianne and I can get married. I'll be able to break that glass like you did. Now, Jesus, drive already. I have to be there at eight sharp." I held my tongue, ignoring the obvious response to "sharp."

"Do I come in or what?" I asked.

"No fucking way. You just wait in the car. Won't take too long," Tom said.

"In that case, I need to stop for something to drink while I wait," I said.

No way I could do this without getting the rest of the boys involved. I parked and went into the 7-Eleven, started pouring my Mountain Dew Big Gulp, and did what any good friend would do. I found a pay phone, called MKat, and told him to get hold of the rest of the guys. As soon as I told him that Tom was going to get his "prick pricked," MKat told me to "get the fuck out of here" and then to "give me the fucking address." I told him where to go, but the line went dead before I finished, "I'll be there in . . ."

It was not yet dusk when we pulled into Kemp Mill, a neighborhood that was home to hundreds of Orthodox Jewish families. Kemp Mill is a sort of "Israel West," just without the desert or the Wailing Wall. It contains dozens of synagogues, Jewish schools, and even a kosher pizza place, the Ben-Yehuda Café, named for one of the big shopping streets in Jerusalem. Sidewalks extend on both sides of the neighborhood streets, connecting an endless stretch of monotone, red-brick-and-black-shuttered ramblers with their overhanging carports. A handful of little Orthodox Jewish boys in their black hats, swinging peyas, and yarmulkes were running around and playing while a few girls in long, modest skirts and buttoned-up blouses sat on a front porch nearby.

Tom got out of the car, thanked me, and said that he would be right back. He walked across the overgrown, weedy lawn and rang the bell. A short, bearded fellow answered the door, and in Tom went. As soon as the door closed, up drove MKat in his grandmother Bertha's old Cadillac. Like a collection of circus clowns,

Baldwin hopped out of the passenger side. Wocky came out one of the back doors, Budweiser in hand.

"Is he serious?" MKat said. "He's going to let some guy snip his dick?"

"Seems to be the plan, yes," I told him. By that point, I had accepted Tom's decision.

In classic form, MKat was already peeling around the back of the house. "Follow me," he said. "This I got to see."

Wocky laughed, grabbed a couple more beers from under the front seat of MKat's car, and we all beat it around to the back of the house.

The four of us crept over a busted-up and overgrown stone patio that bordered on a sliding glass door with no curtains. Inside, we could see the little bearded dude with a yarmulke and prayer shawl, called a tallit, over his shoulders. He was swaying back and forth. Tom was facing him, studying his prayer book, and sweating profusely.

After a few minutes, Tom sat on the couch, then the bearded guy made a motion with his hand. Tom lay back. The bearded guy took out something from a bag. A knife, a needle, did it matter? It was something sharp and shiny. Never much for blood and medical shit, I thought I was going to pass out. Before I did, though, I heard a pop and a hissing sound and an "oh fuck" to my right. Wocky's beer had exploded, blasting creamy, hop-laden foam all over the door like a goddamn volcano. MKat cackled like only he can. Without as much as a look back to see what had happened on the other side of the glass doors, we all scuttled around front. I got back in my car. MKat got behind the wheel and, in what was not exactly an "inside voice," hollered, "Jesus, that dumb motherfucker." He hit the "play" button on the cassette tape player and squealed some

15

wheels. The Caddy was a block away before I could hear the first few bars of Springsteen's "Born to Run."

Soon after, Tom came out, limping slightly around a very large bulge from the ice pack in his pants. Trying to act nonchalant, I opened the door. "So, how's it feel to get a blow job from a guy with a beard?"

"Fuck you, Bro. I knew you would call those guys. Just get me home."

# THREE

It wasn't that Tom was fascinated by death so much as he had
a need to be connected to it somehow. He didn't have a serial
killer bent by any means, but there was a definite sort of obsession
with following the illnesses and deaths of people that he knew or
even had just heard about, no matter how tangential or remote.
The behavior was definitely curious and even mildly unsettling,
but I think that for Tom, there was comfort in being part of something that he viscerally understood: loss.

Looking back, it's clear that Tom's need to be affiliated with the
deceased and those who mourned them started soon after his mom
died, but it wasn't until we were both older and married with kids
that I really caught on. Whenever Tom started a conversation with
*"Did you hear about ..."* I just knew that the question was going to
end with the name of a dead guy. If I got an email from Tom with

someone's name in the subject line, I didn't have to read the note itself to know what it said. Mr. or Ms. "subject" had perished.

"Hey, Bro, did you hear about Tammy Bienstock?" he called and asked me one night.

"Who's Tammy Bienstock?" I asked.

"Don't you remember? She's Bob Bienstock's sister," he said.

"Okay. Who's Bob Bienstock?" I asked, sticking my tongue out between my lips and blowing air out like babies do when they don't want to eat their oatmeal.

"Jesus, Bro. Don't you remember them? Bob graduated a few years ahead of us. Tammy was his little sister," Tom said, sounding mildly taken back that I had no fucking idea who he was talking about.

"Sorry," I replied, just to make him feel better. I might have remembered the last name, but since I had not seen or heard of Bob Bienstock since probably 1979, I just didn't feel all that attached to his family. I had absolutely no memory whatsoever of the dead sister.

"Well, she died. Leukemia. So sad," Tom said.

"Yeah, sad. Terrible," I said, yawning.

"I'm going to send over a platter to her family. Her parents are still living. Want to go in with me? I'll send a nice card so they'll know it's from both of us. It's the right thing to do," he said.

"Sure, Tom. Put me down," I said, knowing that he would but also that he would never ask me for any money. And sometimes later, when I pounded out another mile on the treadmill, I would think silently, who was I to tell him what "the right thing" was?

# FOUR

At Lianne's urging, Tom used a good chunk of the money his parents had saved for him to open his own grocery store, a little spot called Fresh Eats. Tom specialized in locally grown, healthy, organic-type stuff. Anyone with an aversion to gluten or a food allergy, no matter how remote, could find the right foods at Fresh Eats. The aisles were stuffed with breads of every grain, mountains of kale, quinoa, organic starches, and corn meals. There was even an entire section filled with small, craft, organic beers.

Tom opened the first store just as the health food wave started to crest and ultimately expanded to three locations before cashing in and selling the business to a big corporate gobbler. Unlike Mark, he didn't make crazy, buy-an-island kind of money on the deal, but it was more than enough to not worry about where his next mortgage payment was coming from or how he was going to pay for his kids' college education.

After getting snipped, Tom married Lianne in 1989, three years after I married Laurie and right around the time that our first daughter, Sarah, was born. Laurie didn't have much trouble getting pregnant, but she did have a difficult time with the last portion of her pregnancy and was put on bed rest for almost three months. After unsuccessfully trying to get pregnant a second time, Laurie and I decided to adopt, and in 1993, our second daughter, Whitney, arrived. We felt incredibly lucky to have found Whitney and frankly never once gave much thought to the fact that she was adopted and not a biological child like Sarah. As an added bonus, Laurie kept her figure, and we didn't have to wait six weeks after the baby was born to have sex.

At first, I wasn't sure that Tom and Lianne would ever have kids. Soon after they got married, Tom told me that, not unlike Laurie, Lianne had a "condition" that prevented her from getting pregnant. Afraid to dig too deep, I didn't ask Tom about it, preferring instead to assume that if he wanted to tell me about whatever the problem was, he would.

Not long after Whitney arrived, Tom and Lianne came over to our place one Sunday afternoon to talk about adoption. Since Whitney was always going to be a bottle baby, Laurie sat on our brown, leather, sectional couch and sipped a little chardonnay while Whitney snuggled in her arms and happily sucked away on her Evenflo bottle. Tom and I were around the bend of the perpendicular portion of the couch, wolfing down the meat and cheese plate Laurie had put out before they arrived.

Lianne wasn't saying much. She held her wine glass, but as far as I could see, didn't drink any of it. Instead, Lianne had this peculiar flat affect about her. Watching Lianne keep her distance, preferring to observe rather than participate, I was reminded of that unfortunate "those who can, do—those who can't, teach" adage. She had a hypnotized sort of smile on her face, and it obviously was not one of those "oh, she's such a cute baby" looks. More like the baby was a Martian.

Laurie asked her if she wanted to hold the baby, but Lianne wasn't interested.

"Don't you feel differently since she's not yours?" Lianne asked.

I had a hard time finding anything positive in Lianne except that she was married to one of my best friends. I did try my hardest, especially when Tom was around. But really? What was Laurie supposed to say? *"Yes, Lianne. We feel differently. She's not really ours, but oh, I guess she is okay."*

Tom glanced over at me as if to say "sorry about that."

Laurie was not fazed. "No, not at all. What you have to remember is that families can be built a lot of different ways. When she gets older, I will tell her that we fought to get her. We loved her before she was even here. I think she'll understand." Laurie kissed Whitney on her forehead.

I looked at Laurie, her brown hair pulled up in her around-the-house "high pony," holding our baby. In that one moment, I had an unmistakable feeling of pride. All over again, I was reminded of why I loved her.

Following her lead, I jumped in. "I have to tell you, Lianne. It's no different with the girls. I feel the same about both of them. Not one difference. To be honest, I don't even think about one being adopted and one being biological. They are both ours, regardless of how they got here." I looked over at Laurie, who seemed to be both startled and pleasantly impressed with the depth of my contribution to the conversation.

When they left, I was quite sure that Tom was ready to start the adoption process. His wife? With the way she looked at Whitney, I didn't think there was any way that Lianne would ever adopt kids.

As it turned out, I couldn't have been more wrong. Within a couple of days, Tom and Lianne plowed straight into the independent adoption process in much the same way Laurie and I had found Whitney. Never one to rely on others, Tom had no interest in working with an agency to find his child. Instead, he and Lianne hired a lawyer who helped them run "baby wanted" ads in grocery store, PennySaver coupon books throughout remote, lower-income areas of Ohio, Pennsylvania, West Virginia, and elsewhere. After a few months, a woman outside Pittsburgh, who was pregnant with twins, saw their ad and contacted them. Both Tom and Lianne went to Pittsburgh to meet the woman. The visit went well, and Tom paid for her to get a lawyer to make sure everything was legal. When she was ready to deliver, the woman's lawyer called Tom and the two of them drove up to Pittsburgh, just in time for the birth of Tom and Lianne's twin daughters. Laurie went out and bought them cute baby onesies and fluffy, pink blankets. I gave Tom a bottle of scotch and a box of ceremonial cigars. We were in our own special fraternity now, Tom and me, except that it never occurred to me until much later what the initiation had really cost him.

Although we all had years of sitting together at card tables and restaurant tables, telling tales and scoping girls, Tom and I had a different, deeper bond from the other guys, I think primarily because of the way we became dads. Like me, Tom was rubbed the wrong way whenever someone asked if one of our girls was "really ours" or whether they were all "natural born." We kidded each other about the responses we would make to those asinine comments, but we never did respond.

I suggested: "*Actually, the baby is my neighbor's. He came over and fucked my wife one afternoon when I was at work.*"

Tom would counter with: "*Oh, no. She's unnatural? Doesn't sound good. I better do something about that.*"

Years later when the girls had grown into their teens and Tom had sold his business and was casting about for something to do, he went back to his roots—literally. He became a manager at a local Roots grocery store, and, I am sure, loved every minute of it. Ironically, the card game loser did just fine in the game of life, kind of like the guy who finishes fourth in the Olympics—no medal but pretty damn good when you think about it.

A big fan of the TV series *Deadwood*, Tom never used the word "die," instead constantly referring to himself as the one that would be the first "croaker" in the group. After thirty-plus years of card games, Tom finally hit his number. My friend, Thomas Edward Porter, was dead at fifty-two. The rest of us, sometimes despite ourselves, were not. Sitting on an over-buffed, high-glossed, wooden bench in the back of the Danzansky-Goldberg Memorial Chapel, I wondered how exactly that decision got made.

# FIVE

I wasn't really sure what to think or what to feel. Of course, it was sad. Tom was young, at least to a guy the same age. He was married. Although it was not a stellar partnership, he and Lianne had stuck with it, yet I can tell you they don't give out any life prizes for that kind of thing. They had two children. He had run a good business. Tom had all the building blocks in place to fit the cliché "he had it all." Now, those blocks were still there, but he wasn't around to enjoy any of it.

I was sitting by myself, enveloped by the sterility of the windowless chapel, located in the heart of this strip-center funeral home pinched in between the golden arches of a McDonald's and a Best Buy store. Danzansky-Goldberg is the last stop for Jews who are unaffiliated with a particular synagogue, a place where you don't need to be a member to get in. Setting aside its umbrella of banality, there is nothing particularly offensive about the place. Day in and day out, families of mourners file in, sit down underneath the white, drop ceiling and recessed lights, cry, and file back out again. "Ships in the night," my grandfather would have called it.

I pictured Tom sitting in a bar somewhere listening to tunes in an old concert T-shirt, sipping a beer, and thinking about all he had done and accomplished. Do we all get a chance to do that? To look back and say, "Yeah, that was good" or maybe, "I should have taken that job?" I don't know, but it seems like at some point after we're gone, there should be a place to go and "run the videotape," as an old local sportscaster used to say. Like Tom, my place would be at a bar somewhere with a cold beer and an endless bottle of smoky, smooth Kentucky bourbon. After all, I assume you can drink as much as you want when you're dead.

Up until now, I hadn't faced a whole lot in terms of death. I'd had my struggles, of course, some financial, others family-related, but no one had ever died from any of it. My parents are alive, my kids are mostly doing well, and all the really bad shit you read about in the newspaper is still happening to someone else.

It's the usual family stuff that keeps me up at night, but that said, in my home and personal life, by any measure, I really can't complain. I still love the same girl I fell for almost thirty years ago and, for the most part, my four daughters are growing up and happy in their lives. Probably the one place I wish I had taken a different turn was in my career.

I'm a divorce lawyer. That's right. My financial security, my kids' college accounts, my cars, and everything else I have are dependent upon the unhappiness of others. Our family lives in what I like to call "the house that misery built." Every day I listen to the sad, sometimes compelling, but more often mundane bullshit that bleeds like sewage from other peoples' lives. The devastating and sincere, real-life burdens of "she took my kids" or "he screwed my next-door neighbor in our bed" are usually overwhelmed by "she won't give me my aunt Joan's candlesticks back" and "he ate the leftover chopped salad that was supposed to be for my dinner" minutiae.

I engage in regular arguments with judges, witnesses, and other lawyers. I even have to argue with my own clients, who pay a tidy sum to listen to my advice yet rarely follow it, opting instead to lean on the very lack of common sense that brought them to see me in the first place. When people talk to me about what I do, they always seem to ask me the same three questions:

"It must get depressing listening to everyone's problems every day, right?" Uh, yes. That's an easy one.

The sex-charged *"why do people have affairs?"* is my absolute favorite. Without wading too far into the "men are from Mars, women are from Venus" analysis, the answers are definitely different depending upon who is asking the question. In my experience, men are fairly simple beasts. If the husband had an affair, it's a pretty good bet that it was because his wife wouldn't fuck him. As hard as it is to believe, I have seen men who have been married for years, with kids, but after a couple of weeks of no action at home, the guy's bags are packed and he is on his way to a buddy's basement or the local Residence Inn.

Women, on the other hand, are much more complicated characters. While it certainly happens, generally speaking, a married woman doesn't usually cheat just because she's horny. More often, she is bored or sad, sometimes both. In good shape from spin and Zumba classes, wife is dressed in her lululemon workout gear and then looks across the kitchen table. In his rumpled Brooks Brothers suit with pleated pants, there sits her bloated husband, knee-deep into the middle-aged spread and paying more attention to his smartphone or that night's *SportsCenter* on ESPN than to her. She suggests a babysitter and a Saturday date night. If he even hears her over the day's baseball scores or glances up from his email, husband declines and tells her something like, "We don't need to go out. Let's stay home and watch a movie." They do just that, and, not surprisingly, he's asking her if she bought his favorite beer and then snoring in his overstuffed chair by nine. Trust me, that's a woman who is going to find a guy who only needs to invest a few minutes of conversation and tell her she is pretty before she bangs his brains out.

For me, after grinding through this work for almost thirty years, the more difficult one is "*how do you represent someone who is a real asshole?*" This is sort of the divorce lawyer's equivalent to a criminal defense lawyer being asked, "How do you represent someone you know is guilty?" With some fine-tuning, I have developed a slick, patented response in which I compare what I do to the public defender representing a client who just bludgeoned his spouse with a kitchen knife twenty-four times. You just do. It's our justice system, and it's not my place to judge. I then lay on the requisite "everyone has a right to a lawyer" yakety-yak for a few minutes. In practice, I do try to guide people to be decent in dealing with their spouses and kids, but if they don't, it's not my problem. I work hard and do the best I can. The moment the case is over, it's a good, firm handshake, and I move on. At least, that's what I try to tell myself, anyway. In reality, though, this work gets to me. It really does. You can't just lock the office door. People's lives follow you into the elevator; they hover in the passenger's seat as you drive home.

When I was younger, both my dad and my mom's father, Ben, wanted me to be a lawyer (the divorce part is solely my fault). With no interest in science, not to mention my inclination to pass out when giving blood, becoming a doctor was never an option. From as far back as I can remember, both of them pushed me relentlessly to become a lawyer. I would go to college, then law school, and do what neither of them did. Now that I am older, and a father myself, I understand that desire to do all you can to help your children support themselves and even experience financial success. That's not to say that either my father or grandfather were unsuccessful. Far from it.

My dad grew up in Trenton, New Jersey. More than a decade younger than both of his siblings, his own father died when I was young. Although I have no real memory of my paternal grandfather, I do know that he owned a bar, which may account for my seemingly genetic attraction to hanging around in them. My dad went to college, married my mother, and raised and supported his family by selling wholesale gifts and housewares to retailers up and down the I-95 corridor. He now lives a pretty decent life in South Florida, dabbling in residential real estate when he can and playing golf when he wants.

The only grandfather I really ever knew, Ben, was basically a second father to me. We all called him "Peepsie," and he was, to put it simply, a man amongst men. Born into a hardscrabble Jewish family in the mountains of Pennsylvania, he lived through the Great Depression and somehow survived the second Johnstown Flood in 1936. Although he had little education past high school, Peepsie had a certain flair with people that served him well. Long before I arrived, he built quite a modest empire in the dry cleaning business (which he eventually sold to a bunch of equally hardworking Koreans) and went on to become one of those small-scale, self-made, American entrepreneur stories that were written during the middle of the twentieth century.

Even at a young age, I quickly became aware of the way everyone noticed him. Ever the perfectionist, he always dressed impeccably in a sport coat and tie, slacks, and a pair of his prized and polished Johnston and Murphy shoes. Whether he was at home or on his boat, in the basement fixing his radio or on the patio sipping a beer, Peepsie's shirt was always tucked in and his thick silver hair was perfectly combed back. I am sure he would cringe and be none too happy at the sight of me now heading off to my office on a "casual Friday" in jeans and boots much like the ones I wore when I was in high school.

Whenever Peepsie and I were together, his only concern seemed to be about me. How was I doing? Any girlfriends? Did I need money? He was proud of me and never let me forget it. I can't count how many times he would tell me, "You're a lawyer, boy. You can do anything."

From a young age and well into my twenties, I soaked it up, and, as we often do with people we care about, I took him for granted. Then he got sick, and my first pangs of real adult selfishness started to become apparent, at least the first ones I became cognizant of. Peepsie and I no longer had the conversations that we used to, mostly because he wasn't able to and the gaping hole in my character didn't allow me to simply sit and visit, to just be with him. I guess I couldn't bear to look at him and not see that guy I grew up admiring, no longer in control, no longer able to put sentences together or even get his own belt on. Basically, a man who put my life and my needs first now needed me. And I wasn't there. Thinking about it still makes me sick to my stomach more than twenty years after his death. I wish he could have known how grateful I was. I wish I could have told him then.

I am grateful, infinitely so, to both my father and grandfather for the constant encouragement and persistence in guiding me into a legal career. Every kid should grow up with the kind of direction and advice that I was given. Doing what I do has enabled me to have what I have. I'm not digging ditches, driving a bus, or laying tile. I have absolutely no reason to complain about anything.

Still, though, I can't help but wish that I had at least given thought to doing something else. Of course, it could be one of those "the grass is always greener" kind of things, but I do think about what might have happened to me had I even, just once, tried something different. I don't know what, maybe anything—a writer, an actor, owner of a bed and breakfast. Maybe even a bartender. Assuming I ever had the guts, though, I could still give it a shot. There's still time. After all, I'm still young, right? I'm still alive.

# SIX

**F**unerals have always been weird to me. The first time I can recall being at a funeral was in this very spot after Peepsie died. I gave a eulogy that I am sure he would have appreciated had he been around to hear it. I talked about being on his boat and his teaching me to drive and always just seeming to care about how I was and what I was doing. Conveniently, however, I omitted my failure to hit the ball back when it was my turn to look out and care for him. When it was over, I felt as if, once again, I had failed the guy, not to mention myself, by replaying the same old tape. Play it safe, stick to what I know. Don't go outside the box by actually talking about something that is hard. After the service was over, everyone told me how well I spoke, how clearly I painted the picture that was my grandfather. Over and over again, I nodded my head, thanking them and pretending to agree.

I was here again a few years back when a young girl who grew up in our neighborhood committed suicide. I went to the funeral along with most of the other folks who lived nearby.

The place was filled with spit-shined twentysomething friends of this girl, a recent graduate from the University of Chicago who, as they say, had her whole life ahead of her. Bright, pretty, and engaging, Stephanie Wills seemed to be moving through life's inevitable path of good and bad, joy and heartbreak. The same kind of stuff we all experience at one time or another. Her parents had just finished footing what had to be a bone-crushing six years of bills for college, grad school, apartments, and the rest. Stephanie got a job in the city, according to the eulogy given by the requisite rabbi, who never knew her when she was alive but felt a sudden closeness to her now, no doubt after interviewing her grieving parents for all of twenty minutes just a couple days earlier. She had a boyfriend. She had a long and beautiful life to live. Stephanie Wills was good to go. Then again, maybe she wasn't. Unlike Tom, who had no control over his life's last chapter, Stephanie closed her own book at the ripe old age of twenty-six.

So here I am, two years later, sitting in the same polished and pasteurized spot that I last spent an hour listening to a recap of Stephanie Wills's life and times. I found myself laughing just a little about Lianne's decision to have the funeral here, at a "Jew joint" as Tom liked to call all the places with Jewish names, even years after he converted. Pumpernickel's, a long-gone delicatessen that specialized mostly in mediocrity, was a "Jew joint." So was Roth's, the only dry cleaner not owned by Koreans. And, of course, many of our favorite places in Atlantic City, the card game boys' adopted hometown, were "Jew joints," too.

I found out a couple of days ago that Tom's family would not be visiting with guests before the service. Contrary to what most Jewish families do before a funeral, which is spend some moments with family and close friends, Lianne did not want to see anyone and had made it clear in an email blast to several of us that only "immediate family" was invited to sit in the private anteroom, with its heavily carpeted floors and furniture that looked like it had escaped from the local Marriott. My first reaction when I read the email was anger, directed squarely at Tom's bitch of a wife. Widow. Whatever. Now, as it turns out, I am just as happy to be sitting out here in the back of the room, waiting and not having to wear one of those torn black ribbons that Jews make mourners pin to their jackets so that everyone else knows that in the hierarchy of grief, you are a little higher up the food chain.

Trying not to look conspicuous, I watched as the stream of people milled in and filed past, making their way into the rows closer to the front. I saw an older couple that didn't ring a bell to me, arm in arm, bowed from age, and shuffling in unison toward what looked like a section set aside especially for octogenarians. When the fellow's black yarmulke slipped and fell off the back of his head, he didn't notice, leaving it to be trampled in slow motion underneath the soft-soled shoes worn by the trail of mourners plodding in behind him.

Aside from being an all-around decent guy, Tom must have talked to hundreds of people a day in his grocery stores and it seemed like many of them were here. Most I had never seen before in my life and, even if I had, I probably wouldn't remember their names anyway. There were a few that I did recognize, but preferring to avoid the irritating small talk that seems to be unavoidable at these types of gatherings, I blinked and looked away when anyone remotely familiar came into view.

When Loren Jantz walked by, I quickly reached into my pocket and pretended to talk on my phone. She was a local girl that we all met in college. A little chunky but with full, round, milky-white breasts, Loren loved two things—drinking beer and giving hand jobs. Having shared the first and been a beneficiary of the second, I still held her in high regard but did not want a smile misinterpreted as an invitation to relive a couple of quick encounters from years ago.

Tom's night manager at the Rockville store, Miguel, who I knew as Mickey, walked behind Loren. From El Salvador or somewhere down that way, "Meeky" had an annoying habit of referring to himself in the third person as in "Meeky will help you find the coffee" or "Meeky thinks the tuna is very fresh today."

"Meeky sit next to you?" I heard him say to Loren.

Loren smiled and told him sure. With Meeky's eyes firmly fixed on her blouse, the two of them sat down in unison.

With nearly everyone ready and in their seats, a very serious-looking but unknown stranger serving as an usher opened a door to the side of the raised altar area in the front of the room. As Springsteen's "The Ties that Bind" played in the background, Tom's wife and kids filed in and stepped to the first row. Never all that much to look at, Lianne always seemed to be missing her chin, a characteristic that was accentuated by a pie-shaped face that kind of drooped, even when she was younger. From what we understood from Tom, she was not exactly Jenna Jameson in the sex department, either. Not long after they adopted the twins, Lianne told Tom that she really did not like sex and had no place in her life for it. He shouldn't worry, though, she said, promising a good solid missionary-style poke twice a year at least on Tom's birthday and Father's Day. No dice on the wedding anniversary, though. After all, that was as much her day as his, so there would be no action for Tom to commemorate their wedding night.

Any lawyer that does as much divorce work as I do inevitably has to head to court at least two or three times each month for what we call the "uncontested divorce." In Montgomery County, Maryland, where I spend most of my time, an appointed judicial officer almost always oversees uncontested divorce hearings. One step below a judge, those folks are known as "masters." For years, I have wished that a qualified candidate whose last name was "Bates" would come along and get appointed. Thousands of court orders floating around and available online signed by "Master Bates" would serve our judicial system just right.

The master's courtroom, absent of any garnish or elegance, looks more like some midlevel bureaucrat's office than a place where divorces are decreed and families officially fractured. The walls are whitewashed, bathed in fluorescent lights covered with some browned and warped plastic. The ceiling is checkered with tiles that are stained in yellow, reminiscent of a guy who hasn't brushed his teeth in twenty years. Front and center is the master's bench, raised a few feet above and looking out on the rest of the courtroom. Constructed of some inexpensive wood-grain material, it is usually cluttered with papers, a computer monitor, and a thick, burgundy book that contains domestic laws in Maryland labeled the "Family Law Article." Closest to the master's bench are a couple of trial tables for the parties and their lawyers. Rows of worn and scratched wooden benches sit behind the trial tables and line either side of the courtroom.

Maryland is one of the few states that still require live testimony in order for someone to obtain a divorce, even if the basis for the divorce, known as the "grounds," is tagged as "no fault." Set for ten minutes each, uncontested divorce hearings are stacked back to back from 8:30 a.m. to 9:30 a.m. every morning.

I recalled one particularly memorable hearing to the boys at one of our monthly card games.

At about 8:35 a.m., in strode one of the less than likeable family law masters, Miriam Binder. With no perceptible sense of humor and maybe five feet tall provided it wasn't raining outside, Master Binder was built like a midget wrestler. Whenever I saw her, I couldn't help but be reminded of an old kids' toy commercial pitching "Weebles wobble, but they don't fall down."

Master Binder called the first case. A heavyset black woman ambled to the trial table escorted by her lawyer, who was neatly clad in a dark blue suit and striped red tie. His hair was cut short and his small, rounded glasses certainly helped the fellow look like a lawyer and just about made you forget that he appeared young enough to be wearing braces and eating Pop Tarts for breakfast. Once they reached the trial table, both Baby Lawyer and his client remained standing and faced Master Binder.

Glancing over at a pile of files a dozen or so deep, Master Binder was ready to plow through her docket. "Call your witness, sir."

Baby Lawyer called the woman to the stand, she was sworn in, and he began to stumble through his questions, clearly reading them off a single page in front of him in that new lawyer, not quite sure of himself way.

"How old are you?" Baby Lawyer asked.

"Thirty-five," his client answered.

"How old is your husband?"

"Thirty-seven."

"How long have you been a resident of the state of Maryland?"

"My whole life."

"When were the two of you married?"

"December 31, 2001."

"Did you and your husband have any children together?

"No. Thank the Lord." That got some scattered chuckles from those of us in the gallery.

Master Binder just looked annoyed. "Let's proceed please," she said.

Baby Lawyer was a bit flustered and seemed to have lost his place on the page. "I'm sorry. Court's indulgence, Your Honor?"

Master Binder rolled her eyes and heaved a sigh.

Baby Lawyer found his place. "Was there a time that you and your husband separated?"

"Well, sure. That's why we're here." Another smattering of laughs.

From my vantage point along the side, I could see Baby Lawyer's face. His client was not cooperating, using her time on the stand to try out a few one-liners. He was turning a little pale, and maybe just a small bead or two of sweat was trickling down his cheek. With each passing minute, Baby Lawyer looked more and more like he was getting ready not for a routine examination but an execution.

Pretty soon the rest of the lawyers, who were no doubt billing our clients while doodling or daydreaming, perked up and began paying closer attention to what was developing into anything other than a standard uncontested divorce hearing.

Master Binder was nonplussed. "Sir, please continue."

"Uh. Sorry, Your Honor." Baby Lawyer was in trouble. He looked up from the page and at his client, doing his best to get back on track.

I have no idea where he got this next one, except maybe someone mistyped his cheat sheet or, who the hell knows, maybe he just misread the question. Either way, the bombshell was launched.

"Ma'am, when was the last time you and your husband enjoyed sexual relations?"

In that moment it was like one of those television shows where they purposely drop the scene into slow motion for added dramatic effect. I think everyone in the courtroom looked at each other, at poor Baby Lawyer, and then up front at Master Binder. Even she seemed interested in the answer to that one.

"I never enjoyed sexual relations." Kaboom. I broke out laughing at about the same time as everybody else.

Even Master Binder couldn't squeeze back a smile. After taking a few seconds to gather herself and let the commotion subside, she shook her head and looked at Baby Lawyer. "How about I ask the rest of the questions?"

Baby Lawyer was resigned to his fate. He sat down. "Yes, ma'am," was all he said.

When I told that story to the boys it got a good chuckle from everyone but Tom.

To my surprise, though, today Lianne didn't look awful, even without a chin. In a simple black dress, her hair loose over her shoulders Mary Tyler Moore 1970s-style, there was actually a grace to her as she guided the kids and her parents to their seats. In what was surely an unexplainable irony, Lianne somehow looked her best just as her husband was getting ready to go underground.

Tom's twins, now in their twenties, followed behind their mother. Jess and Kasey were both nice kids, who their mom made dress identically like the girls in those old moronic Doublemint gum commercials for years. When they were young it was always cute to go to Tom's house for our monthly game and see the girls in all their "matchies," as Lianne called them. I mean, everything always matched—hair, jeans, shirts, dresses, PJs. Everything. But even as they got older and into their teens, Lianne continued buying them exactly the same clothes. We thought it was inevitable that at least one of those girls was going to simply say "*no mas!*" and give the word "rebellion" a whole new look. So it was not particularly surprising, except to Lianne, that when Jess hit about thirteen or fourteen, she pulled the plug on the matching coats and shoes, opting instead for a "Marilyn mix"—Manson and Monroe. Everything was dark, except for her face, which was made up in brightly colored mascaras and lipsticks. There was something about Jess, though, that always struck me. Even without the biological connection, Jess somehow always reminded me of her dad. It wasn't that they looked alike exactly. It was more that she had this certain sense or feel of her father. Whenever I saw her, I always saw him.

Kasey, on the other hand, was a mirror image of her mom. She wore a basic black dress and some flat-pointed toe shoes that made her feet look way too big. Her hair was Lianne's color, without the touch of gray, and styled just so, exactly like her mother. Jess kept a step or two behind her, hair spiked with a streak of pink, in a tight-fitting skirt, wearing some ridiculously high heels and those sexy black stockings with the line up the back. Although not exactly appropriate for her father's funeral, you had to give the kid some credit for separating herself from the mundane Ann Taylor sameness of her mother and sister.

At the last game at Tom's, he'd spent much of the night lamenting Jess's giant butterfly tattoo on her back as well as a piercing in what he understood to be a place that left the rest of us fifty-something men swinging back and forth between wild pornographic visions of Tom's twenty-two-year-old kid and, of course, serious guilt because a lot of us had grown or nearly grown daughters.

As the family filed in, I took a quick glance around, checking for all the guys.

Wocky was the first of the boys to arrive. He slid into the pew next to me. It didn't take long for him to start yammering in my ear about Tom's daughter having more sex in twenty-two years than her mother did in fifty-one. Then we both tried to look serious and did our best to choke down a laugh.

It was almost always hard to stay serious with Wocky. Years ago, before beginning his career in the medical sales field, he called me late on a Wednesday morning to tell me was "wiped" from having to get up at 7:00 a.m. He said he simply could not believe how many people were out on the roads at that time of day. It took him a while but now, a bit north of fifty, Wock was used to getting up early to pitch the latest cancer drug to any medical professional that would listen.

Dressed in one of his standard work suits and showcasing his hypochondriac tendencies, Wocky loosened his tie and grumbled a bit about how his back was "just not right." When he wasn't looking, I glanced at my old buddy. I'd grown up in two different neighborhoods and two different houses, with him living next door each time. We played "army men" in a weird-looking treehouse his father built and chased each other around a makeshift football field pretending to be NFL running backs during endless games of "tackle-oko," an unrestrained and undisciplined game of backyard football. Through elementary school and junior high, we rode our banana seat Schwinn bikes around the neighborhood together well past dark. It wasn't until high school though that Gregg became "Wocky."

# SEVEN
## 1977

Gregg and I have known each other since soon after his birth, late in 1961. Our early years were spent as neighbors in a sprawling '60s-style housing subdivision as they used to be called. This one was known as Calverton. The only differences between the houses were the colors of the shutters and front doors. My dad called our place "the Vorton Mansion." In reality, it was a smallish split-level house almost identical to others on the street. A scar still remains above my left cheek from falling down the "mansion's" metal-tipped basement stairs.

When we were little, Gregg and I would often head to a small park in the center of the neighborhood and engage in some bruising acorn battles with the semi-retarded kid down the street. I know it is no longer politically correct to call someone "retarded," but that is what we called him in those days. We didn't wear bike helmets and no one used car seats or seatbelts. We played with the plastic bags and bent metal clothes hangers from Peepsie's cleaning empire. Little Pete was a weird-looking stump of a dude who couldn't hit a house with an acorn from three feet away. We pummeled and teased him endlessly. Good times. For us, not for Pete.

In the middle of second grade, both our families "moved on up" to another development, Stonegate—a place with no stone and no gate. It was newer than Calverton and less of a paint-by-numbers neighborhood, with bigger houses and bigger yards.

All in all, Stonegate was a pretty nice place to grow up. Not only was there lots of room to roam on the streets, but the neighborhood had been plunked down almost in the middle of nowhere on what had previously been clear-cut farm fields, it was surrounded by what felt like endless acres of thick woods and makeshift paths to walk, ride bikes, and explore. Our house was on a dead end, boarded by some woods on one side and Gregg's family on the other. He had two younger sisters, and his parents were close friends with mine.

"Big tits don't come with a round, curvy ass," Peepsie informed me when I was about thirteen. "You only get one or the other." It was the same with Stonegate, an outwardly serene and friendly slice of suburbia well north of DC. Lurking in the shadows of the growing shrubbery, Lawn Boy lawns, and brick colonials, however, was another side. *The Rocky Horror Picture Show* had nothing on a freaky neighborhood sociopath in the making, Kenny Conrad. Kenny was the oldest of the nine Conrad kids. His face was pallid and waxy and sat below a greasy, wet mop of long black hair. Tack on a pair of popped-out, bloodshot eyes and a grungy beard that was always toting the remnants of a recent meal, Kenny looked like Jesus Christ might have after a few months of heavy methamphetamine abuse.

Gregg and I steered clear of Kenny. If he was roaming the neighborhood, we would hide out in Gregg's treehouse to avoid any possibility that he would have an opportunity to make good on the threats to take us to his "torture chamber" somewhere deep in the woods. Apparently a couple of the neighbor's cats were unable to avoid the crazy fuck and were summarily executed in the tree-lined chamber, thankfully prompting Kenny's parents to ship him off to a boys' school in some remote corner of Arkansas.

It wasn't long after Kenny left that the neighborhood was rocked with a fresh set of rumors of a smoky sexual encounter between Mr. Talbot, a beer-guzzling loudmouth from down the street, and Mrs. Worgan, whose husband was bedridden with some disease that no one was exactly sure of. According to Gregg, who heard his mom telling the story over the phone one afternoon, one of Mr. Talbot's neighbors was outside on her deck late one night when she spied Mrs. Worgan on all fours and Mr. Talbot lunging at her, pants down, from behind. Although Mr. Talbot told everyone that it wasn't really Mrs. Worgan and that he was really just pushing a sled into his garage, no one believed him. The moving trucks were out front of the Worgans' within a few months; not long after, Mr. Talbot and his family were gone too. I probably should have thought a bit more about that particular story before I embarked on my present career.

When we got close to high school age, our parents did some investigating and became quite concerned about the high school

Gregg and I would attend. Our designated "home school," Westwood, was filled with what they described as "hicks" and "rednecks" and was obviously not the right place for a couple of soft-spoken Jewish kids from the suburbs. About eight miles in the other direction was John F. Kennedy High School. Kennedy was the school that, because of an oddly crafted school zoning map, some of the neighborhood kids were supposed to attend. Sadly, although named after my father's favorite president, Kennedy was also not a place our parents wanted Gregg and me to spend our high school years. Kennedy's halls, according to my parents, were filled with the world's bottom feeders, a scourge known as "potheads." The whole place was apparently infested with these aimless, drug-crazed "lowlifes." Nope. Not going there. So our parents broke some rules and got us both into one of the county's flagship public institutions, Sherbrook High School. Good choice. I was choking down Rolling Rock ponies and Genesee cream ales before my first report card was mailed home.

One summer night in 1977, Gregg's parents went out and left him to his own relatively limited devices. Often happy, generally rowdy, and in many ways absolutely uncontrollable, Gregg had become a fairly fun character to hang with. He was not destined for Harvard but was more than smart enough to know about life and how to enjoy it. Free from adult supervision, the two of us and some other neighborhood kids drank a few too many Rolling Rock ponies to count and gorged ourselves on a bushel of crabs. Our favorite movies around that time were *Saturday Night Fever* and *Rocky*. Gregg was no Sylvester Stallone, but he was pretty big and one of the first guys I knew to start lifting weights. Standing at about six feet, fairly thick and muscular, he was certainly no pushover.

At some point after the last crab was shelled, Gregg stumbled out of his chair and to the refrigerator. He grabbed a couple of eggs and stood behind his mom's fashionable kitchen counter, a muted yellow Formica. Then he cracked the eggs open into a glass, looked at all of us with a wide grin, and shouted, "Who am I? Who the fuck am I?" The rest of us just looked at him, knowing, of course, who he was but not necessarily who he wanted to be. Gregg peeled off his shirt and grinned even more widely at the rest of us, all of whom by this time were becoming a bit concerned about his mental health. Again, he bellowed the same question, "Who am I?" Like Rocky Balboa in the movie, he lowered his head and choked down the raw eggs. Swallowing back a gag and belching up an unpleasant waft of crabs, eggs, and Rolling Rock, Gregg looked up and gurgled, "I AM WOCKY." And so he was.

# EIGHT

Even though Lianne had barred my entry to the family's holding room before the service, I had made sure to get to the funeral on the early side. I wanted to be one of the first at the service so that I could leave quickly and avoid the inevitable and mind-numbing small talk with people I have not spoken to for years, with good reason. Since graduation from high school, I have only grudgingly gone to the various class reunions, primarily because the rest of the boys would be there and in no small part due to Don's position as the unofficial class of 1979 "reunion chairman" for life.

From the time that I met him in high school through college when he was tall and lean, with movie star looks, and all the years and weight gain since, never once has he shaved his moustache off. Unlike some styles, there is nothing that is particularly trendy or striking about Don's moustache. It's just there and no doubt always will be there, like a two-inch caterpillar forever Krazy Glued below his nose.

When it came to attending high school reunions, Don would not take no for an answer. He was always calling and emailing regularly to make sure all of us showed up every five years for lousy food, a cash bar, and, of course, plenty of leering at the same women we used to leer at when they were girls. Reunions, to me, were just stupid. I figured if I really wanted to stay in touch with those clowns, I would not need a buffet at some shithole restaurant like the Golden Bull to do it.

I completely forgot that as a pallbearer, I would be leaving before everyone else anyway. Within a few minutes, more of our card game boys had started to arrive, with Don the next to sit down. Like Tom, Don had married his high school sweetheart. Robyn, however, was everything that Lianne was not—pretty, smart, and all around fun.

Don is smart, decent, and, as a girl he tried to date many years ago once said, "the nicest guy" in the world. Because he's much less boisterous than either MKat or Wocky, it takes a bit more digging and rummaging to discover that Don (real name Eric) is actually every bit as colorful, just in a quiet, subdued, and somehow slightly more disturbed way.

# NINE
## 1977

When I arrived at Sherbrook High School in the fall of 1976, I really knew only two or three people. Seeing a kid named Eric in several of my classes, I got to be friendly with him. Sporting a white dude's '70s version of an Afro, Eric was mild-mannered and polite, and he rarely saw anything but the best in any situation or any person. A born diplomat if there ever was one, he seemed to have an uncanny knack for being friends with everyone from all walks of high school life. But Eric seemed closest with a few guys that seemed to be right up my alley—MKat, Mark, and a skinny, odd-looking character named Steve Baldwin, who bore an uncanny resemblance to Andy Griffith's Mayberry deputy.

It wasn't until the spring of 1977 that I got up enough nerve to approach Eric and ask if I could hang with him and the other guys. I had my license, had access to a car, and could drive. That, as they say, was that. From that night forward, whether those guys liked it or not—and it is quite possible that they did not—I was glued to their sides. Almost thirty-five years later, in a lot of ways, I still am.

Eric is not Eric to any of us. Just as Gregg is forever "Wocky," the only name we ever call Eric is "Don." His father is blessed with the not-particularly masculine name Sheldon. From Sheldon, well, the not-so-creative "Don" became Eric's given name.

As with most high school-aged boys, it was no secret to any of us that we all masturbated regularly. A few guys had certain, shall we say, rituals. Wocky, for example, loaded up on some Neosporin from his medicine cabinet and jerked off into a tube sock. MKat preferred dry humping a particularly bumpy pillow that he kept secretly stuffed under his bed. I had no such restrictions. In the bathroom. Watching TV. Wherever and whenever. As long as anyone wasn't around and I had a spare minute, I would yank it out. The thing seemed to have a mind of its own and, goddamn if it didn't feel really good. By far the most curious of all, though, was Don's lengthy dalliance with his father's electric sander.

Sheldon, I imagine, was annoyed with his sixteen-year-old son's lack of initiative, so he assigned the kid a project to work on. The family had a pretty nice screened porch on the side of the house, and Don was tasked with refinishing a table to put on it. Sheldon showed his boy how to use an electric sander and sent him to work. As Don tells it, one day he was sanding away in his favorite Levi's when he brushed up against the sander and became aware of its vibrating qualities. Immediately thereafter, Don and his sander became inseparable. Several days each week,

Don rode the bus home, raced into the house, and promptly "went to work."

When it was done, one of the table's legs was shorter than the others and it wobbled pretty badly, but Don learned the ins and outs of how to use a sander. He still has it in his garage.

# TEN

While many of the people we knew in high school tuned their car radios to an endless loop of top 40 pop drivel like ABBA or, even worse, the Bay City Rollers, the guys and I were lovers of all things Springsteen. We would listen to the lyrics of every song, from "Jungleland" to "Darkness on the Edge of Town," and debate endlessly what Bruce was trying to say in each line. Tom was also a huge Southside Johnny fan, another, albeit less well-known, New Jersey shore rock legend. Tom turned me on to Southside back in 1977, and we absolutely loved going to see Southside and his Asbury Jukes play. Once the Boss hit the big time with *Born to Run*, it was hard to afford tickets to Springsteen shows. Southside, however, was another story. He packed folks into smaller places and played, sweated, and sang his ass off for hours. Tom and I listened to Southside almost every time we were together, and it was a long-held tradition to see him play whenever he and the Jukes were in town.

It came as no surprise, then, that the music overhead while folks were ushered in to the service had a distinct Jersey shore flavor.

After "Lucky Town" melded into Southside's "I Don't Want to Go Home," I heard MKat behind me. "Jesus, we have to listen to the bowler at the guy's funeral?" MKat always thought Southside looked like a bowler. I don't know, maybe he does, but it never mattered much to me. The guy could flat out sing, and his music made me feel, well, happy. Even here. It took all I had to stay in my seat when he hit the *reach up and touch the sky* chorus.

For a quick second, I think I did try to reach up. Reach up to find my friend.

# ELEVEN
## 1977

Sometime in the spring of 1977, I got my first invite to the card game. I was grabbing some books from my locker on my way home on a Friday afternoon. As I had no real intention of opening them over the weekend, there was no real reason for me to take them. My sole purpose for standing at my locker and slowly packing the things was to try, unsuccessfully as always, to make even fleeting eye contact with one Barbara Barnsley. A day did not go by without me wishing that just once she would walk toward me so I could smile and say, "Hey, Barb," just like all of her friends did. She was an exotic-looking thing; I think her mom was Hawaiian, Asian, something. Whatever she was, Don and I referred to her as "The Tahitian Treat." The Treat was not real tall, maybe five feet two inches, but whenever she walked by me in those clunky high-heeled Candie's and tight Jordache jeans that were all the style in the late '70s, my eyes literally burned. Seriously, I couldn't see. It's very difficult to be cool when your eyes well up and you look like a six-year-old who just got his candy stolen.

There I was, eyes glossed over, when Don walked up, took one look at me, and said, "Come on, man. You got no chance. Wanna play some cards? Wocky's been playing. Silber's coming too." Doug Silber also grew up in Stonegate, just a few blocks from me. We were not all that close before high school, but he would ride around the neighborhood and play basketball with Wocky and me in his driveway at night until my mother called me home.

The good news for me was that Peepsie had taught me poker at a fairly young age, so I at least knew the basics. I'd never played for money, especially since I didn't have much of it, but I figured I could cobble together a few bucks for the big game.

I sighed, maybe a bit too loudly at Barbara as she walked by. The muffled sound of air going out of a bicycle tire was just loud enough to get her to look my way at least. "Sure, I'm in," I told Don.

I got directions from Don to a kid named Tom Porter's house and headed home. After a few hours of hanging around and playing some Ping-Pong against the backstop on my table, I threw on my favorite Levi's 501s, a T-shirt, and my still-out-of-the box-looking Puma "Clyde" black-on-white sneakers. Feeling pretty lucky with about six bucks in nickels, dimes, and quarters jammed in my pockets, I jumped into my used Mustang II and headed out.

Tom's house was easy to find. Not too far from school and behind the church that lit his front yard, the house was a two-story brick-rambler-style with green shutters. Although similar to the other houses nearby, it was easy to notice everything that Tom's father had added on that the other homes did not have—covered, wood, a front porch that reminded me of a beachfront boardwalk, landscaping that was neat and trimmed, and a separate stone-and-brick shed-looking thing off to the side of the house.

The front door was open behind a metal screen door with a big "P" in cursive emblazoned on the lower panel. I knocked; no one answered. I waited a minute or two, knocked again, and rang the bell. Finally, I heard someone yell, "Tell the dick to come in already!" I guess that dick was me.

Opening the front door, I found that the house was much darker inside than out. Off to the right was a plain kitchen with a round dinette-style table and chairs, dark cabinets, and a glossed-up tile floor. Three steps from the front door to the left was a stairway going downstairs from which I could hear a fair amount of chatter.

"Who is this dude anyway, Don?"

"Trust me, he's cool."

"This coming from a guy who jerks off to a sander."

"Better than that fucking tube sock, douche."

About five steps down, I ducked my head to avoid cracking it on the dropped ceiling in the basement, looked around, and said, "Hey."

Seven guys were pinched in around a rectangular metal table, with one of the legs wrapped in some silver duct tape. On top of the table were two decks of cards, one red and one blue, along with a lot of change and some cans of Budweiser.

Everyone has those moments in life that are forever ingrained and charred into their memory. Lasting no more than ten seconds, that glance down Tom's basement stairs remains a snapshot that I can still close my eyes and recreate in my mind whenever I want. A dim woodshop fluorescent tube fixture hung from a wooden beam. Cinder block walls were painted in an off-white eggshell color. Around the table, along with Don and Tom, were the rest of the guys: MKat, Mark, Baldwin, and Wocky. Several beer cans were already littered around along with opened bags of Fritos and potato chips.

Wocky had made his first appearance at the game a couple of weeks earlier, sitting in when Don was stuck at home doing homework. He undoubtedly made the best of the invitation, toting a case of Bud to share with his new friends. Once he tossed in the "I am Wocky" egg-drinking routine, Wocky became a card-carrying member of the group.

Other than Wocky, they had been friends for years, all having grown up within a few blocks of Tom's house. Even with Wocky there, I was definitely an outsider at this little game. But Don stood up, gave me a genuine smile, and slapped me on the back.

"Glad you could make it, man."

I sat down in one of the empty chairs along the corner of the table, between Don and MKat, who had Wocky sitting on his other side.

"Thanks, bro." Not sure why I called him "bro." Dopey.

"You've known the guy for a fucking minute and he's your 'bro?' That's funny." MKat angled his head to the side and looked at me through a pair of bloodshot eyes. He didn't seem annoyed or offended about the "bro" moniker. I wasn't exactly sure how to read the guy. His mouth was half-open, so I was thinking he was going to laugh but no sound came out. He may have thought it was funny. Maybe MKat was confused. Of course, he could've just been stoned.

In what was to become a habit as the years passed, I ignored MKat's comment and shuffled the red deck of cards.

"Your deal, *Bro*," Baldwin said, rocking his head back and forth. It was clear that he was running the game.

"So, you live next door to this moron?" MKat looked at me as Wocky took a major slurp from a can of Bud, then burped and wiped his chin at the same time.

"Yep. Been living next to him since we were kids," I responded.

"Guy's brilliant. A real Mensa candidate." MKat shook his head. Wocky, with his beer in one hand, was bent halfway off the chair and reaching under the table for something, and remained blissfully oblivious to any of it.

"What the fuck are you doing down there?" Tom asked.

Wocky was still fishing around and balancing what was left of the beer where we could see it, but with most of his head having vanished, he was also knocking into the middle leg of the table and causing everyone's coins to run from one side to the other.

"You gonna blow me or what?" MKat nodded his head and smiled.

"I thought Bryna already blew you this morning," Baldwin responded. Bryna was Wocky's mother.

"Oh, yeah. Almost forgot. I banged Bryna while Morris watched from the closet," MKat shot back. Morris was Wocky's dad.

I had gotten the general drift of things and was certain that I did not want any of these characters to know my parents' names.

"Leave my mother out of it. Come on already," Wocky chimed in, his head still under the table.

"That's exactly what your mother told me this morning when my dick was in her mouth." Quick with the one-liners, this MKat guy.

"Walked into that one, dumbass," Tom piped in.

Wocky's head emerged from underneath the table just as I stopped chuckling.

"Found it," he said while holding a quarter up in the air for the rest of us to see.

Wocky turned to me. "And what are you laughing at, JB? Think you're safe from all this bullshit?" Then the douchebag told everyone my parents' names.

Don cut the red deck and slid it back to me. I looked around the table. "You guys ever play Follow the Queen?"

Follow the Queen is a simple seven-card stud game. Everyone starts with two cards dealt face down, called "hole" cards. The next four cards are dealt up with bets in between. For those who have not yet folded, the last card is also dealt down. All queens and the next card dealt up that "follows" the queen are wild. If another queen comes out, then the prior wild card cancels, replaced by the card that follows the last queen dealt. Between the changing wild cards and the "hole" cards, it can be difficult to gauge the strength of the other players' hands. Consequently, someone who looks like he is only holding a pair of threes might actually have a full house or four or five of a kind if he has wild cards that have been dealt down.

"No. Never. Maybe you can teach us Go Fish, too, Bro." MKat's response made it pretty clear that yes, they knew how to play Follow the Queen. Also that sarcasm had a place at the table.

"Yeah, we've played before. Unless it's some ridiculous game like Wocky's Night Baseball or a game with one-eyed jacks, deuces, and "suey" kings as wild cards, chances are we have played it." Baldwin gave me the general rules about moving the deal around the table. Dealer antes fifty cents, deal moves to the right, whoever has the next deal is responsible for shuffling the extra deck so as not to lose any time between hands. Minimum bet was a dime; maximum fifty cents. No check and raise. The stakes were afford-able, and nothing was too complicated.

I tossed in my fifty-cent ante and dealt the cards. Somewhere between the fourth and fifth card, things got sidetracked when Baldwin, having already folded, snubbed out a cigarette and blew some smoke rings into the side of MKat's head across from the other end of the table. "*I can see clearly now,*" Baldwin sang, completely off-pitch, tapping his fingers on the table. Wocky coughed.

"Creedence," Tom belched, thoughtlessly crushing a can of Bud against the side of his head. In those days, the cans were made of a thick, metallic tin, not the lightweight aluminum cans of today. I was impressed.

"Just like with his cards," MKat said. "Folds. King of the losers."

"You mean like the French?" I added. "I surrender."

Tom looked up. "I don't get it. What's with the French thing?"

"He meant that you play cards like France fought in the wars. They surrendered to the Germans. Twice," Don explained.

Tom looked across at MKat, then stared at me. Was he angry? Were his feelings hurt? I wasn't sure.

"History maven douche," he said.

I guessed he was okay.

"*Nyet.* Johnny Nash." Baldwin was apparently the host of this particular version of *Name That Tune*. And he knew a little Russian, too.

Also having folded, Mark spurted from out of nowhere, "I can do twenty one-armed pushups." And, indeed, he dropped to the floor, lifted his left hand, put it behind his back as if giving himself a one-armed nelson, and threw down twenty one-armed pushups. "Okay, who can match?"

"What a bucket of shit." MKat got on the floor next to Mark. He got maybe three of the one-arms in and flattened facedown onto the floor. "Anyone get me a beer?" he asked, not moving.

Don grabbed him a beer, set it on MKat's back, and got up. "I'm out, too. Got to take a piss."

Only four of us remained in the hand. Wocky was nervously pinching his new lucky quarter between his fingers and deciding what to do. I was sitting on a well-hidden low straight and figured I would be able to bluff my way through. Tom was bobbing his head back and forth, which I knew had to mean something but I just wasn't sure what.

"Let the new guy deal. Go ahead, Bro. Deal the fucking cards." MKat stuck his tongue out. He globbed up some spit, made it into a giant *Wizard of Oz* kind of bubble, and blew it at me. It floated about two feet before imploding on its own.

"Tom, your bet." I tried to get Tom's attention, but having gotten sidetracked while the bubble was bearing down on me, Tom was fiddling with an Asbury Jukes *Better Days* cassette tape that needed winding.

After MKat opened the bet for fifty cents, Wocky folded. "Think the fucker's got something good," he said, sliding the cards to the center of the table. I wasn't sure what Tom had, but he sure looked confident. I followed Wocky and turned my card over.

Tom was showing a pair of kings and a queen, giving him the equivalent of three kings. He raised an eyebrow at MKat. "Shit is what he's got. I'll raise you another fifty."

MKat didn't hesitate. "And another," he said as he put his dollar on the table.

Suddenly, Tom looked nervous. I dealt the last card down.

"Last bet's a buck. Three raises." Baldwin was still watching.

MKat, showing what looked like a jumbled mess, was charged up. "I'll bet a buck," he shot over at Tom.

By this time, Tom was into the hand for maybe three or four

dollars, but his uncertainty was palpable. He sighed and ground his teeth. "Fuck, I'm out. Take it. I know. I fold." He turned his cards over and looked at MKat. Full house, kings over jacks. "What'd you have? Straight flush, I bet."

"You don't have to show," Baldwin offered, also looking at MKat.

"It's okay. I don't mind. Read 'em and weep, dummy." Showing a pair of aces, MKat turned over the rest of his hand to reveal that he had absolutely nothing else. Just the pair of aces.

Bluffed and apparently not for the first time, Tom dropped his forehead, tapping it gently on the table in front of him. "Fuck, fuck, fuck," was all he said.

MKat swept in about eight dollars in dimes and quarters. "Nice job, Frenchie," he said, chuckling at Tom.

Tom threw up his hands and cracked a smile. "I surrender," he whooped in a passable French accent.

The deal moved to my right as we all laughed at Tom. With him, too.

After an hour and a few turns around the table with the same seven or eight bucks simply moving from one of us to the other, in bounded my longtime Stonegate friend, Doug Silber, who was more commonly known as Vinnie (and in later years, after we all had kids, as a much more respectful Uncle Vinnie). In a group full of guys with nicknames, he was called "Vinnie" after Vinnie Barbarino, the class cutup in the '70s sitcom *Welcome Back, Kotter*. That Doug could also claim to be on a par with John Travolta didn't hurt.

"Look who's here," he said, looking at me. "How're Marchee's big titties doing?" Uh oh. Didn't take him long to get to that.

"Marchel Marchee, Marchel Marchee." Now he was repeating it, in a sort of annoying, sing-songy way that still made me laugh in spite of myself. My mother, whose name is Marci, has large breasts, and Vinnie had creatively incorporated my mother's generous anatomy into his own little tribute to the mime Marcel Marceau. While cackling like a carnival clown, Vinnie mimicked the mime, rattling his head between a big set of monster breasts and chanting, "*Marchel, Marchee. Marchel, Marchee.*"

"Isn't he French?" Tom asked. "The mime guy, I mean."

Vinnie looked at Tom like a touched cousin. Vinnie is one of those guys who seems to sail through life, never having to worry about anything. Everything about him is outsized: He talks loud, laughs loud, he even breathes loud. In those days, Vinnie rode around in a jacked-up blue Gran Torino. On weekend nights when he couldn't find something in a tube top to hang with, he enjoyed flying through our neighborhood at about eighty-five miles per hour, running over mailboxes. Brash, never shy, and always on, he and Tom were my best buddies in a card game full of them.

Vinnie's family owned a local record store chain. His days at "work" were spent behind the counter, looking like the miniature Great Gazoo Martian fellow from *The Flintstones*—earphones on, listening most likely to Springsteen, while gnawing on Goldenberg's Peanut Chews.

Of course, Vinnie's "Marchel Marchee" did not go unanswered. Much like war plans from the Pentagon, there must be a balance of terror. I hit back with a less-than-classic late-'70s song along the lines of, "*The Sharif don't like it, rock . . .*" and then I added "ANITA." Why? Vinnie's mom's name is Anita, and her maiden name is, wait for it, "Rock." I dropped my hands on MKat's shoulders, and, although we had just gotten to know each about other an hour or so earlier, started humping MKat in the back. Needing no encouragement, MKat joined me in the chorus, now a loud and rousing "*Rock Anita, rock Anita.*"

Never one to back down from a fight, Vinnie dropped his

jeans, shooting all of us a full frontal. He then proceeded to squeeze his penis backwards between his legs so that it looked like, well, it looked like a vagina, and shouted, "How's this, pussy boys?"

MKat and I kept singing and soon enough everyone else joined in: *"The Sharif don't like it. Rock Anita. Rock Anita."* After a couple of choruses, MKat flashed the smile and we all laughed, as Don later described it, like "banshees." I don't really know what a banshee is, but even today, whenever someone does something really loud, it is always "like a banshee."

By the time Vinnie reached into his pockets to start to play, the game was breaking up. Mark was due at work early, Don was up and stretching, and MKat was back on the floor, seemingly asleep in the same spot where he had been unable to keep up with Mark's pushup exhibition. Wocky was finishing his beer when he asked us, "Who's got the next game?"

It's been a long time since that first game. A lot has stayed the same. MKat continues to tease Wocky unceasingly. Don remains the nicest guy I know. Vinnie is still late, if he shows at all. We still play a hand or two of Follow the Queen at every game. Of course, much has also changed. Weekly games are now monthly. Bowls of Fritos and potato chips with French onion dip are gone, replaced with celery, carrots, maybe some Sun Chips. After years of working out, it's MKat who can do the pushups while Mark stays seated in his chair. And obviously, there has been one other change.

Tom, the guy who started the game, is gone.

# TWELVE

**B**y now the rest of the guys and their families, along with everyone else, were waiting for the service to get started. Sitting as far as possible from the front, like I had done in every class since high school, I was anxious for Laurie and my kids to get here. Even Vinnie had shown up too, although he'd largely dropped out of the game years ago. He sat to my right with his wife, Pam, between us. She had her long brown hair pulled back and pinched into a sleek ponytail behind the center of her neck.

"So sorry, Bro," she said to me. "We all loved the guy." She was being herself—sincere, serious, and, as always, in complete control. I looked and thought of her back at the University of Maryland, not as the mother of three that was sitting next to me.

"Wish you were in the pink bikini," I said.

"Me, too," Wocky chimed in.

I got a different, but probably predictable, reply from Pam. "God," she said, smiling. "You guys are all still such assholes."

MKat, the only one of the crew to have gotten divorced, sat behind us and off to the left, looking a lot like many newly single guys over fifty do. He wore a starched shirt and tie under a European, gray, wool designer suit with slim-fitting pants, and a jacket that was just a bit overtailored. His hair, although still long, had an unnatural brown-orange tint, the result no doubt of a salon stylist's "color camo" hair dye. Don and Baldwin were directly behind me and next to MKat, with Don resting his arm on Baldwin's shoulder. Often emotional, Baldwin seemed to be leaning into Don for support, something he had probably done countless times since they were kids. Mark and his wife were in that same row. A real rarity, there was not much chatter between us; in its place was just an awkward emptiness. We saw each other, nodded heads, but no one said anything. I was happy and oddly relieved to see Laurie and my kids come in through the rear entrance. Typically oblivious, Vinnie did not notice the five of them standing at the end of the aisle waiting for some room to open up. It wasn't until Pam rapped him on the side and said, "Move down, doofus," that Vinnie realized he was holding things up. After the gentle reprimand from Pam, he slid down the pew in order to make room for the girls to sit with me.

There was comfort in having my kids with me. Tom had adopted his two girls, and we had adopted our two middle kids. A couple of years after Whitney was born, Laurie got a note from her biological mother saying she was pregnant again and asking if we were interested in adopting Whitney's sibling. Although I was plenty comfortable with two kids, there was no getting in Laurie's way. We adopted our third daughter and then were surprised when our youngest came along "the old-fashioned way" soon after.

Between my friendship with Tom and the adoption connection, our families spent a lot of time together despite the distance that Lianne kept from both Laurie and me. We took summer trips to the Outer Banks in North Carolina, a great vacation in Arizona, and several weekends back and forth to the local beaches. Tom was "Uncle Tom" to my kids. His girls called me "Uncle Bro."

Laurie was never one for much in the way of public affection, so I immediately was conscious of her hand settling on top of mine. Overhead, Springsteen was lamenting another lost love. I had no idea who was in charge of the music, but it sure was a good time to hear "For You." Once the lyrics faded and the song ended, though, I was really ready to get this thing started and done. I needed to get the hell out of there, grab the other guys, crank a little Southside in the car, and just go.

# THIRTEEN
## 1978

In the spring of 1978, we took our first trip to Atlantic City. Resorts, AC's first casino, had opened its doors just a couple of weeks earlier. We were all anxious to break out of the parental basements and try our card playing skills in a real casino, hoping to win someone else's money instead of each other's.

Tom, Mark, and Wocky were squeezed into my Mustang II while everyone else rode in a bit more style with Baldwin in his grandmother's Lincoln. Lodging was covered: MKat had an aunt who ran a boardinghouse near the beach. The rooms were cheap. We had to share a bathroom with everyone who was on the same floor, but that was of no importance to a bunch of seventeen-year-old guys. MKat insisted that we stop on the way at some old-fashioned ice cream place, even though the New Jersey Turnpike would have gotten us into Atlantic City about a half an hour faster.

Sitting on a large, grassy lot, Richman's on NJ Route 40 was a throwback to a time before highways, when people took back roads to reach the shore. It was a massive, city-block-sized white building, fronted by a fiberglass cow and horse-drawn wagon out front, and every year I stopped there, the "C" in the Richman's Ice Cream sign was always broken.

We got to Richman's about seven o'clock on a pretty hot Friday night. There was a long line of people waiting to get in and sit down, so we opted for the walk-up service window where a freckle-faced, redheaded kid, maybe fourteen, took our order. He was right out of a cartoon, even wearing one of those pointy old-fashioned diner hats. "Welcome to Richman's," he said jauntily. "Can I help you?"

Never one to wait for others, Wocky cut in front and took a quick look at all the flavors and options. (Baskin-Robbins had nothing on this place.) After a minute had passed, I could tell he was up to something. Tom, who was between the two of us, along with the twenty or so people behind us, was getting impatient. "Come on, Wock. You're not buying a fucking house."

"Yeah, sure," Wocky said. "I know what I want." He looked the kid square in the face and, swear to God, with not even a hint of a smile, gave his order. "A jism shake, please."

"Oh, Christ. He didn't." Tom was not happy.

"Yep. He did." MKat was giggling, his head straight down, not wanting to see what might be coming next, uh, no pun intended.

That poor kid, I thought. What was he going to do? A line of hungry, family-friendly customers and my dipshit friend was trying to be funny.

"Sorry, sir, we don't have that flavor," replied the redheaded kid. Well, ignorance is bliss, as they say.

Sadly, Richman's closed its doors in October of 2009. I read recently that someone bought the sign at auction. The great ice cream is gone, along with the horse and wagon. Even the fiberglass cow has vanished. Not the jism shake, though. The jism shake springs eternal.

From Richman's we headed east on Route 40 toward our destination. Our unofficial AC historian, Don, was a nonstop chatterbox about all things Atlantic City, including things interesting to us and those well beyond what anyone knew or really needed to know about the place. A budding history buff myself, I read a lot about both world wars and American and British history. If anyone ever wanted a quick trivia test, I could give it to them. I loved it when, every so often, the boys would ask me for a multiple-choice question and try to guess the answer. The winner was always rewarded with a beer or slice of pizza, depending upon what was in reach. Sometimes the questions would go on and on, but that was usually after we were well under the influence of alcohol. As we approached Atlantic City, the car was clamoring for one of my patented trivia questions. Happily, I gave in.

"The first German soldier killed in World War II was killed by a soldier from what country?" I asked.

"United States," Mark answered before the others.

"Nope."

"Had to be Great Britain," Tom said.

"Wrong again," I answered.

"I skipped most of American history class, so no clue," Wock said.

I kept driving, waiting for someone to beg me for the answer.

They were silent. I checked my rearview mirror. Mark and Don were staring right at me, waiting.

"You're going to be surprised." I was taunting them just a little.

"All right already, douche. Who was it?" Tom really needed to know.

"Okay, the first German soldier killed in the war was killed by a soldier from …" A deliberate pause. "Japan."

"Get the fuck out of here. No way," Tom said.

"Yes, way." I responded like a ten-year-old.

"Fucker knows his history. I bet he's right," Mark said.

I did, and I was. I smiled and kept driving.

When it came to Atlantic City, though, Don was the guide. He made sure that we all understood that the game of Monopoly was based on Atlantic City's streets and byways and that the Miss America Pageant started there in the early part of the twentieth century. We were schooled in dozens of other bits of Atlantic City trivia, including that the first boardwalk was built alongside its beach and in the 1930s the town was known as "The World's Playground." The depth of Don's Atlantic City knowledge was unparalleled, something particularly impressive long before the advent of the Internet.

Don's mom, Judy, grew up on the south side of town in the Chelsea area. As Woody Allen would say, she was quite a beauty and won the Miss Chelsea pageant as a high school senior. Don spent many summers as a young kid on family vacations in and around Atlantic City.

Given how much he talked about Tony's Baltimore Grill, the White House Sub Shop, and various other restaurants, his family must have spent a lot of time eating while on vacation. Don was also well versed on the history of Atlantic City's famous 500 Club, known as "The Five," which was apparently home to Frank Sinatra,

Dean Martin, Sammy Davis Jr., Milton Berle, and other entertainment legends. The club burned down in 1973 and was never rebuilt. Sadly, as we headed north on Pacific Avenue, it looked like a lot of the town needed to be burned down. Dark, dirty, and decrepit, Atlantic City of the late 1970s was clearly not the '50s paradise I had pictured. It's come almost full circle back to that broken-down place today. Casinos are folding faster than the gamblers.

The haggard look of Atlantic City did nothing to dampen our enthusiasm. We all hurried up the stairs into Aunt Kay's Brighton House, changed our clothes, and then ran back out to try our luck. Resorts was about eight blocks from Brighton House, making it an easy walk. After a short trek through a not-so-friendly and seedy part of town pocketed with panhandlers and prostitutes, we rolled into the hazy and costume-jeweled palace pretending like we belonged. I wore a belt. Wocky and Tom even had their shirts tucked in. Tom couldn't stop talking about the mirrors, walls of singing slot machines, and all the cameras that were perched above us, watching everyone. "There are hundreds of guys up there monitoring everything we do. Everything," he said.

Mark was not impressed. "Come on, man. You really thinking they're watching you and the fifteen dollars you got in your pocket? Relax." He snagged a waitress who looked like she needed a pail of Vaseline just to get into her cocktail dress. "Gin and tonics for all of us, please," he said suavely (yeah, right). He handed her two quarters.

"Thanks, moneyman," the waitress grumbled through the gap in her front teeth. "Be right out."

Tom was astounded. "You buying all those drinks? Jesus, you won't have any money to play with."

"They're free, dumbass," MKat chirped from next to a spinning roulette wheel.

"Free? Oh yeah!" Wocky cheered and raised his hands above his head as if he had just scored a touchdown.

Once the beauty in the cocktail dress had returned, we took our drinks, each ponying up a quarter tip for her trouble. "Not so bad. She made about two bucks off us," Tom observed.

"Yeah. She's probably giving her notice and retiring tonight," Mark answered back.

From there, we all split up and headed in different directions to make our fortunes. Wock, MKat, and Mark went to shoot craps; the rest of us drifted to various blackjack tables. I found my way through the pillows of cigarette smoke to an open three dollar minimum blackjack table and sat down. I gave the dealer twenty-five, got my chips, and was ready to run with the high rollers. Vinnie and Tom sat at the table with me, Vinnie dropping a whopping fifty bucks down. Tom took out his Wrangler denim wallet and put his fifteen dollars on the table. We were locked and loaded.

Over the next hour, I won some and I lost some. Tom seemed to be doing the same, solidly holding his own. Vinnie, however, was dropping like a stone. His pile of fifty white dollar chips was about gone. A couple of seats to my left, the area of the table in front of him was a little difficult to see, but it looked like he had about ten chips left, all of which he was rubbing and twiddling rapidly between his fingers. After the dealer finished a shuffle, a particularly odd-looking dude who was sitting between Tom and me was given the yellow card to cut the "shoe." This guy had one cigarette in his mouth, another in his left hand, and a pack of opened Camel menthols on the table. He wore glasses that looked like he had borrowed them from Elton John and, as a matter of fact, seemed to be whistling "Crocodile Rock" as he slid the yellow card between two of his smoke-stained finger stubs in his free hand.

While cutting the cards, he snarled at the dealer and mumbled something that sounded a lot like "cocksucker." I tried not to stare and just figured things weren't going so well for the guy.

The next forty-five minutes were magic for me. I was pulling aces, picture cards from everywhere. For every twelve showing, I pulled an eight or nine. Every double down, every split, a crazy ass winner. Of course, at three bucks a hand, you can only win so much, but whatever it was, I was winning it. By the end of the shoe, I looked at the pile of chips in front of me, instantly remembered why they call it "gambling," and grabbed up my chips like a kid standing under a split piñata. I went directly to the cashier and, when all was said and done, I took those poor casino folks for a little over three hundred dollars. It might as well have been a million. I had never had that much money in my hands. Making sure that no one was watching, I jammed the crisp bills into my jeans.

In all my excitement, I had forgotten about Vinnie and Tom. I went back to the table. Tom seemed to be holding the same fifteen or twenty bucks he had started with. Vinnie, however, was gone. In his spot was an older guy in a very bad hairpiece wearing a light-blue polyester sport coat and loafers. The dude seemed to be doing his best Burt Lancaster imitation, trying way too hard to impress the much younger redheaded girl who had taken my seat. I slipped behind Tom, saying, "How you doing?" As if I didn't know. "Okay. Pretty good. Vinnie got killed, though."

Apparently it was too much for Vinnie, who had held at twenty with the dealer showing fifteen only to see his chips be wiped away when she pulled a six. According to Tom, Vinnie grunted, "Fuck this, I'm getting wasted," and took off.

I stood behind Tom as he was dealt two aces. Following the blackjack tip card we had all copied and were carrying with us,

Tom doubled his bet and split the aces. He had all of six bucks on the table. The dealer dealt him two kings and then broke. "Oh yeah," Tom said, flashing a grin. "Let's roll." In about two hours at the blackjack table, Tom had won a princely sum of nine dollars, a whopping good night in our basement card game but not quite enough to buy a round of beers in the barroom big time of a real casino.

After poking around a bit, we found Vinnie near a roulette wheel talking up another cocktail waitress and scarfing down free drinks. I pried him from the girl and had him and Tom follow me into a stall in the men's room where I pulled out my winnings.

"Un-fucking-believable, Bro. Let's get out of here," Vinnie said, pumped. On the way out, I yanked them over to a bar on the outer edge of the casino and used some of my winnings to buy a round of Jack Daniels shots.

"You don't need to spend your winnings on us, Bro," Tom said. "Take it home and save it."

"Fuck that," said Vinnie, punching Tom in the shoulder.

"Yeah, okay, maybe you're right, Vin," Tom said. How about one more round of Jack, Bro?"

Not knowing if I would ever have this amount of money in my pocket again, I could think of no better way to spend it. I pulled a twenty out of my pocket and flagged down the bartender.

A few more drinks later and with a good chunk of the money that I had won having already been given back at the bar, we called it a night. With my two buddies serving as sidemen, the three of us booked from Resorts back to the Brighton House, laughing "like banshees" the entire way.

# FOURTEEN

The music stopped. Finally. After a few uncomfortable moments of shifting silence, the rabbi walked down the middle aisle from the back of the room toward the front. Tom's casket was set just below the podium, a bit difficult to see from my spot in the back, which suited me just fine. I really did not want to look at the thing. It was bad enough that I had to see all the photos of Tom at different ages swarming around his dead body. There were multiple collages of these grouped photos, all neatly arranged left to right by decade in a way that only Lianne could have done: Tom and his mom in the yard, Tom with his dad outside the church, Tom and Lianne, Tom and the kids. Somehow she even found a way to include a poster full of pictures of Tom with the rest of us. There was one person, however, who did not make the photo array. Tom never really liked his brother, Paul. Then again, neither did we.

Paul was two years older than his brother and a senior at Sherbrook when I joined the card game. He and Tom looked a lot alike. Each had gotten their dad's sharp facial features, a sharp jawline, green-blue eyes, and a nose that turned ever so slightly to the left. Where Tom wore his hair hand-brushed across his head from right to left, Paul cut his short so that it stuck up in the front. But the most striking difference between the two brothers was not immediately noticeable—the "likability chromosome," that intangible piece of Tom's personality, whatever it was that Tom had that drew people to him, was missing in Paul. A bit of a loner and probably better off that way, Paul spent a lot of his after-school time working at a Shell gas station in an area of town called Hillandale, not too far from school. As far as I could see, he really didn't seem to do much of anything other than go to school, go to work, and watch cartoons. You heard me right. This never sat well with me or the rest of the guys: an eighteen-year-old high school senior whose favorite downtime activity was keeping up with the comings and goings of Bugs Bunny and the Road Runner.

Paul and Tom didn't really have a bad relationship. They just didn't seem to have any relationship at all. Before their mom died, we played a lot of cards at Tom's house, and every time we inevitably could hear Paul cackling away at his cartoons. His bedroom was adjacent to the basement room where we played, and to get upstairs to the kitchen or the bathroom, he would have to squeeze by eight of us, all crammed around a couple of folding card tables that Tom pushed together and covered with one of his mom's red and green holiday tablecloths. I can't say that I ever heard Paul say as much as a word to his brother. Not one. When he did talk it was usually to spout off endlessly about what he and "his buddies" were doing. It's one thing to be a sad, pathetic sort of guy; then we might have felt sorry for him. But Paul didn't come across that way at all. He was a big, loudmouthed, bragging dickhead. Even worse, we all knew that every story about him and his buddies was utter bullshit, created in Paul's own self-absorbed fantasyland. Whenever he would come in and get going, we usually listened, nodding our heads and trying as hard as possible not to laugh, all the while knowing full well that the only buddies the asshole really had lived inside a television set.

We all knew that Paul had a major love jones for a girl in our class named Kristen. Sadly for him, Kristen had a thing of her own, but the thing was for Vinnie and MKat, or MKat and Vinnie, whichever way you wanted to look at it and depending on who was telling the story. Kristen was a nice enough girl. She didn't have much to say, but she was very pretty in an untouchable cool blonde sort of way. Knowing that the entire male population of school would run into traffic just for a chance to roll around in the grass with her, Kristen had about two hundred wallet-sized photos made of her class picture and handed them out to almost anyone who asked. That way, when any of us opened our wallets, there she was, smiling with that feathered blonde hair tussled around her face and washing over her shoulders. Paul did not get a picture.

One Friday night just before our junior year ended, we met up at Tom's for some cards and beers. As the host, Tom provided the cards, the basement, and his all-time favorite, Pringles Newfangled Potato Chips. Pressed and stacked into a can, Pringles tasted to me like salty wood chips. For some reason, Tom could never get enough of them, and you could count on a few cans of Pringles for every game at Tom's house.

Since Lew's Market was directly on the way to Tom's from

Stonegate, Vinnie, Wocky, and I were tasked with grabbing a couple cases of beer. Aside from location, Lew's had two legs up on the competition. Not only was the beer so cold that the cans stuck to your fingers when you pulled them out of the refrigerator case, but Lew, an aging mongrel of a guy with cheeks that wrinkled and drooped below his neck, could not care less how old you were as long as you could pay in cash. He also had a way of running all the words in a sentence together without taking a breath, making it nearly impossible to understand what he was saying. That is, until he told you how much you owed for the beer. That was clear as a bell.

As always, Lew was on a wooden stool behind the register as we bounded into the store.

"What's happening, Lew?" I asked.

"*Nahamuchwhuabowyoufellaz?*"

No idea.

Vinnie and Wocky went to the back, looking for what was on sale.

Always a little nervous that he might try to card us, I did my best to have a conversation with the old fucker. "Been busy?"

"*Aaahpreedygoodahthinknotsurenotcounteddumoneyyeh.*"

I nodded.

Vinnie and Wock were up front in no time, each with a cold case of Budweiser over their shoulders.

Lew looked at the two of them. "Twelve-forty with tax."

That I understood. I dug into my wallet and paid the man, and off we went.

After a few hours of cards at Tom's, Paul came out of his room in some burgundy Sears Toughskins jeans and a collared shirt tucked in with a thick, black leather belt pulled way too tight. We were all flying pretty high by that time, having sucked down a couple of

Buds each, when Paul started ranting to us about how he was going out to see Kristen and a friend of hers. At least a few beers in, MKat decided that he just was not having it tonight. "Really," he said, pausing to make sure Paul could not miss the sarcasm. "Where you two going?"

Paul looked at him and said nothing.

"Seriously, cartoon man, what are you and your girlfriend doing tonight? You're a big fucking talker, so fill us all in."

Paul still said nothing.

"What, no story?" Nothing about you and your boys? You and Kristen heading out so you can get laid? Nothing?" MKat paused. "Bullshitting motherfucker."

"Fuck you, man," Paul shot back. "It's none of your fucking business." From overhearing many of our card game discussions, no doubt, Paul knew Kristen was, shall we say, spending some quality time with both MKat and Vinnie.

He was pissed, but not pissed enough to do anything but go back into his room. We heard the door lock click, then an "*eeebuduh, eeebuduh, eeebuduh. That's all, folks.*" The *Looney Tunes* theme was blaring.

The rabbi, whom I actually recognized from my last Danzansky-Goldberg Memorial Chapel funeral a couple years earlier, leaned over at the first pew and said who knows what to Lianne and the girls. Then he stopped for a second or two and bowed his head as he passed Tom on the way to the podium. Once he got there, he paused and fumbled with the microphone. There was a quick pop of that squeaky feedback sound followed by a generic welcome that this guy seemed to have down pat and a few prayers in Hebrew, then English.

"Tom Porter was a good man. He loved his wife. He loved his children."

Christ, I thought, here we go again. Patented speech number nine.

The rabbi continued. "As you all know, Tom's parents died when he was in high school. He went to college, met and fell in love with Lianne, and made the choice to convert to Judaism. Tom and Lianne raised two beautiful children. He was a successful businessman."

Actually, now I was starting to develop a certain appreciation for this guy. A person's entire life—front to back—in about four sentences. Impressive.

After another seven minutes reminiscing about Tom (or Bill or Steve or whomever), the rabbi-in-a-box opened up the floor.

"Anyone who wishes to talk about Tom and his life is free to come up and do so. It is only appropriate, though, that we begin with Tom's lifelong best friend and the person he looked up to as a young boy after his parents passed."

Well, now I was interested. Which one of us was his best friend? It could have been Vinnie or me. Possibly one of the other guys. But who was Tom's mentor? Certainly not me. I never had much to say by way of guidance. I'm embarrassed about this now, but I don't think that I ever talked to Tom about his parents' deaths or his new life at his uncle's house. How did it feel when he had to pack up and donate his parents' things? I had no idea. In fact, for all the time over the years that we spent playing cards, running the streets of Atlantic City, and travelling on our annual golf trips, I can hardly remember more than a handful of serious, real-life discussions. I recalled making fun of each other a lot; swapping stories about sex; talking sports, mothers, girlfriends, and more; but shockingly little that concerned business, loss, kids, or marriage troubles. Nothing of the sort. We knew. We saw. We abstained. It was almost as if we all understood that our time together was not to be penetrated by life's difficulties. No decision or rule was made or articulated. I think we all just knew that our time was just that—our time. Whatever problems, pressures, or conflicts we all were experiencing in our day-to-day lives, well, they didn't have a seat at the card game. Now I wondered if that was right.

The rabbi continued. "But not for this man, Tom may have never found his way to a fulfilled life of love and family. Paul, please come up and talk to us about your brother."

Needless to say, a literal chorus of whispered commentary erupted all around me.

Vinnie: "Get the fuck out of here."

MKat: "If the guy wasn't dead before, you can bet he is now."

Mark: "Well, that's odd."

Don: "Shhh. It's his brother."

Baldwin: "Yeah, but Tom hated the guy."

Wocky: "We all hated the fucking guy."

Vinnie hummed the *Looney Tunes* theme.

MKat giggled.

I blew out my breath and waited.

# FIFTEEN

Paul walked up the steps to the podium from the left, opposite Lianne and the kids. He sauntered up in a gray suit, from the Men's Warehouse no doubt, and a tie so perfect that I just knew someone else had knotted it for him. The Windsor knot did nothing to hide the obvious—draped over his narrow shoulders, the suit was clearly off by a couple of sizes. He still had the same odd way of walking where his back swayed, his neck was sort of spindly and straight, and his head stuck out at an angle like a groundhog looking for his shadow. Though he hadn't said a word, there was no doubt in my mind that he was still the same pompous bullshitter who made up stories while squeezing past us as we played cards in metal folding chairs.

Sure enough, Paul stepped behind the microphone and rested both of his hands on the podium as if ready to give an address to Congress. As he reached into his pocket and pulled out a wad of papers, I looked down into my lap and amused myself, half expecting to hear some loopy story about how Paul made it with a gorgeous girl on his boss's desk in the office.

After unfolding the notes in front of him, Paul peered over his reading glasses, scanned the room, and smiled. For a second, the smile was a lot like Tom's, sort of crinkled, with just a sliver of top teeth showing through. The smiles were also different, though. Where Tom's crooked grin always exuded friendship and sincerity, Paul's smile put me in mind of the bad guy who inevitably gets killed in the shootout at the end of a Western. As he looked around, it was clear that he finally saw MKat and the rest of us in the back. He made a weird grimace, let out a kind of "humph" noise, and began to speak.

# SIXTEEN
## 1978

**W**henever we played at Don's house, we could trust his mom to take care of us. Always looking like she just stepped out from under a massive dryer at an old-time beauty parlor with a head of thick, lightly frosted hair and friendly, big brown eyes, Judy Hoffman greeted everyone with a smile. Just inside the front door, the walls of the small foyer were decorated with several pageant photos from her days as Atlantic City's Miss Chelsea. Years had passed since she had won her crown, but she seemed pretty to me, in a "mom" sort of way.

"How you doing, Bro?" she asked as I walked through the front door around ten that night. I always loved that a lady called me "Bro." Still, the fact that everyone really liked Don's mom didn't qualify her for a pass in the never-ending "I want to fuck your mother" conversation. By the time I got there, most everyone else was already sitting down in the kitchen inhaling the plated assortment of chicken salad, tuna, and turkey sandwiches she had made.

"Boys, there's plenty more in the fridge, so don't be shy," Mrs. Hoffman said to a room full of silent swallowing.

"And if anyone is drinking beer, you just stay here the night. I don't want anyone driving. You can all sleep downstairs." She said goodbye and left for her bedroom. A small split-level house, it was easy to hear from the kitchen when her bedroom door closed. As soon as it did, we started in. Tom was first, modifying an old Bobby Sherman tune just a bit and singing, "*Judy, Judy, Judy, do you love me...*"

Baldwin countered, "Mmm, Miss Chelsea. I got another pageant for you to win..."

"I don't know why she thinks we would be drinking beer," Wocky said as he opened up a Rolling Rock pony.

"I'm in for staying over," Tom said.

"There's a shock," Mark put in. "Free dinner, free breakfast, and the hope that Don's mom will come down in the middle of the night and jerk you off."

"I'm in for that," I said.

"Me, too," said Wocky, "but only if she wears her crown."

"Come on, guys. That's my mom," Don pleaded. "She can hear us."

"Yeah, okay, but the question is whether she wants to fuck us," Tom said.

"Jesus, Tom. Really. Stop." Don was still pleading.

Recognizing that Don was at the end of this particular rope, Baldwin finished shuffling both decks. "Let's play, boys," he said. "My deal."

Sometime just before midnight, Vinnie and MKat came bopping in. Both were smiling uncontrollably, like one of them just hit a big number on the roulette wheel. They each sat down and grabbed a beer, both still grinning ear to ear. Neither said a word. Done singing, Tom was the first to ask, "Yeah, so? What's up?"

More smiles. More silence.

Looking at the two of them, we just had to laugh. We had no idea, but whatever it was got us all laughing just looking at the two of those morons.

Tom tried again. "What the fuck? You going to tell us?"

At that point, MKat just stared and grinned. Vinnie could contain himself no longer and tried to spit it out, laughing loudly as beer came out of his nose. "He called her Amy," he squealed. MKat picked his head up, tears in his eyes from laughing, and nodding in a way that made it clear to most of us that yes, MKat called another girl by his girlfriend's name.

Tom, however, was still not getting it. "What do you mean? Who called who Amy?"

"Listen," Vinnie started. "Here's the deal." The rest of us shut up and listened.

It appeared that Vinnie and MKat were due to have a double date with Amy and Kristen. Although the rest of the school was aware, Amy must have missed the memo. She had no idea that Kristen alternated her free time between Vinnie and MKat. Amy got sick and told MKat she couldn't make it but invited him over to watch a movie. Not exactly the king of empathy, MKat declined, telling her he was just going to go to bed early. He didn't want to catch whatever she had, after all.

Vinnie and Kristen picked him up around 7:30 p.m. with a couple of six packs of Michelob but no plans. "No plans" to those two often meant a ride over to the golf course at Indian Spring Country Club. Not real fancy like some of the higher-end clubs, there was no gate to block the entrance after hours. From the brightly lit "INDIAN SPRING COUNTRY CLUB" sign, it was about a mile or so of dark blacktop service road to the top of the hill to a fork that led to a clubhouse to the left. If you took the split off to the right, the road extended back down a hill, behind some tennis courts, and to the edge of the golf course. According to Vinnie and MKat, it was a great place to take girls. The golf course was dark, remote, and completely empty at night. The rest of us only knew about the golf course because MKat and Vinnie told us. They were the only ones that were ever lucky enough to take girls out there.

When MKat got in the car he asked Kristen if she had been out with Paul. She responded with, "Uh, sure. When my tits fall off."

Vinnie parked near the bottom group of tennis courts and the three of them walked out to a secluded spot behind a big sand trap next to the seventeenth hole. After a few beers, Vinnie had to pee, so he took a walk around the back of the green into a cluster of trees. Gifted with great situational awareness and most definitely touched with attention deficit disorder long before anyone knew what that was, Vinnie got sidetracked and spent about twenty minutes trying to catch a box turtle in the dark before heading back to the MKat and Kristen. He no doubt figured twenty minutes was long enough.

"I was coming back to the hill," he said, "and it was pretty quiet except I could hear some, you know, fucking around noises." He was smiling again.

"MKat and Kristen? You left them there?" Tom asked. I think he was taking notes.

"Uh. No," Vinnie said. "Not exactly." Like a commando, Vinnie tucked himself behind a bush. "An azalea, I think," he said. "Anyway, Kristen was on top of MKat with her top off. She was riding him like fucking Roy Rogers."

My boy Vin sure knew how to tell a story. "Actually," he told us, "I started jerking off. Just over my pants, though."

"Whoa," Mark said, clearly as beside himself as the rest of us. "Hold on a minute. Let me get this straight. MKat is fooling around with her. You're watching the whole thing and rubbing your dick from behind a bush?"

"It was more like a tree," Vinnie said. "Jesus. And it's not like I yanked it out. Like I said, it was over my pants, for Chrissake. "

Somehow, to Vinnie, the fact that he was masturbating while watching his friend have sex was okay since his penis was still in his pants. Fair enough.

"Any more questions, fags?" Vinnie continued. "So, yeah. After a few minutes, they're really going at it. MKat is all over Kristen's breasts like a madman. I can't even see them. Then out of nowhere, I swear to Christ, I hear this big grunt and then, 'Amy, I love you.'"

"Aaah!" We were all in hysterics, laughing and crying at the same time.

# SEVENTEEN

"**M**y brother, Tom," Paul began, "was my best friend."

"*Oy*. And he banged Kristen in the ass, too," MKat whispered. His disgust toward Paul had not faded over the years.

"After Dad died, Tom and I were inseparable. We did everything together throughout most of high school. Tom had some good friends, but we were best friends."

I turned my head, nodded at MKat, and whispered, "Don't do it."

"Yeah, yeah, yeah." His teeth were clenched.

Vinnie leaned forward and chimed in, "The guy is still a douche, Bro."

Paul continued. "When Dad died, it was really tough on both of us. Tom pretty much stayed home a lot and hung out with Mom and me. For a while, we were okay. Mom cooked at nights for us and helped with homework. We even took a trip, just the three of us, to

Disney World. It was great. Tom and me rode Space Mountain over and over again. Mom was scared of roller coasters, so she waited outside. It seemed like we would be okay. But then Mom started drinking. First, it was with dinner, and then before you knew it, she was pouring something into her juice in the morning. One time she accidentally gave Tom her orange juice. Tom spit it out, saying it tasted horrible. Turned out it was half-filled with vodka. From there, the drinking just got worse and neither one of us could really watch it. I got a TV for my room and stayed in there a lot. Tom buddied up with a bunch of guys. They all played cards and went out together. Sometimes I went along, but I think Tom wanted to just get away from everything at home."

Mostly Tom wanted to get away from him, I thought.

"He talked a lot about his friends, the stuff they did together, going to Pop's and places like that. They made fun of me a lot for staying in my room. I knew they were just joking with me, though. Right?" He paused and looked up from his notes, straight at us. He seemed angry. Really angry.

# EIGHTEEN
## 1978

**B**y our junior year in high school, it was not at all difficult to find places that would serve alcohol to just about anyone who had facial hair. One of those places, Pop's Pizza, was located in a dark and partially paved parking lot near the intersection of two main arteries, Georgia Avenue and University Boulevard, running through Wheaton, Maryland. Bipolar in nature, Wheaton was a sprawl of single-family homes and new townhouse collections intermittently dotted with fast-food joints, gas stations, and tire stores. With its main attraction a bowling alley known as the Wheaton Triangle Bowling Lanes, it was not really a town so much as a place that you had to go through to get somewhere else.

On one of those "we got nothing better to do" type of nights, MKat, Don, Tom, and I finished some duckpin bowling at the Triangle, rode around for a little while, and discovered Pop's, partially hidden behind a circa-1960s strip center that featured Fannie's

Fabrics as its anchor store. Not only did Pop's turn out to be a great spot for cheap, thin-crusted pizza, dumpy waitresses, and cold beer, it immediately became the place for us to just hang out, talk about girls, and, surprisingly, do some very bad singing.

Back then, Friday night was boys' nights out and Saturday was date night. Of course, most of us often couldn't find dates and those of us who did made sure to end things by midnight so there would be enough time to meet up at Pop's before last call.

At the time, I was in the midst of an inexplicable relationship with a very pretty girl from another local high school. Like some mystical creature from a kid's fantasy book, Maggie had fiery auburn hair and cat-green eyes. She was one of those girls that just made a kid's neck hurt. Every time she walked by, you just had to turn and look. I had met her at a party a few weeks earlier and, for some reason, probably boredom, she seemed to enjoy being with me.

Although I had no idea what she was thinking, spending time with me (at five feet ten and one hundred and thirty pounds, with boots on, I was no one's idea of a stud), I tried not to give it too much thought. I just figured I would enjoy the ride as long as I could, knowing full well that my "Maggie clock" was ticking. Sure enough, when Maggie found out that I went to meet the boys at Pop's after dropping her off that night, the bell tolled and my run was over.

I got to Pop's around 12:30 a.m., parked, and entered, as always, through the swinging hollow wood doors. Most of the guys were already there. Tom, Don, Wocky, and Baldwin were at a corner table. Their waitress, whom we dubbed "The Scarf" because, of course, she was always wearing one around her neck, was taking orders. The Scarf was about five feet five inches and a solid one hundred and eighty pounds. She had one of those scraggly, roly-poly types of faces and cheeks that looked like they were always full of applesauce.

Mark was hovering over the jukebox, dropping in quarters. A few empty beer mugs and a drained pitcher or two littered the table. I sat down and gave a nod to The Scarf. "We got three large pies and four pitchers coming, Bro." Baldwin, as usual, had it all under control. The Scarf crinkled her forehead and looked at me. "You eighteen?" she asked.

"Yup. Same as last night, ma'am." I was not trying to be too big of a smartass, but I could afford to be a modest-sized one. The Scarf had stopped asking to see our IDs a long time ago.

Vinnie was not there, so Tom happily ordered extra cheese. The man loved cheese on just about everything and was always handcuffed when Vinnie was around. Long before anyone knew what "lactose intolerant" meant, Vinnie would frequently run— and I do mean run—to the bathroom after downing a few slices of Pop's pie. It would be another year before he took to toting around little plastic baggies of what he called "cheese pills" and washing about a dozen of them down with a cold beer whenever we put our orders in.

Mark was a drummer and loved banging his fingers on the table like makeshift drumsticks. He also fancied himself a musical director of sorts and made sure all of were ready whenever the Doobie Brothers' "Black Water" started to spin. Just like on the record, Don would use his silverware to make a wind-chime kind of sound to get the song going. The raft would be "floatin'." Then as if on cue, Mark joined in, *"Oh Mississippi,"* drawing out the "i." After that, Baldwin took the lead. *"Black Water keeps rollin'."*

I really could not sing a lick, but it didn't matter. None of us held back and we belted out the chorus.

It never failed. Midway through, everyone in the place was singing along. By the time we got to *"oh pretty mamma,"* even The Scarf was humming to the Doobies as she dropped our pitchers on the table.

# NINETEEN

Paul had much to say about his relationship with Tom. He even seemed sincere when he spoke about how he felt bad when they went their separate ways once their mother died, not really seeing each other once they moved into their uncle's house. "Even though we didn't spend as much time together, Tom always talked to me. I loved those times when no one else was around—none of his buddies, no girlfriends, no one."

Another shot at us boys, I guess.

For no reason I could think of, Paul's little eulogy then took a religious turn. "Even though Paul technically converted to be a Jew, I think in honor of our Catholic upbringing, he would want me to offer something from the New Testament. In the Book of Wisdom, the Bible says, 'The Righteous One, though he die early, shall be at rest ....'"

Aside from the "converted to be a Jew" comment that was all

by itself irritating to me and, I am sure, slightly offensive to most everyone in the place, it was at that point I was sure that Paul must have felt this was his "fifteen minutes of fame." He was going to stand up there and say whatever he wanted, no matter how off-putting to those of us prevented by Danzansky-Goldberg Memorial Chapel's etiquette from throwing our prayer books at him. Maybe recognizing that many in the place were Jews, including his dead brother's wife and kids, Paul calmed the Catholic undertow and went back to talking about himself again.

"Tom knew everything about me. I told him how I felt about Dad, that I hated him for leaving us and blamed him for making Mom sick. One time I even think I told Tom that I thought it was Dad who really killed our mom." That comment led to a collective and extended gasp from everyone listening.

"What a fucking asshole," MKat hissed.

"Yeah, that's great," Mark said. "The guy blames his father for killing his mother at his brother's funeral." It felt even more awkward, put that way.

Oblivious, Paul plowed ahead.

"Tom talked a lot about his friends, the fun they had together. Maybe I was jealous, but I was proud that he was able to move on a bit and make his own way. It wasn't easy for either of us."

He took a breath, looked up, and then focused on Lianne and the girls. "He told me about this girl he loved, that he knew he wanted to marry, even in high school. Lianne, he loved you since he was seventeen. There was never anyone else." To his credit, Paul seemed to be digging out a little from the earlier hole.

Okay, this was nice, but personally I'd long since been ready for Paul to tie things up. Then he said something that smacked me and, I'm sure, the rest of the guys, square across the face.

"He has a lot of friends here. Everyone that knew Tom liked

him. But no one knew him like I did. We didn't just hang and laugh all the time about nothing. That wasn't us. There was more to it than that." Shot number two.

"We helped each other through tough times, the real tough times. We helped each other after our dad died and after our mom died. When he and Lianne had trouble in high school, it was me who helped him get through it. I was the *only* one there for him.

"Just him and me," he continued. "He loved me, and I loved him. That's why he came to me when things got tough." He peered over those reading glasses and stared our way.

"What the fuck?" Wocky elbowed me in the side.

"You got to be kidding," MKat whispered.

I knew what he meant. So did Vinnie and Don. We kept quiet.

# TWENTY
## 1979

By mid-fall of our senior year, I had built a little muscle and gotten a better haircut, and began to draw more than passing interest from The Tahitian Treat. It also didn't hurt that all the other guys in school had aged out. The Treat wasn't going to date a junior.

It began with a smile and a few across-the-hallway stares at each other, but I had such a limited amount of experience to draw on that I had no idea what to do about this coveted, newfound attention. I didn't really do anything. I mean, she smiled and I stared back, but the thought of actually going over and talking to her never even crossed my mind. After a good couple of weeks of the flirty, non-conversational back-and-forth, though, it was Barbara who made the first move. She walked over to me one Friday afternoon. "You going over to Pop's tonight?" she asked me.

I didn't even know how she had heard of Pop's. Somehow I was able to pinch out the word "sure" in response.

"Well, me, Carla, and a couple other girls are heading over too. Maybe I'll see you there."

"Uh. Yeah. Sure. Great." I must have sounded like I was on headed home on the short bus with the rest of the special-ed kids.

She tossed a purse over her shoulder and walked down the hallway.

"Smooth, steed," MKat said. He had observed the entire painful episode, and, having replaced "stud" with our own inside sarcastic version of the word, he chuckled and put his arm around my shoulder. "Let's roll."

Except for Tom, the rest of us played cards at my house for a couple of hours that night, then went over to Pop's. Lianne had decided she didn't like being alone every Friday night, so the two of them were supposed to head out to see Tom's favorite movie, *Animal House*, probably for the fifth or sixth time.

We got to Pop's around 10:30. Having gone to the early movie, Tom and Lianne were already there, holding the big table near the jukebox. "Thought I would join in on your boys' night," she yapped, obviously pleased with herself and using that annoying nails-on-the-chalkboard voice that drove me nuts.

"Sure. Great," Mark responded, not meaning a word of it.

"Absolutely. Happy to have you," Don chimed in and, as the "nice guy" he is, meant every word of it.

We sat down. The Scarf nodded from across the room and dropped a few laminated menus on the table. As usual, the menus were hard to read, the print having faded and the plastic browned from, well, I am not really sure. Not that we needed them anyway.

Per our tradition, Baldwin started ordering for everyone. Somewhere between "large" and "pepperoni," Lianne cut him off. "We'll also have a large Italian salad. What kind of dressing do you have?"

She placed her hand like a muzzle on top of Tom's. Tom looked at us with sort of an "I know, I'm fucked" look but said nothing.

Even The Scarf looked annoyed. "Salad dressing? We got oil. We got vinegar."

I think she was being sarcastic but couldn't really be sure. After all, no one ever ordered a salad at Pop's.

Right about then, Barbara and a few of her friends came in through the double doors across the restaurant. Tight jeans, high heels, and a scooped Bee Gees T-shirt, she looked fucking amazing.

"Hey, JB," Barbara called out. "Mind if we sit with you guys?" Backed by a few beers' worth of courage, I was topped with a lot more confidence than I had exhibited at school earlier in the day. I took a deep breath, waved them over, and grabbed the girls a couple of chairs. Barbara skipped past the chairs and squeezed in next to me on the red plastic booth seat.

A couple of hours went by in what seemed like a couple of minutes. Barbara and I talked, we flirted, and we stared. At some point during my lust-clouded haze, she leaned in and asked, "Want to go somewhere?"

I was up and handing Baldwin some money before she finished the question.

"Oh. We'll come, too." Lianne screeched, yanking Tom's arm.

"Aw, fuck," I thought to myself. Not exactly what I had in mind.

I opened the Mustang's door and Barbara slid into the front seat while Tom and Lianne scrambled tightly into the back. Before I could get out of the parking lot, Tom and Lianne were going at it behind me. I hit the gas and pushed that little four-cylinder Ford as fast as I felt comfortable. I knew exactly where I was going. When we got to the golf course, I remembered what

Vinnie and MKat told me and drove down the darker road toward the lower tennis courts. Lianne and Tom jumped out, ambled through some bushes and over the hill into a fairway. Barb got out of the passenger side of the car and we essentially tackled each other on the still warm hood of my car. Within a few frenzied minutes, her jeans were off and the Bee Gees top was inside out on my windshield.

Even now, I still get horny whenever I hear any song from *Saturday Night Fever* on the radio.

Yanking off my boots was no easy task, but we were persistent. Pants down to my ankles, I was still a gentleman, laying my jacket under Barbara as she lay back onto the hood. It was over in just a moment, but it was a pretty great moment. For me, anyway.

Once my golden retriever-like panting died down, I stood up and pulled her naked body into me, wrapping my arms around her. The Tahitian Treat and I had just had sex and now we were about to ...

Sadly, the moment came to a crashing halt when I saw a flashlight and heard what I thought was a golf cart coming down the path toward the car.

"Shit. Tom," I called, doing that yell-whisper thing. "Get your ass up here. Someone's coming."

I could barely make them out coming up the hill, Tom in just his white underwear, Lianne, with no shirt on, breasts bouncing as she ran toward me. Even though I didn't care much for her, that didn't stop me from admiring the view.

Aware of my attention and as pleasant as ever, Lianne jumped into the backseat and shot me an annoyed look. "Come on, idiot. Put your adolescent eyeballs back in your head," she said. "Let's go."

All in the car, we drove up the hill past what I assumed was a security guard. "Fucking Vinnie," I whispered to myself. I had done exactly what he told me. He said there would be no one around.

While we were heading back out and toward the club entrance, my jeans seemed really tight and were riding up my crotch. I figured it was what just what was left of my post-intercourse erection until I looked at Barbara, who still looked spectacularly sexy while grinning and reaching around to hook her bra. She looked in my eyes then down at my lap and laughed for a quick second. "You want to give me my jeans back?"

Not unlike our fleeting moment on the hood of my car, my relationship with The Tahitian Treat came to a rapid conclusion. She and I never got together again. We smiled when we walked past each other in the hallway and gave a quick hug at a party here or there. Unfortunately, there was no more sex on the hood of my car, or anywhere else for that matter.

For a couple of weeks, Tom and I kept the events of that night between us. With both of us having lost our virginity at the same time, we proudly high-fived and nodded our heads whenever we passed each other in school. The shine wore off about two and a half months later, though. Lianne was pregnant.

One Friday night after our golf course excursion, I was sitting around a table at Pop's with Vinnie, Tom, and Don, waiting for the others to show up.

"What the fuck?" Hearing the story for the first time, Vinnie was apoplectic. "Pregnant? Your first time and she gets pregnant? Why couldn't you just pull out like the rest of us?"

Tom was clearly distraught, compulsively running his hand through long blond hair that waved right to left across his forehead.

"What am I going to do? She's really upset. She doesn't want to tell her parents. If they find out, I'll never be able to see her again."

After a few seconds of silence, Vinnie chimed in. "Well, there's your silver lining."

I had to agree. "Got that right," I said, nodding. Despite the sincere upset and worry on his face, and even though I was acutely aware that this was a moment he really needed some support, I couldn't help but think that Tom would be better off without Lianne.

Even Don, ever the one with more sincerity than the rest of us combined, let the moment pass. "Fucking steeds, you two," he said.

Vinnie got up and put his arm around Tom, half-nelson style, and gave him a big noogie. "You guys will work it out."

However Tom worked it out, we were not a part of it. Sometime after, Lianne had an abortion.

The four of us didn't talk about it again. Not then, anyway.

# TWENTY-ONE

Paul removed his glasses from the end of his nose and put them back in his jacket pocket. After folding up the papers from his speech, he peered our way one more time. It was a weird and smarmy sort of look. I couldn't tell if he was truly sad that his brother was dead or in some twisted way jacked up about laying a big boomer on a few of us. He stepped down from the podium, kissed Lianne and the girls, and then lumbered back to his seat at the end of the first pew.

No one else walked up to speak.

After a few moments of painful silence, the rabbi moved back behind the microphone. "Anyone else? A lot of you were Tom's friends. This is a wonderful time to share your stories about him. Doing so is a *mitzvah*, a gift to his family."

I looked at Wocky, then at MKat. Nothing. Vinnie was quiet.

Steve was crying. Don was patting his back and rolling his eyes. "All right, all right, Baldwin."

Mark was annoyed. "It's not like someone died or anything." Bad joke. Always a guy who enjoyed his own jokes, he laughed and stood up.

"Fuck," he said. "I'll go next. Pussies."

The man squeezed through the aisle, buttoned his jacket, and strolled toward the microphone like he owned the place. Come to think of it, maybe he does.

Mark put his hands on the side of the podium and leaned into the microphone. "I knew Tom Porter. Tom Porter was a friend of mine." We all knew where Mark was going. The man loved to parrot great movie lines, impersonate famous actors, and imitate those special moments in history. He looked up, pointed at no one in particular, and did his best Senator Lloyd Bentsen debating Dan Quayle: "You people are no Tom Porter." I am not sure it was really all that funny, but Mark sure did break the cloud of gloom hanging over the place after Paul finished. Everyone cracked up.

# TWENTY-TWO
## 1979

In the late spring of 1979, the Sherbrook High School Senior Class loaded into six Trailways buses and ventured south to Daytona Beach, Florida. This annual rite of passage for high school graduates, the "Senior Trip" was at least as important to a high school experience as graduation itself. At Sherbrook, we even formed a Senior Trip Committee more than a year in advance. Tom, Mark, and I had immediately signed up, having finally found an important way to spend our valuable free time, and became the committee's official "cochairmen." We were both impressed with the sudden explosion of school spirit, hoping that it would lead to us enjoying a few other explosions of our own once we got down South.

Our committee immediately went to work. Many afternoons were spent with Tom, Mark, and me playing blackjack for a dime a hand while two other guys we didn't know hunted for hotel rooms on the phone.

Ultimately, we found a Holiday Inn willing to host the trip if we could commit to one hundred students and, something we had not thought of, faculty chaperones. *Ruh roh.* The three of us thought we were sunk.

"None of our teachers is going to be dumb enough to skip their vacation," Tom said. "Let's just forget it."

Mark was equally despondent. "Sounds like we will be spending a lot of time at Pop's," he said.

I almost agreed with them. It was hard for me to believe that any teacher who spent his life with high school students would actually give up a vacation to spend thirty hours in a bus and a week in Florida with those same students. Three months prior to our departure, we had only one faculty chaperone. The outlook was grim, but I was not ready to pack it in. Mark, on the other hand, held up a white flag and left the group. "I'm out" was all he said when I called one afternoon to find out why he wasn't at one of our afternoon get-togethers.

After much thought, Tom and I went out and did what any natural leaders would have done in our situation. We begged. Literally. We went to our principal, good old Dr. Stephen Mitchell, and told him of our plight. A true '50s caricature, Dr. Mitchell wore thick, black-rimmed glasses, a suit with pants a bit too short, and jet-black hair greased back with a fistful of Brylcreem. The funny thing about Dr. Mitchell was we all knew he was there, but no one ever saw him. Except for an assembly here or there, he was kept out of sight, a lot like a crazy relative.

There was a spindly old wooden bench just outside his office and to the left of the "Dr. Mitchell, Principal" sign. I knocked on the locked door and promptly heard a muffled woman's voice through a tinny speaker on the wall telling us to take a seat. After a few minutes, the woman, presumably his secretary, opened the door. She didn't say anything, just peered at me with a "you're wasting my time" expression on her face. The secretary pushed the door open a bit and turned back into the office, leaving it to me to open it the rest of the way and let Tom and me in.

The first thing I noticed as I walked toward Dr. Mitchell's office was its obsessive neatness. His metal and oak desk wasn't just clean; it showed no evidence that a person actually worked at it. Besides a pen canister with a pencil or two inside and a shiny silver water pitcher, the only things on top of the desk were Dr. Mitchell's hands. Without saying anything, he tipped his head toward the two chairs in front. I tentatively took this as an invitation to sit down. We sat. Tom didn't seem to want to say anything, so that left it to me to make the pitch. Before I could say anything, though, Dr. Mitchell started to speak.

"Son, we are here to educate young people, get them to graduate, and, for many, make sure they are ready for college," he said, hovering above me even from behind the desk as if to accentuate the differences in our positions. Dr. Mitchell was a high school principal with a lifetime career in the academic world. He was responsible for the well-being and academic progress of two thousand or so high school students. He was an important man. He had real-life adult responsibilities. He had a big desk.

My credentials were not quite as impressive. I just wanted to go to Florida with my friends and get laid.

Dr. Mitchell finished his thought, not that I didn't already get his drift. "I don't give a hoot about some trip to Daytona Beach. These days, though, those PTA folks say I have to give students a voice, so here's your chance to use yours. Say whatever it is, and then I'm going to smile and send you on your way. Understand, son?"

I understood.

I also understood another thing. This guy in front of me, in his suit and thick glasses, was no failure. Putting two and two together, I decided my best bet was to convince Dr. Mitchell that if a few hundred Sherbrook students missed out on this trip, it would be his failure, not ours.

Unbeknownst to me at the time, it was right there in Dr. Mitchell's office that I would give my first closing argument. Never the smartest or deepest thinker in the room, I was not destined to serve on the law review or graduate from law school with any kind of *cum laude* on my diploma. Like Vinnie and MKat, who excelled at hooking and reeling in smiling seventeen-year-old girls, however, I have always had a certain aptitude for telling people what they need to hear in order to get them to do what I want them to do. I leaned forward in my chair, put an elbow on his desk, and got to it.

"Dr. Mitchell, I know how important it is for you that your students are successful. Am I right?"

I looked straight into those thick glass lenses, expecting a response. I got none.

Not deterred, I kept going. "But being successful as a human being requires a balance. Success in the classroom and success out of the classroom. Right?"

Still nothing.

I pulled my chair closer to his desk and leaned in, my head craned toward our principal. "Here's the thing, Dr. Mitchell. There are a bunch of other schools around here. Their principals don't have anywhere near the experience that you have." In honesty, I had no idea who the principals of those schools were or anything about their experience, but what the hell, I was on a roll.

"My parents wanted me to come here. To your school. To Sherbrook. Not one of those other places. And do you know what the seniors at those schools are doing for spring break? Nothing. Their parents, their faculty, their principals, they don't trust them. They're not putting in any effort for their seniors. Those kids are going home for spring break. To roam around unsupervised. To drink alcohol and get into whatever trouble teenagers find when they are home for a week unsupervised with nothing to do."

He was still stone-faced, but at least I had his attention and he hadn't thrown me out yet.

"You have a chance to show something to all those parents and all those kids at the other schools. You can send a real message to the other principals and those folks down at the Board of Education. You can show them that Dr. Thomas Mitchell is a different kind of principal. That Sherbrook is a different kind of school. That Sherbrook is a place where students are not only taught, but they are trusted."

Not realizing until I was done that I had stood up at some point, I sat back down. I looked across the desk, not exactly expecting applause but certainly hoping for some response that would validate my position or maybe even recognize my budding oratorical skills.

He nodded, rubbed a nostril with his thumb, and swiveled his chair around so that his back was facing me. "Good day, son, and thank you for your input" was all he said. That was it.

We left.

A day or two after my meeting, I got a note from our assistant principal, Ed Finninger. This guy, we did see a lot. Some of us actually saw him a bit too much. He was always around, peering in lockers, showing up like a ghost in the back of classrooms, and roaming the halls, often breaking up the sloppy hallway kissing that some students seemed to enjoy. Not that I had any problem with kissing and making out, I just never understood the necessity of doing it with a chemistry book in your hand while a couple hundred high school kids walked past. Poor Wocky, who was caught one afternoon trying to head out for a couple of beers between classes, felt Finninger's personal wrath when he was suspended from school and unceremoniously banned from going on the Senior Trip.

I, on the other hand, learned early on to avoid this pudgy, balding school administrator with his too-short tie and badly-in-need-of-some-dental-work teeth. I generally steered clear of trouble as a rule, and when Finninger came my way, I immediately and gently skulked into the shadows.

Thankfully, Finninger's note was brief and sweet. I was instructed to come to the main office the following morning. After the early announcements, I would be given ninety seconds, and only ninety seconds, over the public address system to make our case to the faculty and try one last time to rustle up enough of them to volunteer to chaperone us. Finninger's note went on to say that if we did not have the requisite number of faculty volunteers by the following day, the Senior Trip would be cancelled.

Tom followed me into the office. Not much of a public speaker, he left the pitch to me. I don't remember what I said that next day after the Pledge of Allegiance. I do remember staying up much of the night before worrying about it. I also remember that it worked. A loud cheer filled the halls of school a couple of mornings later when, during the announcements, we were all told that enough faculty members did volunteer to chaperone and, yes, our Senior Trip was a go. I was, in essence, a class hero.

Our bus left for Daytona as scheduled. We were sharing a

double room that would include all of us except, of course, the blackballed Wocky. On the way down south, we decided upon a little competition. We would put together a large tally sheet to keep in our room and award points for our sexual exploits with the women of Daytona Beach. Other schools, after all, would be in Daytona that same week, which meant we were headed to a beach full of girls who didn't know us and had therefore never rejected us.

During the first few days in Daytona, most of us picked up some scattered points here and there. Not Hall of Fame numbers but enough to keep the competition interesting. An obvious favorite, MKat led the pack. Apparently, women found his mind-numbing chatter and seemingly sincere smile irresistible. He was firmly at the top of the leader board by midweek.

Then there was Brother Don, whose strategy and approach with girls was to be their friend. He was certainly successful at making friends, but unfortunately there was no slot on the tote board for friendship. Don was planted interminably in the cellar, not deriving too much comfort from the number of girls who told him he was "such a nice guy."

I would like to say that I was real threat in this competition, but that was not the case. Even with a little muscle, I was still a long shot, with odds much longer than those of MKat and Vinnie, who both had a God-given knack for striking up an interesting conversation, pouring on the perfect compliment, and smiling at just the right time. With competition like that, in fact, I was rarely getting noticed. I struggled.

By Thursday, I did catch a bit of luck on the beach when MKat and I met up with some girls from Kentucky. One of them, Kim something, seemed to like me. She had that sexy southern way of drawing out certain words and adding syllables to them. "*Can you get me a co-old bee-yuh from the coooooluh, JB?*"

I spent a full day on the beach just passing her cans of beer and listening to her talk. It didn't matter what she said, and the fact that I could see her nipples through the white bikini top didn't hurt matters either.

The girls invited us up to their room later that night. With MKat by my side working her roommate and drinking from a bathtub full of some alcoholic creation they called "Kentucky hooch," I was able to rack up a few points.

The next night, Tom got into another argument with Lianne. Earlier in the day while the rest of us were slathered with Bain de Soleil "sun jelly" and frying on the beach, Tom took her up to our room, hoping to score a few for himself. Lianne saw the tote board, blew a gasket over our immaturity, and told him that they were through. By the time we got back, Tom was gone, but none of us even thought about it, focused as we were on the latest tote board results.

No doubt crestfallen after Lianne's latest rejection, Tom drifted in and out of a couple of happy hours and ultimately ended up at a hotel pool party at the Howard Johnson's next door that was hosted by a senior class from Columbia, South Carolina. Depressed, dejected, and alone, Tom evidently attracted a South Carolina girl who was anxious to hear his troubles. Never one to focus on details, Tom told us they went back to her room and, after about an hour, he came back. He worked a few angles and calculated that he had put up a nine-point night. No one questioned him, and Tom leap-frogged to the top of the leaderboard.

On Friday, the class took a side trip to Walt Disney World. Left completely without supervision, we were free to roam the park for about twelve hours and then return to our bus by 9:00 p.m. Around 8:45 or so that night, we all piled back onto the bus. Well, all of us except one. When one of our supervisors, Mr. Pine, completed a head count, we were one body short of a full load. (Mr. Pine, another of those caricature-looking teachers of the time, showed off his academic prowess by teaching classes in typing and coaching the golf team.)

We all looked around and ultimately realized that Mark was the missing body. After replaying the day's events, MKat remembered Mark meeting up with one of the Kentucky girls in the park. Much like a Western movie hero as the film fades to black, Mark was last seen somewhere in Frontierland as the sun set.

Several of us were dispatched to go back, get into the now closed amusement park, and attempt to hunt down our missing comrade. Our efforts were unsuccessful, and we returned to the buses after about half an hour. Mark was nowhere to be found.

Making what would be a very expensive decision in today's litigious world, Mr. Pine instructed the bus driver to head out and drive us back to Daytona. Not that we all weren't worried about our friend; we were just tired. Everyone slept the entire bus ride back.

Back at our hotel, we trudged up to the room, each with a different theory about Mark's fate. Had he fallen asleep somewhere? Fallen off a roller coaster? No one knew.

We'd only been back in our room for a few minutes before the phone rang. MKat answered. We all listened in. It was Mark.

"Where the hell are you guys?" he thundered.

"Where are we?" MKat laughed. "Where are you?"

"I can't believe you left," Mark said.

Obviously, that wasn't fair. "We looked all over the fucking park for you," MKat told him. "Where'd you go?"

"Tell Tom he lost again," Mark replied. "It's Boz Scaggs time, douche. It's over, it's over now, baby." He sang and cackled more than loudly enough for the rest of us to hear it through the phone. At that moment, I could picture Mark in the lobby of some hotel, using a house phone, with his feet up on a coffee table, grinning away.

"I scored a lot of points..." Mark finally said, as though he hadn't been clear enough.

Winner, winner, chicken dinner.

# TWENTY-THREE

Mark ended his little eulogy to smiles and appreciative laughs around the room. He walked back to his seat amid a smattering of "nice job" and "short and sweet" comments. After Mark sat down, Baldwin popped right up and cleared his throat, a visual message that it was his turn to speak. Baldwin and I made some eye contact as he squeezed through the far end of the aisle past Vinnie, Pam, and a couple of other people I didn't recognize. Knowing that this kind of thing made Baldwin nervous, I nodded and mouthed, "You'll do fine." He didn't look so sure.

When he was younger, we sometimes referred to Baldwin as "Knotts" because he had more than a slight resemblance to the squirrely TV actor, Don Knotts. He hated the nickname, and no one wanted to be responsible for increasing his therapy bills, so, for the most part, we just called him "Baldwin." Having become addicted to running and weight lifting over the last ten years or so, Baldwin's body hardly resembled the gaunt and pale kid he used to be. The third of four tranquility-challenged boys, Steve was the only Baldwin brother who would ever shut up.

In high school, while we were friends and saw each other regularly at all the card games, Baldwin was not one of my go-to guys like MKat, Tom, or Vinnie when it came to my finding things to do on a Friday night. It wasn't until college and even later, after I married Laurie and he had married his first wife, that Baldwin and I actually developed a relationship outside the card game.

Baldwin married Jackie early in 1987, six months after Laurie and I tied the knot. They lived just a few doors down from us in a little garden apartment condominium complex called Jocelyn Mews, tucked off Route 29 near the White Oak Shopping Center in Silver Spring. Tom and Lianne were engaged but constantly swinging back and forth between talking about a wedding and breaking up. With Baldwin the only other married one in the group and living so close, it was easy for us to hang out together.

Having just graduated from law school, I was working at my first real lawyer job down in Langley Park, Maryland, a town stuck somewhere between the white-bread 1950s and a 1980s influx of a new, young, and more blue-collar Hispanic community. The entire town of Langley Park was essentially comprised of an intersection between two main commuter roadways, New Hampshire Avenue and University Boulevard. Further south on New Hampshire was the DC line; east on University took you to College Park, home of the University of Maryland. Langley Park was a pass-through.

Laurie was in grad school working toward a master's degree in social work. While registering for classes a month or so after we got married, she met an older woman who had decided to start on a career outside the home now that her children had grown. Always inquisitive and sincerely interested in learning about people's lives, even strangers', Laurie found out that the woman's husband was a partner at a law firm near where we lived and was looking to train a young lawyer to specialize in family law. A random encounter in a course registration line, a couple of conversations, and my fate was sealed. Becoming a divorce lawyer was never part of any master plan of mine—nor was carrying someone else's briefcase around for a year or so—but I needed a job and was willing to work for anything those folks were willing to pay me. I got an interview and, whether it was my natural ability or my unique willingness to succumb to slave labor for a while, I don't know, but I got the job. Factoring in the two workweeks I was required to squeeze into one five-day span, I was earning about two bucks an hour.

Despite the low pay, the firm gave me more courtroom experience than most other new law school graduates. While many of my friends, several of whom were on law review and were making more in a day than I did in a month, spent their days in law library cubicles like turtles in a shell, heads down and rarely coming out except to pee or find another book on the shelf, I was racing off to one courthouse or another several times a week. Not that any of the cases I was given required a lot of skill or what smooth-handed lawyers generously refer to as "heavy lifting."

One of my early "trials" was a case in which my client, who was paying the princely sum of ten dollars a month to his baby mama pursuant to a family court child support order from 1976, was being hounded by the local child support enforcement office to increase his monthly payment.

These "child support modification" cases, as they are called, were all scheduled in the afternoons, back-to-back from 1:00 p.m.

until the end of the courtroom day, generally about 4:30 or so. The parties had to be present, and often some poor sod working for an agency called the Office of Child Support Enforcement represented the parent who was looking to get more money. Although one would think that the lawyers for the OCSE would be young newbies out of law school, in fact the opposite was true. Most of these folks were lifers and spent each and every day for decades moving through endless piles of child support cases, trying most of them in fifteen minutes or less, rarely even looking at the file or talking to the client before the afternoon began.

There are no longer that many court fights over child support since most states now have child support guidelines in which income and other numbers are plugged into a formula that then spits out what the child support payment should be. Today, all a judge needs to be able to do is type numbers onto a computer screen and push "calculate." In the '80s, however, there were no such guidelines in Maryland and, therefore, the courts decreed that in order to show that an increase in a parent's child support obligation was warranted, the party asking for the increase had to provide evidence that there was a material change in circumstances justifying the increase. Such a burden was not usually too difficult as most things tend to cost more as time goes by and kids usually get more expensive as they get older.

The economic needs of a family are often expressed in the courtroom through the admission into evidence of a simple and straightforward financial statement, a document that every litigant in a child support matter is still required to submit. A smart lawyer (and I like to think that I fall into that category) looks not only through the financial statement that is being offered now, but also closely reviews any that were filed in prior hearings in the same case.

I got to the courthouse a couple of hours early in order to review the court file in my case. What I found in the mom's financial statement from 1976 when the baby was born and child support was first established had me chomping at my lawyer bit. I made a copy of the old financial statement to use as an additional exhibit, found my client outside the courtroom, and waited for our case to be called. Third or fourth down on the list, we waited about a half hour before Judge McCullough called out my client's name and the case number. Retired for some time, Judge McCullough was back on the bench earning a few extra bucks by helping to move cases from a bloated courthouse docket.

Although I did not have any cases with him before his retirement, I had asked some folks back at the office about Judge McCullough so that I would know what to expect. I got some good advice.

"Wear a white shirt, blue or gray suit, and a red or blue tie. Nothing else," one of the lawyers told me.

"Say what you have to say and sit down. He hates young lawyers and, even more, hates guys who think they are Perry Mason," said another.

"The guy's a moron. You're fucked," someone else said.

After Judge McCullough sat down at the bench and called the case, the OCSE lifer put the mom on the stand, handed her the financial statement, and asked her the customary questions necessary for it to be admitted into evidence.

"Do you recognize this document, ma'am?" he asked.

"Yes," she answered.

"Is this your financial statement that you prepared a few moments ago in my office?" A leading question, but I did not object.

"Yes."

"Does it accurately reflect your income and expenses?" he continued.

"Yes," she answered again.

"And it fairly includes and represents the needs of your son. Is that correct?" Leading again, but it didn't matter. I was ready to pounce.

Same answer. "Yes," she said.

The lifer walked around the trial table, approached the mom, and took the financial statement from in front of her. "I would offer the plaintiff's financial statement as exhibit one," he said, handing it to the judge's clerk.

"No objection." I could barely control myself.

"Exhibit one is admitted." The judge looked at me. "Any questions, counsel?"

I almost jumped out of my chair. With my best card game poker face, I said, "Just a few, Your Honor."

I had the 1976 financial statement marked as an exhibit and handed it to the mom. Unlike when asking questions in a direct examination, the lawyer can lead the witness in cross-exam.

I pointed to the bottom of the page. "This is your signature, correct?" I asked.

"Yes," she answered.

"And it's dated December 12, 1976, is that correct?"

"Yes."

"This is the financial statement that you, under oath, said was correct when you were last in court, correct?"

She looked at the page again and then back at me. "Yes," she said.

"So, in December of 1976, this was a fair and accurate summary of your income and your expenses, right?"

"Yes." She had no idea where I was going.

I then retrieved exhibit one from the judge's clerk and handed it to the mom. "If you would, please put these side by side so I can ask you some questions about both."

"Okay," she said, seeming confused.

I looked over at the lifer, who was thumbing through the pile of other case files on the table and did not seem to be paying much attention to what was coming.

"Take a look at your income in 1976 and your income in the financial statement that your lawyer submitted today," I asked.

"Okay," she responded.

I looked at Judge McCullough. "May I approach the witness, Your Honor?" I asked.

He looked at me, maybe an ever-so-slight smile turning up from his mouth. "You may," he responded.

I walked up to the witness stand and pointed at the income line on the financial statement. "You are earning twice as much now as you did in 1976, correct?"

"Yes." She still had no idea.

"Now, let's take a look at your son's expenses. Your financial statement shows that you spend less on food for your son than you did in 1976, correct?"

"Yes."

Your financial statement shows that you spend less on clothing for your son than you did in 1976, correct?"

Another yes.

I continued down the statements, back and forth, over and over again, all the way down to the bottom.

I looked her straight in the eye, preparing to put a nice exclamation point on this brilliant cross-examination. "So, just to be clear, ma'am, you earn more money today than you did in 1976, yes?"

"Yes," she answered quietly.

Knowing that she likely had no help whatsoever preparing either financial statement from the OCSE team of legal eagles, I polished her off. "And based upon the two financial statements, both of which you signed under the penalties of perjury, you spend less money on your son now than you did in 1976, isn't that right?" I asked, still not taking my eyes away from hers.

"Yes, that's what it says." Obviously resigned to her fate, the mom now was keenly aware of what was coming, even if lifer was still not paying attention.

"Any redirect?" Judge McCullough asked the other lawyer.

Painfully oblivious and otherwise occupied with the rest of his docket, the lifer answered, "No, sir."

I immediately moved to dismiss the case as the mom was unable to meet her burden of proof. She made more money now and she spent less. There was no change in circumstances that would support an increase from the ten bucks a month my client was paying.

"Motion granted. Case dismissed." Judge McCullough looked at me and nodded. I am not sure if it was silent praise for the job I had done for my client or contempt for the complete lack of assistance that the county employee had provided the mom. Either way, it was a win, and I was, after all, there to win.

Out in the hallway, my client was ecstatic. "That was great, man. Give me some cards."

I pulled six or eight cards out of my wallet and handed them to him. "Fucking great, really. I appreciate it. I'm going to tell all my friends to call you. Great job." He almost shook my hand off before bopping down the hallway.

Still feeling pretty proud of myself, I stuffed the file into my briefcase and started over toward the stairwell. There was the mom with her young son, maybe twelve or thirteen. His pants were too short and the coat he wore was large, probably a hand-me-down or something picked up at Goodwill. The mom and I looked at each other briefly as I walked past. She looked numb, her face unresponsive and blank. I put my head down and kept walking, trying not to think about what I had just done to her and her boy.

While I was making a name for myself as a guy who could keep deadbeat dads from having to put food on their kids' tables, Baldwin had just started a check cashing business in the District. Since we didn't have much money, those early "double date nights" often included a drive to Langley Park and the Hot Shoppes for the famous "Mighty Mo." Long before McDonald's came out with the Big Mac and its jingle, it was the Mighty Mo that was built with "two all-beef patties, special sauce, lettuce, cheese, pickles on a sesame seed bun." We ate these with a side of oversized, extra-crispy onion rings.

Baldwin could eat onion rings for every meal. He always buried them like a dog with a bone under a half bottle or so of Heinz ketchup. After dinner, we would usually take a quick jump across the street to Weile's, an old ice cream parlor that was on its last legs, a sort of Richman's wannabe. If all the cracked and faded black-and-white pictures on the walls showing lines outside the place and standing-room-only crowds of bobby-soxed college students inside were real, Weile's popularity peaked around 1958. That didn't matter much to me, though, as the ice cream was still spectacular. I always ordered a dusty road sundae, a couple of dollops of cement-thick hot fudge slopped on top of a mound of vanilla ice cream, topped with malt powder. Just too damn good. (Laurie usually took a few tastes of mine, just to be sociable.) Baldwin always ordered one of the big-name desserts like the Eiffel Tower, with eight scoops of ice cream and eight maraschino cherries piled into a tall glass bowl with four toppings and about a quart of whipped cream. Or he'd ask for the glutton, ten scoops of ice cream, five toppings, and walnuts all crushed and mashed together into a silver mixing bowl that were then buried in whipped cream and cherries. He knocked this stuff back by himself. As a diabetic, Jackie avoided the ice cream altogether, but she was a pretty good sport about our regular jaunts for dessert. From there, it was back to one of our apartments to watch a little *Saturday Night Live* and have a drink or two.

No more than five feet tall, with short blonde hair and smoky green eyes, Jackie was a sexy, good-looking girl. She was always dressed in short skirts and heels, something you didn't see much of at the Hot Shoppes, where the average customer's age hovered somewhere north of seventy. We didn't have too many other "couple" friends, so Laurie tolerated her, but Jackie never had much to say and was not destined to be on my wife's best buddy list. Fortunately, Tom would tag along with the four of us on the weekends that he and Lianne were "broken up," something that happened with alarming frequency.

Always big on the anniversaries, Lianne was none too happy if Tom missed what she thought to be a relationship milestone: "It's the three-year anniversary of our first kiss" or "the one-year anniversary of the first time we spent the night together."

Baldwin and I always rode Tom pretty hard over her irritating obsession with anniversaries. "When's the anniversary of the first time you dry humped her on the couch?"

"Yeah. That would be one to celebrate. Have her add it to the calendar."

Tom usually ignored the comments, probably because, in his

heart, he knew we were right. Not that it mattered. He loved her, or at least he thought he did. The fact that she was an absolute loopy bitch to the rest of the world was simply irrelevant.

While I am sure there was real love early on, back in high school, maybe through college, and probably even for a few years into their marriage, at some point I think his relationship with Lianne became more of a tedious familiar routine than anything else. Tom had a business. Tom had a house. Tom had Lianne.

As insane as it seemed to the rest of us, Tom did in fact keep a little calendar for marking off all the special days that were so important to Lianne. Actually, what he had was one of those small two-by-three-inch spiral notebooks (long since replaced by smartphone technology) that you could buy at the drugstore back then. That little notebook was bent and squished from him constantly pulling it out and making a note about some forgotten occasion he would need to remember to avoid an argument.

Inevitably, though, Tom would forget something, and Lianne would call it quits. Down he would go into a dizzying tailspin of despair until I assume Lianne figured no one else would put up with her and she would give him the green light to get back together.

Both our date nights and Baldwin's marriage to Jackie came to a screeching halt one night after we finished dessert at Weile's and headed back to Baldwin's apartment in Jocelyn Mews. We arrived and settled in. Baldwin grabbed a half-empty bottle of Cuervo for the three of us along with an open bottle of white wine from the fridge for the girls to share. Drinks in hand, all of us except Jackie headed out onto Baldwin's six-by-eight-foot cement slab that served as a porch to have our drinks and listen to music.

Jackie excused herself, saying she was going to change and would be out in a few. After about fifteen minutes, we finished our drinks, but Jackie's glass was still full, beads of moisture sweating down the outside. Laurie offered to go look for Jackie and see how she was doing. Instead, Baldwin got another round for everyone and said he would check on her. After a couple of minutes, we heard a screech from inside. A girl's screech.

"What the fuck?" Baldwin yelled.

Laurie, Tom, and I ran in, assuming Jackie was hurt.

We went into their bedroom. Baldwin was standing outside the small walk-in closet. "I can't believe you," he was yelling. "You're going to fucking kill yourself. We talked about this. Jesus Christ." His hands were wrapped around his head, and he looked at the rest of us in disbelief as if we somehow knew what was going on.

One by one, Laurie, Tom, and I peered into the closet. Jackie's face was smeared in something brown. Seeing her like that, in her push-up bra and a pair of shorts, my first thought, frankly, was that she had shit herself. But as soon as I saw the crumbs on her hands and a crushed Entenmann's chocolate cake box next to her on the floor, I realized that Jackie was having a bit of a problem with her sweets. From the tone of Baldwin's voice, coupled with the fact that there were several candy wrappers strewn around and more than a few lunch-sized Hostess cherry pies poking out from underneath some clothes, this was clearly not the first time Jackie had secretly gobbled masses of sugary supermarket baked goods, obviously ignoring the advice of her doctor as well as her husband.

Jackie moved out a couple of days later. Baldwin's parents were still both working; his father was a judge and his mom a state senator. In high school, they were rarely around, and his house was a good place to spend time after school. I always found it a bit funny that while Baldwin's parents were writing and enforcing laws, he and the rest of us were in their house breaking them. In any event, soon after Jackie left, Baldwin's dad must have called in a few favors at the courthouse to grease some wheels. Unlike everyone else in Maryland who has to wait at least twelve months, Baldwin was divorced before the year was out.

And Tom was engaged to be married.

Although not much of a public speaker, Baldwin is a sincere guy, and his six or seven minutes at the podium were most definitely from his heart. He talked about how he and Tom first met in middle school and played boys club basketball together. With Baldwin's parents busy, often out running from one political event to another, Tom's mom drove the two boys to practices and was usually the only parent at their games.

The wistful reminiscing done, Baldwin then related one of our more memorable nights together when Tom was at the center of the insanity.

# TWENTY-FOUR
## 1980

"Jesus, I hate that thing," Tom said. He was staring at the enormous cross his father had built years earlier as we were stopped at the New Hampshire Avenue traffic light with St. Paul's on our right and Sherbrook High a half mile down to the left.

"Don't guess he much liked it either," I told him.

"Huh?" Tom was confused. "Who? I mean he spent like two years working on that thing."

"Not your dad," I said. "I meant Jesus. Doubt he liked the cross either is what I mean."

"Oh. Yeah. Funny," Tom said, but he was not laughing. "Every fucking day I have to look at that thing. After he died, I looked at it every day from my room. I know it sounds shitty, but in some sick way I was happy when my mom died too. At least I got to move out of that place. But, still, every day in high school I walked by it.

Shouldn't I be proud? Happy? Feel something good anyway? I just hate it..." Tom's voice trailed off.

We were on a semester break in our freshman year at Maryland. With me living at the dorm and Tom at his uncle's house and commuting to school, we had not spent a lot of time together, so it was good to be back hanging out. I didn't know how to respond, though, and I've always had a hard time with any uncomfortable silence even between friends, so when John Cafferty's "On the Dark Side" came on the radio, I turned it up. I wasn't a big Cafferty fan, an obvious Springsteen wannabe with his Beaver Brown Band, but this was a great tune. I cranked it way up. Tom and I sang along, me banging the steering wheel, Tom slapping the top of the dash.

On the dark side. Oh yeah.

"Hey, Bro," Tom said. "Does Tracey still work at the Big Boy? Let's go over."

"I don't know," I told him, "and I have no interest in heading over there. No thanks."

I definitely did not want to see that girl. After The Tahitian Treat, I spent most of the rest of my senior year in high school doe-eyed and way too dedicated to Tracey. In return, I was pummeled with a merciless cocktail made up of equal parts flirt and "fuck off." I seemed to have a thing for short and curvy girls, and Tracey more than fit the bill. She was pretty enough and had some really white teeth, long before Crest White Strips hit the market. I could never put my finger on the weird hold she had over me, but I'm sure her smoking body and the seemingly effortless way she had of using it had absolutely nothing to do with it.

Toward the end of our senior year, Tracey and I were talking near the trophy case in the main hallway at school. Right in the middle of our conversation and out of nowhere, she smiled in that mean girl way she had and announced that she was going out that weekend with some guy that had graduated a couple years earlier. Holding my tongue, I just turned and walked away. About fifteen feet and fifteen seconds later, Tracey beaned me in the head with her right shoe. I turned, looked back at her, and kept walking. Presumably sensing that she had pushed even me a bit too far, she ran down the hallway, jumped onto my back, yanked my head back a bit, and kissed me on the cheek. I knew I needed to ignore her and keep walking, but instead I turned and wrapped my arms around her. Like Charlie fucking Brown, I kept trying to kick the ball for the rest of the year. True to form, Tracey kept pulling it away.

"We're going," Tom said. "Let's get Baldwin."

Tom made a U-turn toward Baldwin's house and headed back toward the Big Boy. Baldwin was in the front yard, so as soon as Tom pulled in the driveway, Baldwin jumped in the backseat, clearly pumped up. "We going to Big Boy?"

"That's the plan, yep," Tom responded.

"Yes!" he said triumphantly. "I want some of those onion rings." Baldwin, rail-thin, with jet black hair flopped over his eyes, loved the Big Boy. He ate nonstop and never put on a pound; the man was always hungry. Of course, that might have been the result of his more-than-mild recreational pot-smoking habit.

We got to the Bob's Big Boy, patted the hamburger on the Bob statue for no particular reason as we'd done for years, went inside, and slid into a booth. Just my luck, Tracey was working the counter. She looked over at me and flashed that way-too-familiar smile. She swapped stations with her friend, Karen, bounced over, and announced that she would take care of us. Ugh. We ordered some Cokes, a few Big Boy combos, and two large baskets of onion rings. Baldwin moaned with pleasure, anticipating the rings, no doubt.

"Come with me, Baldwin," Tom said as he basically pulled Steve up, leaving me sitting alone in the squishy booth seat looking up at Tracey. She seemed in full control of things, just like she always was before we broke up six months earlier. Undoubtedly expecting some emotional response from me, she started droning on about what she was doing that weekend and the guy she was going to see on Saturday night. She'd gotten used to pressing that particular button in high school, ending with a flippant, "Maybe we can catch up sometime next weekend, JB."

Sadly for Tracey, though, I was slightly smarter and definitely stronger than when she last toyed with me.

"How about you get that order in?" I said. "Baldwin is hungry." I looked right at her and tried to give her my best "hit the bricks" smile. I wasn't sure she got the message. I looked out the window at Tom and Steve. "What the hell are they doing out there?" she asked me. I had no idea. Tom looked like he was trying to measure the Bob's Big Boy statue while Baldwin was on his knees, apparently trying to determine how Bob the Big Boy was bolted into the cement.

"How about our food, Trace?"

She shot me "the look" and took off for the kitchen. Good to see Tracey hadn't lost her touch.

Within a few minutes, she slammed our drinks down, presumably for special effect. I was proud of myself. I ignored her. When she walked away, though, I couldn't help but watch. That amazing, hip-swinging little walk, well, she still had that, too.

The boys sat back down. "No way we're doing it," Baldwin

said, seemingly adamant, but then again, maybe not. You never really knew with that guy.

"Uh, yes, we are," Tom assured him. "Get Wocky to bring the station wagon. We'll do it tonight." Tom most definitely had his mind set on whatever it was his mind was set on.

"One of you crackers want to fill me in?" I asked. They both looked at me and smiled. Tom was the first to respond. "We're going to do a little decorating at St. Paul's, that's all." I had no clue what he was talking about or what he wanted to do at that big old church. He looked through the glass at Bob, the Big Boy statue.

Suddenly, I figured it out. "Shit."

"These rings are so fucking good," Baldwin said. "Pass the ketchup." He was shaking his head and smiling, either at the food or Tom's plan. Probably both.

We met at Tom's around 11:30 that night. Wocky brought the big green wagon. One by one, Don, MKat, Mark, Vinnie, Baldwin, Tom, and I piled in. Vinnie had his toolbox. Mark had the rope. Bob's closed at 12:00 that night, so we waited around until about 12:30, knowing it would take a while for the folks inside to clean and close up. We realized that with all of us in the wagon, our guest was not going to fit, so I hopped out and followed in the Mustang II.

There was no one in the lot when we pulled in at about 12:40 a.m. With the swift precision of a SWAT team, Mark, Baldwin, Tom, and Vinnie hopped out of the wagon with their tools. MKat got behind the wheel of the wagon and pulled next to me, and we waited for the signal. Neither of us had much going in terms of mechanical skills, so we were in charge of driving the getaway cars.

It was only a minute or two before I saw someone wave at me from the front of the restaurant. MKat and I hopped out of the cars and ran over. By the time we got there, Bob was on his side. It took

four of us to lift him up and shove him into the back of Wocky's
station wagon. Mark tied down the trunk. Everyone hopped back
in the cars, and off we went, laughing, of course, like "banshees."

The job was done long before the morning rush hour started
meandering south along New Hampshire Avenue. Tom, Baldwin,
and I were sitting across the street in someone's front yard looking
over at the church where the ebullient Bob the Big Boy was tied
to Tom's father's cross. I was smiling. Baldwin was smiling. Bob
the Big Boy was smiling. No worse for the wear in his blue shoes,
checkered overalls, and smushed-in nose, Bob was holding his
glossy burger aloft in his right hand as if it were a holy offering or
a bovine sacrifice.

Tom just stared. At one point, he nodded his head, no doubt
particularly impressed with himself. "That's what I'm talking
about" is all I heard him say.

# TWENTY-FIVE

**M**y wife is a smart girl. More than that, she's a hustler and one of the hardest-working people you're ever going to meet. I didn't know her in high school, but my understanding is that she didn't pay too much attention to school, choosing instead to spend her time on friends and boys. Her grades weren't great, and it was thanks in large part to the summer remedial program that the University of Maryland used to offer to graduating high school seniors that she got into college at all. But she went to the summer program, got the grades she needed, and enrolled at Maryland. Four years later, she graduated, magna cum laude, with almost a 4.0 grade point average. She went on to get her master's degree in social work and now runs a successful practice as a therapist for kids with learning disabilities.

As terrific is she is when talking to absolutely anyone directly and face-to-face, it's just the opposite when Laurie has to speak to a larger group. With more than twenty-five years of working in the divorce wars, I still enjoy standing up in a courtroom full of people, cross-examining witnesses, and giving closing arguments. Laurie, on the other hand, feels about public speaking the way I do about giving blood: It's hard for me not to pass out at the thought of it. So, I was more than a little surprised when Laurie stood up to speak after Baldwin was done telling the Bob's Big Boy story, minus the ambiguous ending, but definitely hitting the clear Bob's Big Boy crucifixion imagery.

"Are you sure?" I asked her.

Though I was definitely confused, I knew that public speaking was like everything else in her life—she wouldn't let her own struggle stop her from trying to improve. For the last couple of years, she had attended the local Toastmasters club every other week, giving speeches and critiquing others who were also trying to get better at talking to groups.

"Yeah. I liked Tom," she said. "And Lianne is a friend. Kind of. Plus, Baldwin just finished. Can't be all that much worse, right?"

I smiled. "Right. And you look much better than him in those heels anyway. You'll be great."

"Mmmm-hmmmm." She straightened her skirt and turned toward the podium.

Laurie has a certain way about her, just something, a look in her eye, maybe, that makes people like her. She's endlessly curious about people and their lives and always interested in what anyone has to say. Couple this appeal with the fact that she still has all the curves exactly where they are supposed to be and it's really not surprising that people paid attention as she started to speak.

"I met Tom the night I met my husband, JB," she began.

Yes, she did.

She had my attention without saying anything, and now that

she made reference to the night we met, I sat up a little firmer. I was curious about what sliver of Tom's life she was going to talk about. She spoke for just a few minutes, but Laurie's turn at the microphone was like most anything else she does when she sets her mind to it. Memorable.

"Lianne, girls, let me tell you a story that shows what kind of guy your dad was." She looked over at the three of them and started talking like they were at a sleepover, comfortably sitting around in pajamas.

"When I was about twenty-four weeks pregnant with Sarah, my oldest daughter, I started having contractions and went into what they call preterm labor. I called my mom to take me to the doctor's office for a sonogram. With the usual dose of Jewish pessimism, my mom basically had Sarah killed off as soon as I got into the car. Fortunately, she was wrong, and both me and the baby were okay."

At the time, with Laurie's and my first child on the way, I was working sixty-hour weeks, traveling from courthouse to courthouse, still trying to make a name for myself in a town with a phone book that had fifty pages of lawyers. Laurie had to go onto bed rest, which essentially meant that she couldn't leave her bed at all for the remainder of the pregnancy other than to go to the bathroom or the doctor's office. She was allowed just one shower a week. Before shoving off to work each morning, I would fill a cooler full of snacks, drinks, and a lunch with all the major food groups.

When I got home at night, I made dinner, usually fell asleep exhausted, and then woke up to do it all again the next day. During most days, Laurie had a fairly steady stream of guests, so I left a key under the front mat so folks could get inside to visit.

"One of the people that came to visit me pretty often was your dad," she continued. "He knew I loved Diet Apple Slice soda, and it was impossible to find at the local grocery stores. I can't tell you how many times he showed up during those six months with a six-pack of Diet Apple Slice and some kind of snack for me to eat. JB didn't care at all that Tom was over a few times a week visiting, sipping that apple soda, and just talking about your mom and wanting to have a family, wanting to be a dad. Of course, if it was MKat stopping by every day, well, that probably would have been a different story."

Although no one else in the place really got the reference, the bunch of us were nodding in agreement and laughing. We knew that given a little alcohol and the right set of circumstances MKat wouldn't hesitate to try to fuck any one of our wives.

"That's not true," MKat said in a tone just above a whisper. We all looked over at him. "Well, probably not, anyway," he said. "You guys are dicks."

We all smiled and turned back to Laurie.

"One afternoon your dad was over at about four. We were watching *Oprah* on my little TV, and I told Tom that I really had a craving for one of those big fat cinnamon rolls from Cinnabon. 'Yeah, me too,' he said right away. He hopped up, ran down the stairs and out the door. About forty-five minutes later, he was back with a box of three Cinnabons, with extra 'gravy' of course."

"When JB got home that night, there was one Cinnabon left on the counter. He came upstairs and said he just knew it was your dad who had gone and gotten me Cinnabons that day."

Laurie walked down and hugged Lianne, then each of the girls. The older folks and relatives were wiping their eyes a bit.

"Fucker never got me Cinnabons," MKat muttered.

# TWENTY-SIX
## 1981

I was the only one who lived on the Maryland campus. Tom was still a few years away from having access to his inheritance and the other guys also stayed at home, their families opting not to spend hard-earned money on room and board for their sons to sleep in an eight-by-ten dorm room with linoleum floors and no hot water only a few miles from their free suburban bedrooms. Living in dorms with new people—and even girls—inevitably led to me hanging out more with other students who lived on campus too.

Through the first half of freshman year and into the spring when I decided to pledge a fraternity, I spent less and less time with the boys. Rarely making a card game, I was hardly seeing them at all. Maryland was a big school and, as I went down one path with new faces, they travelled together down another. When I was with them, it was strained; there were new jokes and stories about people

I didn't really know and, as a result, I was no longer sewn into the fabric of those stories or on the inside of the jokes. A new guy, Stu, now was a regular at the game. From New Jersey, a lot taller than me, not to mention a much smoother talker when it came to the female side of the population, Stu seemed to have taken my spot. There was no mistaking it—Stu was in, Bro was out. My relationship with Tom, MKat, and the rest had changed and, without a second thought, I knew it was entirely my fault. I was an ass. I neglected and ignored guys who I literally had spent almost every day of my life hanging or at least talking with since tenth grade. It was inexcusable. To this day, I still think about what a jerk I was to my best friends.

One night late in 1981, I got a call from Tom. He was in AC with the boys, calling me from a pay phone inside Tony's.

"Hey, Bro. Got someone who wants to talk to you," he said. A lot of loud laughing ensued, and then a strange woman's voice came on singing: "*I wanna fuck your mother...*" Tom got back on the phone, and more cackling filled the background.

"You should be here. Dick." He hung up.

Even before I got to Maryland, I always knew I wanted to be in a fraternity. I wanted to live in a frat house with a bunch of guys and be part of something, a brotherhood.

Once I finished pledging and was installed as a brother, I got a room in Phi Kappa Upsilon. The house, fronted with Georgian columns, big double wooden doors, and an end-to-end cement porch out front, sat in the center of a horseshoe-shaped driveway that made up Maryland's Fraternity Row. My window looked out on Route One, a four-lane speedway that was none too safe for the endless flow of college students who had to navigate across it get to classes at the main area of campus.

My roommate in the fraternity was an outgoing and muscular guy who had pledged with me. Frank was athletic and strong, and he never saw a female he didn't try to fuck. Any girl, as he artfully put it every day we lived together, that had "two tits, a hole, and a heartbeat," was fair game for Frank.

Tuesday nights were frat nights at the Rendezvous Inn, a stone-front, dark hole of a college bar a couple of blocks away from Fraternity Row and our house. "The 'Vous" featured cheap beer and rock and roll music that got louder as the night got later. The floor was covered in an inch or two of decades-old spilled beer that had long ago congealed and hardened, leaving a gummy and sticky brown coating on top of the beige cracked tile. As a result, everyone knew to leave their nicer footwear at home and instead to wear "'Vous shoes" whenever visiting the joint. Mine were an old pair of what were originally white canvas Converse low tops that, after a few visits worth of mud, beer, piss, and puke, now looked like two blackened and rotting rodent carcasses tied at the ends of my legs. As bad as they looked, they smelled worse.

Aside from frequent opportunities to feel up any number of loose and willing drunken nineteen-year-old girls, my favorite moments at the 'Vous were always around 1:45 a.m. at last call when the DJ would spin "Mack the Knife." It didn't matter how much beer the packed crowd had ingested up to that point. As soon as the needle on the record hit "Oh, the shark, babe," the Vous started to shake.

One Tuesday night, after about eight hours of slurping two-dollar pitchers of Bud at the 'Vous with some of my fraternity brothers, we stumbled back down to Fraternity Row and into the house. The plan was to head up to my room and watch a few old reruns of *The Bob Newhart Show* while playing a house drinking game creatively known as "Bob." The game of Bob had just one simple rule: Every time a character said "Bob," everyone had to drink. One time I counted seventy-eight separate times in a twenty-three-minute sitcom that "Bob" was included in the dialogue. That was an exciting night.

As soon as we became roommates, Frank and I had devised a simple yet brilliant system for us to let the other know if we were in the room with a girl: put a rubber band on the doorknob. Not that I needed it much, but I never left the frat house without a rubber band in my pocket.

We got to the room and I opened the door and started walking in when I heard a female voice yelp, "Hey, get out!"

I flipped on the light. Frank was lying on his back, naked, looking over at us. Some girl, who definitely met his three minimum requirements, was sitting on him, reverse cowboy style, breasts up and at attention, staring at us.

"Rubber band. Rubber band. Rubber band," Frank said, repeating the mantra in a voice that was especially calm given the circumstances.

"There was no rubber band on the door, Frank," I said, but it felt weird to have a conversation with him while his dick was firmly planted deep into whatever her name was.

"I couldn't find one," Frank told me, "so I put a sticky note on the door." He was calm, exhibiting an admirable ability to multi-task.

"A what?" I kept looking at him. The girl didn't move, her breasts still exposed, Frank still inside her.

"A sticky note. One of those yellow sticky notes," he said. "I put it on the door."

"Uh, okay."

I slid the door back open and looked down on the hallway floor. Sure enough, on the floor was a yellow sticky note. Scribbled in pencil on the note were two words: "rubber band."

I started laughing. The whole scene was hysterical, from end to end. I backed out of the room and closed the door, turning to see the guys who were in the hall with me. They had to be as broken up as I was.

No one was there.

In that moment, I looked down the empty fluorescent-lit hallway. I slid down the wall, plunked onto the floor, and laughed for a few seconds. By myself.

It was right then that it hit me. I didn't need a fraternity house or some stained sweatshirt with Greek letters on it to know who my friends were.

# TWENTY-SEVEN
## 1983

For some reason I will always be grateful for but will never fully understand, once I finished my junior year and was done with fraternity life, I slid easily back in around the card game table. No one ever said a word. My self-imposed exile was over. I was just back.

One Saturday night early in the spring of 1983, Vinnie called and said he was heading out from work and "grabbing up some of the dumbbells" to go to a fraternity party in College Park and then downtown to one of our regular bar stops, Abbey Roads or Rumors. More than likely, both.

By then, Vinnie and I were sharing a room in a Springhill Lake apartment. A sprawling complex a few miles northwest from school, Springhill Lake was the off-campus residential destination for a lot of Maryland students at the time. Even though the apartments were dirty and old, they were still a step up from dorm or fraternity house life. Since everyone had to sign a twelve-month lease, people tended to stay and live there during the summer. With a pool on either side of the complex and plenty of young girls renting apartments, Springhill Lake was a twenty-two-year-old's version of paradise.

Actually, when we rented the place, it was considered a "Florida room," whatever that meant. One thing it did mean was that there was no closet, no wall, no door, and obviously no privacy. After we rented the place, I called Peepsie to see if he would help us build a wall between the Florida room and the rest of the common living space in the apartment. Having grown up in the mountains of Pennsylvania and worked in dry cleaning plants much of his adult life, Peepsie was good with his hands and always carried a toolbox. I was certain that he could put together a makeshift dividing wall that we needed to give us at least the illusion of having our own room. Vinnie and I were tasked with lugging all the materials from the hardware store into the apartment, and Peepsie built a pretty decent wall, encased in some prefabricated wallboard with a sliding door in the center. There was no lock, but that was just fine. The room was, at most, seven feet long and about twelve feet wide, with enough space for a twin bed on either side and a small table in the middle. On the table, Vinnie and I shared an eight-inch, round, space-helmet-shaped white television that, with a little aluminum foil twisted around the antenna, enabled us to tune in to couple of channels, so long as it wasn't raining outside. The back wall was actually a sliding glass door that we left open for Tom to climb in to sleep on the floor whenever he wanted.

It was when we were roommates that Vinnie fell hard for a tiny sweet thing that roamed the west side pool in a barely there pink bikini and heels. It took a couple of years before "little Pam" even spoke to him, but the work paid off. Eventually, she fell for Vinnie's charms, whatever they were, and they have been together since.

It was about nine on this particular night when Vinnie roared into the apartment with Tom, MKat, Wocky, and Don in tow. "Let's roll, cocksucker!" he called to me through the wall. I reached across my bed and yanked open the sliding door. Vin was looking "de-boner" as we called it, dressed in his standard weekend wear, poly-blend flared slacks, Italian-looking loafers, and a long-sleeve, clingy, button-up shirt that was hardly buttoned. MKat and Don were, as usual, neat, cleaned, and ready. Wocky and Tom, well ... weren't. They wore their usual old baggy jeans, way too bright white tennis shoes, and plain T-shirts, Tom in a big red one and Wock in a big blue one. Both cleaned up by tucking their shirts into their jeans and lopping on some Polo cologne. Looking at those two, you couldn't help but laugh, which I did as I pulled on my beat-to-hell brown Frye boots.

Vinnie had heard that one of the fraternities was having a casino night fundraiser to support some local charity.

"Charity, my ass," Vinnie said. "Probably looking to raise money to restock the kegs."

"Probably, but who gives a shit?" MKat was making more of a statement than asking a question.

"Bet they'll have mixed drinks, too," Tom chimed in, seeming pretty excited about the possibility of drinking something other than beer.

"Yeah, they might." Vinnie looked at him. "Maybe you can get a little straw and an orange slice."

"Dick" was all Tom could mutter in response as we left.

The main floor of the fraternity house was definitely set up to look like a casino night, with six blackjack tables and four or five roulette wheels. There were three bars around the room. In those days, the drinking age in Maryland had just gone from eighteen to twenty-one, but if you were eighteen before the law changed you were golden. We were golden. Not that anyone checked IDs at the Phi Delta house.

Drink tickets were two for a dollar. Drinks were two tickets each. To us mathematicians, that meant drinks cost a buck. Having taken an advance on his salary from his father's record store, Vin was flush with cash and plunked down two twenties. Tom stared at those twenty-dollar bills like they were naked women.

"Really?" he said. "Where'd you get that kind of cash?" It was a lot of goddamn money to the rest of us. Vinny shoved a handful of tickets in Tom's chest. "Go drink, dick." A man of few words.

Wocky and Don headed over to a blackjack table with about six gin and tonics between them. Tom went to spin some roulette. MKat, Vinnie, and I were looking for luck in other ways. There were a lot of girls roaming around this place, but I couldn't compete with two of the best talkers in the business. My plan was to stay back and trail all night in hopes of grabbing up a nice girl left behind in the wake.

After a while, MKat ran into a girl from his Alfred Hitchcock film class and introduced me to her. Nice and friendly, Sue had a big smile and a bit of a round face. Not really my type. As if anyone with a vagina wasn't my type.

Behind Sue was a dark-haired, brown-eyed beauty sipping a cocktail out of her clear plastic cup. Laurie was drop-dead great looking—to me anyway. Great legs, hair that went just everywhere, and some amazingly sexy hips that made me stare, probably a little too much. We exchanged a few smiles. Once I was able to gather myself, I shoved past MKat and started up some mindless conversation.

I got us some drinks with Vinnie's tickets, two for Laurie and two for me. Gin and tonics all around. Soon, I was out of tickets, so I borrowed Vinnie's keys to get some money from my wallet in the car. Gone for maybe forty-five seconds—I ran like an Olympic sprinter from the house to the car and back—I found Laurie in the same spot by the time I returned, but the cups were drained. She flashed a big smile, and the words "Spoil Me" glared at me from the light reflecting off her gold-plated necklace.

"Sorry," she said. "I was thirsty." I liked this girl.

A few watered-down cocktails later, Tom came over with Vin and announced it was "time to roll." With Wocky still hovering over the blackjack table and obviously not "rolling" anywhere until he was out of money, I told Tom and Vin that I was going to stay. Leaning in, I whispered to both of them, "I'm staying. I think I can fuck her."

Tom smiled. "She's cute."

Vinnie's response was not quite as well-mannered. "She's wasted, Bro. Any one of us could fuck her."

Well, they didn't. I did. Four kids and twenty-seven years of marriage later, the rest, as they say, is history.

# TWENTY-EIGHT

Once Laurie was done, the rabbi stood up and moved back to the podium.

"So many of you have spoken about Tom," he said. "I'm hopeful that we can hear some more stories about this wonderful man and his life. For now, though, Lianne asked that we play one of Tom's favorite songs."

"Here comes the bowler," Vinnie groaned.

Knowing we had to hear some Southside Johnny and Lianne was choosing the song, there was no doubt that "Hearts of Stone," originally a Springsteen tune, was getting cued up. Johnny's version was Tom and Lianne's first dance song at their wedding, and I always thought it was a strange pick. After all, the song was about a couple having trouble, leaning into a breakup, and reminiscing about the way things used to be between them. Certainly an odd way to begin a marriage, but even more than that, Lianne was never a big fan of Southside, Bruce, or any of the other music that really mattered to the boys and me. When I asked Tom how he was able to get Lianne to agree to come out and dance to "Hearts of Stone," he basically told me that music was the only component of the wedding he had any control over.

"Listen, Bro," he said. "The wedding is Jewish. The food is Jewish. It's at a synagogue, and the party will have all that traditional Jewish bullshit. You know, the candles, the grandparents, all the fucking blessings and prayers and shit. On top of all that, I had to get my dick stuck by some smelly Orthodox dude in his family room and then go to Hebrew school with a bunch of twelve-year-olds for about six months. When I told her I was picking the first dance song, I think she knew I wasn't fucking around."

I had a newfound respect for my friend; it was good to know he could put his foot down and put his lovely bride in her appropriate place. If only I had been there to see it.

# TWENTY-NINE
## 1987

After a year or so working from a makeshift conference room, the firm decided I was good enough to keep, at least for the Third World wage they were paying me. I got my own office that came with a laminate desk, high-back, burgundy vinyl chair for me, and even two chairs for clients to sit in. The same worn-out and dispirited diplomas and certificates that now sit in a box in my basement gathering dust proudly hung on the wall behind me so that all could see that I was in fact permitted to practice law in the great state of Maryland. It didn't matter that I had to prop eight or so business cards under the back right leg of the desk to keep it from tipping, just being able to say, "I'll be in my office" gave me a gleaming sense of satisfaction.

My secretary buzzed me on the yellowed plastic speakerphone

late on a Monday afternoon. Getting ready to head home for the day, I was thankful that it wasn't a lawyer or client.

"What's the good word, Tom?" I asked, in that worn-in-shoe way friends have with each other.

"Hey, Bro. Want to go to the Bayou this Saturday?" Tom asked. "Southside's playing and we can still get some tickets. Two shows, seven and ten," he said.

The Bayou was a music venue that occupied a tattered brick building on K Street in Washington, DC, with old-style air-conditioning units that poked out of the second-story windows like rusty, metal-framed eyeballs. Cars and trucks hummed by endlessly on the Whitehurst Freeway that hung overhead. It was opened originally as a jazz club, but by the time I was old enough to get in, it featured mainly rock and roll acts, some of which went on to grab a national audience, like Kiss and Foreigner. To ensure that folks could not make out the degree of its disrepair, the owners kept things as dark as possible with only knee-high wall lamps or a hand on your friend's shoulder to help you navigate the place. The best spot to see a show was from the catwalk area above the stage, a cold beer in one hand and the creaky guardrail gripped in the other.

Southside had a good following, but he wasn't a headliner type, so the tickets were just affordable, assuming I brown-bagged PB and Js for lunch for a week or two after. With the newlywed shine behind us and with it Laurie's willingness to touch my penis almost every time I asked, it sounded like a pretty good way to spend a Saturday night.

"I'm in. Laurie will come, too," I said. Biting my lip enough to hurt but not actually draw blood, I asked Tom if he wanted to ask

Lianne to come along. Knowing she couldn't stand loud music, or me for that matter, I was sure he would come without her.

"Yeah, sure. Great idea," he said.

"Fuck me," I said to myself, holding the phone far enough away so he couldn't hear.

With the early show sold out, we got tickets for ten o'clock, arriving an hour or so early to be sure we could get our spots over-looking the stage.

We made a beeline for the upstairs bar where Tom bought a round of Budweiser drafts for the four of us. Although it was clear and warm outside, Lianne's clothes were hidden by a black trench-style coat that was belted tightly at the waist; her hair was yanked so far back into a pony tail I thought her face was going to tear off. She turned her nose up at the beer and made what Laurie and I secretly called the "puss face" not once but twice, first when Tom handed her the cup and again when she took a sip.

Not a real beer drinker, Laurie was still a proponent of the "when in Rome" philosophy. Like me, she wanted to get away from the puss face. She slugged some of the beer down and grabbed my hand, and we walked to the rail, leaving Tom to fend for himself.

"Ladies and gentlemen, the world's greatest good time band, Southside Johnny and The Aaaaasberry Jukes," blared over the speakers.

I quickly got lost in the music. We bounced and danced in our spots to "Take it Inside," "Talk to Me," and "Trapped Again." When Southside used his hand to spread the sweat from his forehead through his hair and dug into a slow and sexy soul cover of "Walk Away Renee," I wrapped my arm around Laurie, tucking my hand into the hip of her jeans and pulling her tight.

"Where's my wine?" Southside playfully asked the audience but to no one in particular. A girl standing below us and to the right of the stage handed him a cup. "Thank you, darlin'. This one's for you," he said and counted off a "one-two-three-four," leading the Jukes into a throbbing "Angel Eyes." It was about then that I noticed Lianne was nowhere to be seen. Tom was still standing next to me on one side of the railing, but when I leaned forward to look past him, she was gone.

"Where'd she go?" I mouthed, knowing that there was no way he could really hear me over the Jukes' booming four-piece horn section.

Tom waved me off and looked down toward the stage, blinking back whatever it was he was feeling. Anger, sadness, frustration. I wasn't sure. I remember hoping that at that point he knew what the rest of us had known for years. "*Let her go. Get out. That woman is not for you,*" I thought.

I was wrong. He didn't know.

# THIRTY

Despite the endless hours we spent together from high school and college through marriages, kids, and jobs, the daily grind of life as well as its tragedies usually stayed on the outside during the game, hovering at the periphery of our friendships.

Tom's dad died. His mom was a drunk and then she died too. While we were in college, Don's sister got in a bad car wreck and, although she survived, she still walks with a cane and has some kind of brain injury that kept her from finishing school. Baldwin had a brother that got hooked on heroin and overdosed one winter all alone in a remote beachfront motel room at the Delaware shore.

A year or so before Tom died, we were all at his house about an hour into the Monday night game. Everyone was there but MKat, who had called Tom earlier in the day and told him that he would be late getting to the game.

MKat made it to Tom's after dinner was over and just as Baldwin was shuffling the cards for the first deal of the night.

"Nice of you to show up," Vinnie said.

"Fuck off. Tom you got any beer other than this light crap?" MKat asked.

"Not really. Sorry." Tom was making a slight effort to watch his weight, but with no intention to give up the foods he loved, the options were limited to an assortment of clear, bubbly, and tasteless light beers.

"Jesus, I can't drink this," MKat said, visibly agitated. His forehead was wrinkled and his eyebrows were pointing sharply toward the bridge of his nose. To me, it seemed that his mood was being affected by something other than Tom's sissy beer selection.

"What's the problem?" I asked.

"Oh, Jesus. He's fine," Vinnie replied quickly.

Tom offered another option. "Vodka in the freezer. That good stuff from France. Grey Goose. Help yourself."

"Get your drink and let's play already," Baldwin said.

"Don't know why you buy that overpriced French shit," Wocky jumped in, sending the discussion down a different direction.

"What do you mean? For you, I'll get that Kamchatka Vodka, Wock. Three dollars a gallon. Have as much as you want," Tom replied.

While the rest of us laughed, MKat filled a highball glass close to the top. No ice. He took a fast swallow, downing about half the glass without a breath.

"Uh, maybe go easy on that. Work tomorrow, don't forget," Baldwin said.

"Fuck work," MKat answered.

"Okay, what's going on? Run into one of your old high school girls again?" Mark asked.

MKat made it a habit of telling us whenever he saw a woman he dated back in high school. The same ones that fucked him in his car, at the golf course, or in his parents' bed were now plumped from having babies and wrinkled from raising them. The way they looked depressed him and, I think, got him looking in the mirror more closely than he had in a while. While we all handled hitting fifty with differing degrees of insecurity, MKat seemed to take it the hardest, going from diet to diet to try to fend off middle-age spread and sag while also dying his hair in an effort to slow the insidious spread of gray on his head. Although I never saw anything myself and certainly wouldn't testify to it, I just had the sense that he was bored and looking like some men do for the excitement of the "old days."

MKat sat down. "Me and Amy. We're separating. I moved out."

At that point, we all kept our heads down, looking across the table at each other, hoping that MKat wouldn't notice.

"That sucks," was all I could muster.

"Yeah. Sorry, man," Don said. He put his arm on MKat's shoulder.

"She asked me to leave. Said she needed a break. Can you believe it?" I think the question was rhetorical. Even if it wasn't, no one answered anyway.

"That sucks." Not much for words, Baldwin repeated my thoughtful response.

In the midst of a quick speck of silence, Wocky stuck his finger in his mouth, then screwed it into MKat's left ear and hissed "Wet Willie" at MKat, extending out the third syllable. "Wet Wil-lieeeeeee."

"Dick," MKat yelped as he pulled his head away from Wocky's saliva-coated finger.

"Five-card stud. One buy, one community card." Baldwin started dealing.

As the cards were dealt and the chips changed hands, MKat's mood improved. He laughed with us and laughed at us. He made fun of Wocky. Like most of our games, the rest of the night was spent laughing, drinking, and talking about nothing that anyone can remember much of days or months later.

It's been said that the lawyer who represents himself has a fool for a client. While certainly true, the bigger dope is the lawyer who represents a good friend in his divorce. Although I knew at the time it was a bad idea, I didn't hesitate when MKat asked me to represent him after he and Amy broke up.

"It'll be easy," he told me. "We have it all figured out."

If only I had a dollar for every time a client has told me that over the years.

Although Amy's lawyer was not all that difficult to deal with, MKat was nearly impossible. Between the after-hours phone calls at home, just when I was settling in for some time on the couch with Laurie, as well as the constant barrage of single-spaced, hundred-line emails giving me "advice" about how to deal with his wife and her lawyer, MKat was driving me nuts. The issues in MKat's case were not much different and certainly no more complicated than most of the others I handled. What struck me was that despite having known him for so long, I really didn't know anything about him, particularly about the problems he and Amy had for years, issues with their youngest son, who had been in and out of different drug programs, and MKat's financial troubles. Until I became his lawyer, I didn't know any of it. "*How could I not know?*" I asked myself more than once.

As I sat through a mediation session with Amy, her lawyer, and a retired judge who we engaged to try to help us settle the case, I tried to focus on the issues between my friend and his wife. Custody and visitation, alimony and child support, how to divide the assets that the two of them had accumulated. In law school, we were all taught to "think like a lawyer," whatever that means. Although we were ultimately able to resolve the case at mediation that day, all I could really think about was how little I really knew about what went on in MKat's life. The life he had away from the card table.

Although I have never been a fan of forms, like the preprinted intake sheets some lawyers use during an initial consultation, I do go through a consistent and regular litany of questions that I ask everyone. "Are there any third parties involved?" and "When did you and your spouse last have sexual relations?" are sandwiched between questions about ages of any children, estimated annual income, and separate bank accounts. Some people are short and terse, popping out little more than yes or no answers. But others treat intake like a massive therapy session. I sit at my desk with a yellow-lined pad as complete strangers spill their innermost lives to me ten minutes after shaking my hand and looking at the pictures of my kids that surround the perimeter of my office. I get long discourses on personal slights and bedroom inadequacies. The failure to be taken to Aruba and having to settle for a beach block timeshare in Fort Lauderdale. Sometimes I get wives whose husbands have blown their retirement on a mistress, on a blackjack table, or up their nose. Or husbands whose wives have jumped the pool guy. The worst is when it takes me twenty minutes just to pull someone from the rabbit hole of an argument with her spouse that happened when she was pregnant with their third child ten years earlier. I spend my life asking questions, answering questions, and waiting for more questions.

Even now, though, I still have to remind myself to ask the guys about their lives outside of our own four-hour bubble. After almost every game, I get home around 11:30. Laurie's in bed, buried under blankets and pillows. "How was the game?" she asks.

"Great time" is my standard, and accurate, answer. Sometimes I'll repeat a funny line or conversation before she nods off to sleep. Most of the time, she'll ask me a question about one of the fellows, their families, or their lives: "How's Wocky's dad?" or "Did Baldwin's daughter start back to college?"

Regardless of the question, she generally gets the same answer from me every time. "I don't know. Didn't ask." Both responses are absolutely accurate. And, although it may not seem right, in some weird way, it is.

# THIRTY-ONE
## 1988

**A**s with most Sunday mornings, Laurie was up early, off to get some exercise and then head to the mall with her mom and sister. I was perfectly fine with being left to my own devices, which usually included sleeping in, lusting through the month's *Playboy* magazine, and watching whatever game might be on.

After a morning cup of coffee and bowl of Cheerios, my one-on-one date with the Playmate of the Month was rudely interrupted by a phone call. It was before the days of inexpensive cordless phones, so I had to set Miss April down, pull some shorts over the big fella, and amble awkwardly into the kitchen.

It was Tom.

"Hey, Bro. Want to be my best man?"

"For what?" I didn't even know that he and Lianne were getting married. Of course, I knew they were serious, and I was aware that he planned to ask her, but there was the whole religion thing and, after all, Tom hadn't told me when he was going to ask her to marry him.

"Funny guy," he said. "We're getting married in September. Just say okay, then I'll get you the details."

"Okay."

"Great. Also, I couldn't decide so I asked Don to be my best man, too. No problem with that, right?"

"Right."

"Something wrong? You seem like you're out of it."

"No," I said. "Just got this month's *Playboy*."

"Shit. Sorry to interrupt. Give her a tug for me. Sorry. That sounded gay. You know what I mean. Talk to you later."

He hung up.

Having already been married for a couple of years, I certainly knew the basics of what a best man was supposed to do. Don and I immediately got to work on the most vital responsibility—the bachelor party. This one could *not* be a little one-night get-together at a hotel room or some dumpy strip club or someone's house. We were going to make a weekend of it, and there was not much discussion as to where we would go. We were headed back to Atlantic City.

The nine of us piled into three cars on an August afternoon and headed north to our home away from home. Although we all had jobs, none of us were exactly loaded at the time, so we were booked into the Brighton House for the weekend. Don, Tom, and Mark drove with me. They sucked down some cold Rolling Rocks as I spun Springsteen's *Darkness on the Edge of Town* cassette. "Badlands" boomed out. We all knew the lyrics and sang. Loudly.

By the time we got to Richman's, Don and Tom were decidedly drunk. The two of them stumbled out of the car toward the outside tables. As if on cue, both of them suddenly bent over neighboring benches and redistributed the morning's beer and breakfast intake all over the grass. Mark and I watched, but I got disgusted and turned away. Mark, however, seemed gleeful about being one hundred percent dandy while the other two looked like they needed a week in detox. Tom's and Don's faces were a weird elementary school paste color, and neither of them could stand.

Mark laughed as he walked up to them, a big smile across his face. "This is a family restaurant, fuckers," he said, and then he went inside to grab an ice cream cone.

Eventually, Tom and Don got up and staggered into the restaurant. Mark came out and hopped back into the car. The other guys had already left and were on their way along Route 40.

"Where are those douchebags?" Mark asked.

I had no idea.

I was about to go in and look for them when they both came out of the place, double dips in hand. I couldn't believe it.

"You guys are eating ice cream?"

Don looked at me as if I was from Mars. "Bro, it's chocolate chip!" he said and shoved Tom into the back before climbing in behind him. Off we went.

Once in AC, our first stop, as always, was at Tony's Baltimore Grill. Originally opened in the 1920s as the Baltimore Grill, the restaurant moved to its downtown location on Atlantic Avenue in 1966. It's still an unmistakable Atlantic City landmark of white stucco and red shutters. At nighttime, you can see the bright red, white, and blue "Tony's Baltimore Grill" sign from blocks away. If the outside is a throwback to the 1960s, the inside is a downright time warp: dark-brown wood paneling, red leatherette booths, and wood-laminate tables with diner-style chairs.

On the wall in each booth, a mini-jukebox offers a schizophrenic choice of tunes. Press B-75 and you might find Aerosmith's "Dream On." Flip a couple of pages to D-19 and it's Sammy Davis Jr. singing "The Candy Man." Even the waitresses, each one beefed up and past their prime, are in uniforms straight out of *Happy Days.*

If it's Tony's décor that sets the table, it is the food that keeps us coming back, trip after trip, year after year. We always order up the same king's feast to share: oven-greased thin-crust pizzas with a sweet red sauce, fried shrimp pounded flat and wide, and sides of spaghetti with meatballs the size of one of Jupiter's moons. My favorite, the Tony's Seafood Special, is a mountain of fried shrimp, clams, and scallops, and a crab cake with a side of fries and coleslaw. Wash it all down with a couple of dollar drafts, and you'd better be ready to loosen your pants on the way out.

From Tony's, it was over to the Brighton House where the inevitable debate over rooms began. This was still a boardinghouse, not a hotel, so there were bedrooms on each floor but only one common bathroom. My walnut-sized bladder usually compelled me to scamper up the stairs before the others and grab the room closest to the can. Baldwin, a relatively quiet sleeper, especially compared to a few of the monster snorers in the group, was my preferred roommate.

Unfortunately, I had roomed with Baldwin on our last trip, and borrowing some of his father's judicious Solomon-like skills, Baldwin felt it only fair that he room with Don. That left me in a triple with Tom, one of the gang's bigger slobs, and MKat, the undisputed heavyweight snoring champion of the world.

Once we were showered and ready, we grabbed a couple of cabs and headed down to Margate, a sleepy little beach town just south of Atlantic City. The nine of us bounded out of cabs in front of Lucy the Elephant, just next door to our first watering hole of the night, the Greenhouse.

"Lucy" is no ordinary elephant. She's six stories high and listed on the National Park Registry of Historical Landmarks, having been in Margate, New Jersey, since 1881. I'm still not sure what to make of her besides being fairly certain that there isn't another beach in the world with a giant metal-and-wooden elephant perched on the sand.

The Greenhouse, though much shorter on history than the elephant next door, is a classic beach bar. It offers cold beers in Solo cups, summer cliché drinks with umbrellas floating in them, and the requisite Jersey rock blaring overhead. If the Greenhouse had showers, I could live there.

As usual, the place was packed with young women just off the beach, most of them still sporting bikinis and major suntans. Our job was to find a last date for our boy, Tom, before he was relegated to the ignominy of spending his days as "Lianne's husband."

For some time prior to the engagement, we'd all noticed that Tom wasn't the same guy when Lianne was around. Easygoing, funny, and a chain smoker whenever we were away together, Tom was just Tom when he was with us. Whenever Lianne was in the mix, however, the world spun a different direction. Tom didn't eat much and drank even less. He might drink a light beer or, if he was really out on a plank, indulge in a glass of chardonnay. Even when he talked to her on the phone there was a noticeable difference in the way he spoke. Vinnie tactfully called it the "fag voice."

Just a few hours earlier, Tom had used the Brighton House phone to call Lianne, hoping to avoid the requisite "good night, hope all is well" call late at night when he presumably would have difficulty enunciating any word with more than one syllable. His voice when talking to Lianne was hard to describe and, as a male, even harder to listen to. It was higher pitched, a bit on the whiny side. All in all, Vinnie's "fag voice" description was on the money.

After a few minutes of "love you honeys," Tom hung up, walked out onto the deck, and lit a cigarette. He grabbed my warm bottle of Rolling Rock and finished it off.

Vinnie couldn't contain himself. "Jesus, man," he said. "It's like you're two different people. One with her and one with us."

"And believe me," Tom said, without hesitation. "The two are never going to meet."

The three of us laughed out loud. At the same time, though, I just couldn't understand why my buddy wanted to marry that woman. I looked at Vinnie. He rolled his eyes. He was thinking the same thing.

Try as we might, we were unable to find Tom any companionship for the night. From the Greenhouse we walked the five blocks toward the bay and meandered through a few outdoor, dirt-floored bars in Margate, grabbing a beer or two at each stop along the way.

Today, Margate is littered with sushi bars and new condos, but back in the '80s it was known as the Barbary Coast because of all the drinking and the carousel of sexuality that spun from bar to bar. At the Harbor Inn, it was ten beers for a buck, all in small plastic cups that cracked and leaked beer if you squeezed them even a bit too hard. From there, we walked bayside to the Elbow Room where a guy named Geeter the Heater frequently referred to himself as "The Boss with the Hot Sauce" between spins of Springsteen, the Ramones, and Bon Jovi for the folks in the bar and a live radio audience. Next door peanut shells were scattered on the floor of Maynard's, where the music was just as loud and the beer almost as cheap. Maynard's also served some great hot sandwiches off a grill in the back, assuming you were able to burrow your way through the sweaty crowd to get there.

Having no luck finding a girl for Tom and without the patience to wait for food at Maynard's, we went back to Atlantic City where Vinnie and MKat continued unsuccessfully to push some girls Tom's way. Finally, around 3:00 a.m., we decided to wave the white flag and head back to Tony's for some chow and beer.

By the time we caught the cabs to Tony's, the Atlantic City prostitution industry was humming away. A couple of short-skirted African-American women dolled up for their night on the town shouted at us from across the street. Tom looked over and lit a cigarette. "What the fuck?" he said. "Might as well."

Before we could stop him, Tom was across the street chatting it up with the two ladies. MKat and I ran over, but by the time we got there, the transaction was complete.

"That's a bad idea, man," MKat said. "I'm telling you, don't do it."

"I'm just going around the back into the parking lot," Tom said. "Plus, I already paid her. Half in advance, anyway. The other twenty when I'm done."

I wasn't really sure what he was getting for forty bucks, but I was afraid to ask. We waved at the other guys into Tony's and told Tom we would wait outside for him.

Tom trailed the taller hooker and off they went. MKat and I waited for what seemed like way too long for a guy that had fairly limited experience with women to that point. We were actually worried.

"Maybe we should go check on him?" I said, although I really didn't want to risk seeing anything.

MKat was less hesitant. Sure," he said. "I'm hungry. Let's go grab his ass. Unless she is." He grinned.

"Christ, you go," I said. "I don't want to see that." I really didn't.

"Sure you do. Come on," MKat answered.

I followed MKat around the back of the old building. As we curled around a couple of parked cars, I could see the woman. She was standing next to the trunk of a white Chevrolet. Tom was lying face up on the car, his pants yanked down just below his knees. She was facing our direction. In her right hand was a lit cigarette that she puffed on intermittently. With her left hand, she was yanking on Tom's johnson and looking noticeably bored, like she was filing her nails.

MKat and I had the same thought at the same time. We cracked up, ran back around the building, and flew into Tony's to find the rest of the boys. In the little time it took us to tell them about Tom's late-night parking lot hand job, Tom bounded in, a fresh cigarette lit, looking frustrated.

"Twenty bucks and she didn't even make me shoot."

MKat and I remembered the contract price. "I thought you paid her forty," I said.

Before Tom could answer, his "date" plowed past the hostess stand and toward us. "Hey, you, motherfucker. You owe me twenty bucks." She was pissed.

"I don't owe you shit. You didn't get the job done." Tom looked at me, grabbed a few fries off Vinnie's plate, and tried to ignore the train wreck that was coming his way. "Pass the ketchup, Bro."

"That's because you can't come, man. Not my fault, bitch. Pay up."

Here we go, I thought.

"Yeah," she continued, laying it on. "You a little boy that can't come. You a dead dick. You a dead dick. You a dead dick, Tom. That's who you are. Dead Dick Tom!"

"Can I have the ketchup back, Dead Dick?" Vinnie loved it.

So did we. And so did the rest of the restaurant full of customers. One guy from the back hollered, "Pay her, Dead Dick."

Another chimed in, "Yeah, Dead Dick Tom. Pay the girl."

Even the kitchen staff joined in, with one moppy-headed dude bent over the order window and screaming, "No food for you, Dead Dick Tom."

The woman was standing at our table with her hand out. By now, most of us had developed a sudden fixation with our food and were trying to ignore the spectacle that was erupting a few feet away. Mark, however, apparently made some eye contact at an unfortunate moment.

"What you looking at little man?" she asked. "Bet your dick don't get hard at four in the mornin' either."

"Not for you and that hand it doesn't," Mark answered, shoving a meatball into his mouth.

"Pay her the fucking money already," MKat said, snickering.

"Fuck," Tom said. "Fine." He tossed a crumpled twenty dollar bill at the woman.

"Atta boy, Dead Dick." MKat grinned, grabbing a shrimp.

Duly embarrassed, still drunk, and more than done for the night, we stumbled back to the Brighton House and to our rooms. I dropped into bed and fell to sleep right away. At some point during the night, though, Tom woke me up, presumably in some sort of half-awake fugue state.

"Bro," he said, "I got to pee."

"Okay. Great. What do you want from me, for Chrissake?"

"I can't get into the bathroom. The door won't move."

I peeled my one eye open and looked at Tom.

He was a little frantic. "Seriously, I can't get the door open. I'm going to piss myself."

"Okay," I said, "Let's go."

I followed Tom to the hallway bathroom. The door was slightly open and the light was on. I pushed the door and, while it moved a little, there was definitely something in the way. Another shove and I was able to open it just enough to get my head in. I looked down to see what was blocking the door. It was a foot. MKat's foot. He was passed out and naked except for a pair of boxer shorts with the right leg pulled up and his dick in his hand. Not that it came as a total surprise, but it was clear that MKat fell asleep while jerking off.

I pulled my head out and looked at Tom. "Here, you take a look."

Tom stuck his head through the door. "Nice. And he calls me Dead Dick. Guess I'll go downstairs."

# THIRTY-TWO

After a couple of friends of the family stood up and talked generically about Tom and his life as a father, Wocky lumbered toward the podium for his turn. Wock's lost a lot of his hair, and most of what's left has been shaved down. He hasn't spent too much time in the gym for a few years and, as a result, the muscled-up dude from the '70s and '80s has been replaced by one with rounder shoulders and a softer, but still pretty solid over-fifty frame. He remains a chronic hypochondriac, always suffering from some nick or cough or cut. He doesn't swallow too many raw eggs anymore, but on our annual weekends away he can still call on his amped-up crazy self of years past.

The two of them were buddies like the rest of us, but I don't think Wocky ever really got over Tom's part in the dastardly prank phone call made during one card game years ago.

For his part, Tom could never quite understand the animosity.

I must have heard Tom say, "Shit, I wasn't the only one there that night," more than a hundred times over the years.

Looking back, I think that Wock expected me, Vinnie, and MKat to be morons. But Tom was, in a lot of ways, a more decent guy—not Don-decent, but he had a much higher moral code than most of the rest of us. The fact that Tom engineered the entire event has just continued to stick in Wocky's craw for more than twenty-five years.

# THIRTY-THREE
## 1988

When we were back in high school, all of us at some point found our way into Miss Darling's math class. Miss Darling looked about ninety-six and probably weighed about the same. Her hair was a greenish-white, and she wore long dresses that we all figured she'd gotten secondhand from a Pennsylvania Dutch family. Her glasses were exceptionally thick, so much so that you really had to look hard to see if there were actually a human being's eyes underneath. Worst of all, she could hardly speak. Her voice was so quiet and soft, it was next to impossible to hear anything she ever said. A normal whisper sounded like a train whistle by comparison.

Needless to say, the entire group of us, and we weren't the only ones in a school filled with about two thousand students, made a blood sport out of torturing Miss Darling. Vinnie was the worst offender of all. With Nazi-like precision and planning, he unleashed an endless rash of pranks at Miss Darling that would have sent any normal person into early retirement. It's always been a wonder to me how that woman didn't end up over the wall at St. Elizabeth's or some other mental institution after withstanding three years of mind-numbing attacks from my boy Vin. One day he might sneak into the back of the classroom, wait for perfect silence, and then drop a two thousand-page textbook thunderously onto the floor, garnering a frightened shriek from his aged waif-like target. Another day, he snuck a little water gun into school, and when Miss Darling had her back turned and was writing on the chalkboard, he yelled, "Remember the Alamo" and showered her with an ice-cold stream right in the back of her neck.

My personal favorite gag started with Vinnie standing outside the classroom, waiting for total silence. At just the right time, he would stick his head into the room and yell "Miss Daaaaaarling" at the top of his lungs before running away down the hallway, cackling mindlessly. Scared out of her wits, Miss Darling would let out a yelp and turn to the back of the room only to see no one there. Like the lucky thief who gets rich and keeps on stealing, Vinnie never— not once—got caught. His ability to elude the school's security and administrators remains one of the world's great mysteries.

Even through college and deep into his twenties, Vinnie continued to torment the poor lady. Years after graduation when Vinnie somehow learned that Miss Darling lived with her mother, who by my count would have had to be about one hundred and fifteen years old by then, the smoldering fire was reignited.

Tom was hosting the game at his house in late December of 1988. He and Lianne were newlyweds, but with no interest in visiting with us even then, she was out for the night. A big fan of lighting up his charcoal grill during any season, Tom cooked some burgers, tossed a restaurant-style salad, and baked a damn tasty cherry pie from scratch. All that, a few cold beers, and, as usual, we were in our zone. There was nonstop chatter about our upcoming high school reunion, which girls would still look good and which of the former high school football players had blown up to John Candy-size proportions.

It was around this time that Tom took over the responsibility for bringing small bills and change to the game. No one ever assigned him the task. It may have been because he had easy access to cash at the store. I'm not really sure. He just started doing it. With the rest of us needing to break fives, tens, or twenties, Tom brought several rolls of quarters along with some other change and maybe a hundred singles in his money bag. Whenever the game was ready to start, usually a few minutes after dinner, Tom would hold the old canvas money bag up in the air. Then he would smile, start bopping his head back and forth, and look around at all of us. "Who needs some?"

We tried to ignore him, but he would persist. "Who needs some?" Since we couldn't play without the change, one of us ultimately would give in. "I need some."

That was Tom's cue and he would do this stupid little dance, holding the money bag over his head singing the O'Jays: "*money, money, money, money…*"

I can say with absolute certainty that no one ever, not even the first time he did it, thought it was funny. The guy couldn't sing for shit. Cats mating had better harmony.

Once Tom finished his monthly "sound of Philadelphia" ode to the O'Jays, we could finally start playing cards. During a particularly long game of what we called "the Big Wheel," Wocky folded quickly and went to the bathroom.

The Big Wheel is a seven-card poker game. The difference between it and other poker games is that you have to buy and build your hand. You get two cards from the dealer, dealt face down so no one can see. The dealer turns one card over so everyone at the table can see. If you are directly next to the dealer on the left, you get to take that card for free. If you don't want the card, the dealer turns over another and, in our game, if you want that one, you have to pay fifty cents. If not, you get to see a third card, but this one costs you a buck. If you still aren't interested, you are faced with a small-time card player's conundrum—fold your cards or pay two dollars for another card known as the Big Wheel. If the player springs for the Big Wheel, the card is dealt down so no one gets to see what he paid for. This pattern repeats itself around the table, then everyone bets and the dealer goes around again until the last card, which is free and dealt down to whomever has not yet folded.

At some point during the second or third turn around the table, both Tom and Vinnie dropped their cards, folded, and got up. Realizing that I was once again on the losing end of a hand, I followed, surrendering and standing up from my chair. It was about then that I noticed Vinnie and Tom, heads bent and whispering to each other. They were leaning against the wall with Tom's kitchen phone between them.

"Let's call her!" Tom was particularly animated.

"Call who?" I had no idea what they were up to.

"Quiet, Bro," Vinnie said. "We're going to call Miss Darling." Vinnie's eyes were popped out, he was smiling, and his face was exuding something more than his usual mischief, more of something just, well, wrong.

Keep in mind that this was before anyone had caller ID. Prank calling an elderly lady at this point in our lives might have stretched the bounds of decency, not to mention maturity, so I tried to stop it.

Just a little. "Aren't we too old for this shit? Jesus, you're almost ten years out of high school. Still prank calling that hag?"

Tom pulled MKat and me aside and let us in on the joke. We were lawyers, guys in business, guys who should have known better. And we did it anyway.

Like the old game of telephone, we discreetly passed the plan along to Don, Mark, and Baldwin.

"Miss Daaaarling!" Vinnie was pumped. "And. Bro, I'm only twenty-eight, so fuck it."

"I'm in! Wocky had returned from the bathroom, happily counting his winnings and refilling his tank with Tom's homemade cherry pie. A chunk of the cherry goo dripped out of the corner of his mouth.

Time to tee him up.

"You want to talk to her, Wock?" Tom asked.

"Fuck, yeah. That old bitch. Gave me a D—twice."

"You never went to class," Baldwin reminded him.

"You never even got the book," Don added.

Wock was not deterred. "Who gives a shit? What's the big deal? Everyone got a C, right?"

"I didn't," Baldwin said, lowering his head.

"What are you going to say, Wock?" Tom asked as he dialed.

"I don't know. Just give me the fucking phone already."

Mark turned away. "I can't watch," he whispered.

MKat leaned in to Don, trying not to smile. "Oh, Jesus. Here we go."

Tom made the call and handed the phone to Wocky. "Here. She's on."

He grabbed it out of Tom's hand and slapped it against his ear. Then Wocky yelped those words that would forever be enshrined in the Card Game Hall of Fame: "I wanna fuck you in the asshole!" He slammed the phone down.

We were hysterical, all of us, laughing uncontrollably. Baldwin was on the floor, doubled over. Don had tears in his eyes. MKat's hand was on Don's shoulder, trying to prop himself up and keep from going down on one knee.

Wocky was laughing right there with us, thinking he had just told old Miss Darling that he wanted to fuck her in the asshole. Watching him laugh, not knowing what he was laughing at, was just too much for us to take and, by this time, I was bent toward the floor, my stomach wrenching from laughing so hard.

Finally, Tom broke the news. "Wocky, that was your mother."

"What?" He looked around at the rest of us, barely containing ourselves. Wock's laughter stopped as if someone had clicked the TV onto a different channel. "That's not funny."

Oh, yes, it was.

# THIRTY-FOUR

**W**ocky finished his talk with his head down. "And, Tom, man, I forgive you." He looked up and then out at the rest of us. "Not you guys. Just him." No one else in the place knew what he was talking about except for us. I looked around at the boys. We were all smiling, with maybe even a tear or two here and there. Wocky got back to our row and sat back down next to me.

Vinnie leaned forward. "Really? You forgive him?"

"No. Not really." Gregg grinned. We all heard it, and more than one of us nodded our heads.

"Good," Vinnie said and sat back.

Forty-five minutes into the service and I was still trying to decide whether to get up and say something. In the last couple of days, I'd made some notes about Tom and what I wanted to talk about, how I wanted to say goodbye to my friend. I must have spent two or three hours writing and then rewriting just a few ideas down, much like I do when I'm going to court. Some trial lawyers write out their closing arguments; others who have terrific recall often don't even use a note. I fall somewhere in between and generally write out a few bulleted points that I want to make sure to cover, figuring that my brain and some natural momentum will carry me the rest of the way.

I reached into my jacket pocket, retrieved the latest version of my notes, and took another look at what I was going to say. It was embarrassing. My notes were filled with a lot of shallow platitudes but nothing special about this guy who had been such a constant part of my life for the last thirty-five years. As I read them over, I felt like I would sound like the rabbi, just talking to talk, with no real understanding or feeling about the guy that I was talking about. It just didn't seem right.

"Fuck." I meant to whisper, but maybe was a bit louder. I crumpled the pages and stuffed them back in my pocket.

I squeezed my forehead into my hand. How in the hell was I supposed to sum up this guy's life? All the things we did together, all that was said and so much that didn't have to be. I wondered what Tom would say if the roles were reversed; if I were the guy in the box at the front of the room. What would he say about me? I looked down the aisle and then craned my neck quickly at the fellows in the row behind. What would they say if it were me?

"Are you going up?" Laurie asked, her hand suddenly on my shoulder.

"I don't know," I said. "Not now anyway."

"You should. You're a good speaker. Tom would want you to say something."

I really didn't need the push and probably jumped back at her a little too sharply. "I'll say something, okay? I just don't know when or where. I don't know if it should be *here*."

Then I sat on my hands and waited for someone to take a turn. Anyone. Anything to keep me from having to make a decision about whether to wing it and hope something would come to me.

Thankfully, MKat got up and walked to the front.

# THIRTY-FIVE

"Everyone knows what a great guy Tom was," he said. "Yeah, yeah, yeah." MKat had a certain engaging way about him, even in front of a room of strangers.

"He loved Lianne, Jess, and Kasey. We all know that, too. But what the man really loved was to eat." I could hear Tom's girls laugh.

"Seriously, I don't know how else to say it, and I know I'm not telling you anything you don't already know. Your dad was an inhuman eater. A couple of years ago we were down at the boardwalk in Rehoboth Beach. It couldn't have been more than an hour. He had fried chicken and mashed potatoes from that dump, Gus and Gus. You think your dad was finished?" MKat looked down at the girls. They were shaking their heads.

"Nope. Your dad told me he was still hungry. Any idea where we went?"

I'm not sure if MKat was really asking anyone or if the question was rhetorical, but the girls knew the answers.

"Go Fish for a codfather sub, right?" Kasey guessed, referring to the walk-up fish-and-chips place, not the kids card game.

"Grotto's for a slice," Lianne put in. Even she was getting involved in MKat's game of call-and-response. His little spiel was starting to remind me of a revival meeting.

MKat smiled and nodded. "Yep. You're both right. He ordered his codfather from Go Fish, and since it was going to take a few minutes to fry it up—and I mean just a few—your dad had a slice of pizza from Grotto while he waited."

MKat looked down at the twins once more. "And a little dessert right?" he coaxed.

"Right!" Jess and Kasey spoke in unison this time.

"No doubt. Tom had to have a snow cone, just to help get it all down, I guess."

Again, we could hear some pretty solid laughter from the front of the room. Everyone was twisting and stretching a bit to try to see the girls' faces.

"And here's the funny part," MKat went on. "We stopped about an hour later and, while I was getting gas, Tom came out of the Royal Farms chewing like he had a wad of tobacco in his mouth." Imitating their dad, MKat held his hands up in the air and started exaggerating a weird chewing noise that sounded especially awful over the tinny microphone. "Your dad had packs of Goldenberg's Peanut Chews in both hands. He told me they were gifts for Vinnie, but I'm pretty sure both packs were long gone before I dropped him off at the house."

MKat stepped down from the podium. Lianne and both the girls stood up and gave him a hug. I thought to myself how perfect MKat's few minutes were up there. He didn't say much about Tom but didn't really need to. It was a funny story, a true story. MKat captured Tom in a way that everyone who knew him, regardless of how they knew him, could appreciate. Tom Porter could definitely eat.

# THIRTY-SIX
## 2006

"**H**ey, Laur. Bro home?" Tom, dripping sweat, was at my front door.

"Sunday night. *The Sopranos* are on. What else would he be doing?" Laurie asked.

She was right. Although Laurie and I would share most of the kid duties after dinner, with baths and stories and all that, we had a deal that I was left alone for one hour on Sunday nights so that I could recede into the mob fantasyland that was Tony Soprano and his family. From the previews, I had a feeling this was going to be a great episode; Tony had just been shot by that bastard, Uncle Junior, and was in the hospital fighting for his life. Just as Christopher and Paulie were arguing about who should be in charge, my buddy with the bad timing was ringing the doorbell.

"Everything okay?" I heard Laurie ask. "Everything good?"

It was a strange time for a visit.

I tried not to move from the couch, gritting my teeth and hoping Tom would decide to leave and, like the rain, come back another day.

"No. Everything's great. Got some good news. Some news, anyway. I figured I'd get some exercise, go for a run. I was hoping he wanted to have a quick beer and maybe have him drive me home," Tom said.

"I'm sure it's no problem. It is a long run back in the dark," Laurie said.

It was ironic that a guy who could run like Tom had such big feet and was sort of a lumberer when he was just walking around; you could always hear him coming. I liked to joke that his feet got into a room about five minutes before the rest of him showed up. In his size thirteen Brooks running shoes, it was not hard to tell that he was coming my way across the hardwood floor of the front hallway and into the family room, where, by now, I had slunk as far under Laurie's beige afghan as I could without blocking my view of the TV.

I felt him standing above me from behind the couch. Still holding out some faint hope that maybe he would go away and I could stay on the boat to see some of Tony's coma-induced hallucinations, I remained quiet.

"What's going on, man?" Tom asked.

"*Sopranos*. Want to sit and watch?" I asked quietly as not to miss the banter between the boys on screen.

"Let's have a quick beer. Got something to tell you. It's HBO, Bro. They will replay the episode ten times this week."

He was right, but I was still annoyed when I clicked off the TV and got up. I grabbed a couple of beers and followed him outside to my deck.

"Sure. But I hope it's something more than your running into that twit Dina from Mr. Cliff's class," I said, dropping down into a plastic wicker chair.

Dina was short and chunky with spiked brown hair, a little like Blondie's Debbie Harry. Having transferred into Sherbrook as a senior, she was in Tom's twelfth-grade English class for a while but left after only about three months amid rumors that she had given Mr. Cliff a hand job at detention after school. In the short time that she was there, Tom swore that she stared and smiled at him every day in class, but he was never able to gather up the courage to even talk to the girl.

"I should have gotten that hand job," Tom said.

"Yeah, yeah. I know." I looked at him, nodding my head in that way we both knew meant, "here he goes again."

"Seriously, Bro. She liked me." Tom was still ruminating over the long-lost hand job.

"Must have liked that creep Cliff a bit more, I guess," I replied. "Anyway, what's the big news?" I twisted open the two Rolling Rocks, handing him one, trying not to look at his booty length runner shorts that had crept up above and wrinkled just below his crotch.

"I sold the stores. Deal is done." Tom took a swig.

I knew that one or two corporate grocery chains had approached Tom in the last year or so, but other than some off-the-cuff legal advice, we never talked much about the details.

"All cash, just like you said." Tom took another drink. Bigger swallow this time.

"Get the fuck out, man. That is unbelievable. You're all set." In that moment, I was really happy for him. For years, Tom was up by 3:30 a.m. or so each morning and off to one of his stores, unloading produce and stocking shelves, as if he were a six-dollar-an-hour employee and not the owner of the place. While he did get the money to start the business from his parents' estates, it was years of his sweat and hard work that made the stores successful.

I sat up a bit in my chair and reached my beer over toward his.

Tom gave me a halfhearted clink. "Yeah, I guess" was all he said, staring forward across the deck and out into the woods, his legs now splayed out in front of him.

"Okay, first of all, it's hard to take you seriously when your one nut is hanging outside those hot pants of yours. Second, you don't seem too thrilled about it. What's the problem?" I asked. I sat back in my chair, shaking my head at a guy who seemed more than a little troubled after just hitting the big time.

Tom slipped the runaway testicle back into the nylon liner of his shorts. For a little while, he didn't say anything, just sat there looking like a guy who was one digit off in a seventy-five million-dollar Powerball.

Tom's attitude was particularly annoying to me although I tried to keep my feelings to myself. Here he was, set for life financially. Not yet fifty years old, he didn't really have to work and, while maybe not one of the world's richest men, he could spend the rest of his life running on cruise control and for the most part doing what he wanted. We should all have his problems, I thought.

As we continued to nurse our beers, I think we were both waiting for the other to say something to get the conversation restarted. If he wanted some kind of sympathy from me, he was not going to get it. It was about then that the tide of my selfish, jealous side washed in and took over. Here I was, stuck in a job that I really hated but needed if I was going to keep up with my family's ever-increasing need for more. More lessons, more clothes, more vacations. More. I had no way out. I wasn't going to be retiring on the sale of my bound editions of the collected statutes of Maryland family law. If only I had Tom's options. Poor me.

"Yeah, well, it's not so great, Bro." Tom finally broke the silence.

"Sure," I said, unable to contain my annoyance. "You have more money than most anyone could hope for. You can stay home, not work, and do whatever the fuck you want. Sounds awful. I don't know how you are going to manage." I was laying into him pretty good.

"You don't get it. I came here because I figured you were the one guy that would. If I wanted to get hammered on, I would have gone to see Vinnie or MKat," Tom said.

"At least then I would have seen what happened with Tony," I reminded him.

"Like it's going to be some mystery, for Chrissake. It's *The Sopranos*. He gets patched up, wakes up, and gets better. Not too tough to figure out that plot line," Tom said.

Of course, that was exactly what would happen. We laughed and drained our beers. I got up, went inside to grab two more cold ones, and sat back down.

"Seriously, what's the problem?" I asked.

"Bro, how much longer you think I got? Both my parents died around my age now. My wife won't fuck me." Tom shook his head.

I wasn't sure which was worse. Thinking you were going to die soon or living without sex. Neither sounded appealing to me. And lots of people ended up in my office with thick file folders over the second. I kept listening.

"And you know the worst part? Lianne hates Jess. I mean hates her. She's tough, I know, but really? How do you hate your own kid? She says it all the time. When we are out and people start talking about their kids, she only talks about Kasey, never about Jess. It's like she has one kid and the other doesn't even exist." Tom banged the bottle of Rock on the table and wiped his mouth.

"She doesn't really hate her," I replied. "We all say stuff about our kids that we don't mean." That seemed like pretty decent insight to me.

"I know you don't like Lianne. None of the guys like her. None of that used to matter to me. But this thing she has with Jess, I just don't know. It's hard for me to even look at her sometimes. I try to talk to her about it. She just blows me off. Says there's nothing she can do. She feels the way she feels; that 'it is what it is,' whatever that means."

I kind of got the "it" part.

For their birthdays a few years back, Tom and Lianne had rented a party bus to take the twins and some friends down to a Japanese-style restaurant in DC. They were going to one of those tacky places that teenage girls seem to love where everyone sits around a circular table watching the chef in the middle toss knives in the air while all the major food groups sizzle and conglomerate in a cast-iron skillet like some strange slice 'n' dice floor show.

Since the party was billed as a "girls' night out" and Lianne was chaperoning the kids on the bus, Tom and I made plans to head out after the girls left for some pizza and a few beers. When I got to his house, the pink party bus was in the driveway, blaring some Britney Spears drivel from the speakers. Fighting the urge to cringe, I gave a perfunctory wave and head nod to the girls on the bus and started walking toward Tom's front door.

Like his dad before him, Tom kept his lawn in prime condition, the freshly mulched flowerbeds popping in pinks and purples, grass cut at what I assumed was a mower-measured three inches.

Once I got far enough away from Britney's sexually infused nails-on-the-chalkboard moaning, I could hear Tom and Lianne going at it pretty good. Tom was facing his wife, whose back was to the door. Neither of them noticed me.

"She needs to get out here now or we will just leave without her," Lianne said.

Having seen Kasey on the bus, I figured she was talking about Jess.

"She's coming." Tom seemed to be pleading.

"Every fucking time we plan something, we're always waiting for her. It's her party and she's still late." Lianne was pissed.

"I know, but none of her friends could come. Everyone here is for Kasey. She's upset. Just give her a minute," Tom said.

"Friends? Yeah, right. She doesn't have any friends. Don't you get it yet? No one likes her," Lianne said just as the door opened behind her. "I don't like her. I can't stand her. She ruins everything. She fucks everything up. I'm not letting her wreck this party. Not this time. You want to stick up for her again, that's fine, but I'm not staying around to listen." Lianne spat out it all out in one unbroken continuous sentence as she turned and brushed past me toward the bus. Not surprisingly, she didn't acknowledge my standing right there, having just witnessed her tirade.

"Ready to go?" she asked the girls inside.

As she walked away, Jess stepped forward and stared at her mother from the doorway. Although she looked pretty, in a light-colored floral dress and sandals, there was a certain awkwardness to her, as if she had picked some clothes from her sister's closet to be sure she would fit in with the rest of the girls. Staring ahead and blinking away tears, Jess didn't say anything as she backed her way inside the house and out of view.

Tom was running his hands through his hair. "Sorry, Bro. Think I'll have to pass tonight. I'm gonna hang with Jess," he said. His face was flushed. His hands were moving in that absent way of ex- or almost ex-smokers, fumbling for the absent lighter and filter tip.

He may have been craving a smoke, but Tom already had his hands full. Behind his wood and beveled glass front door were two kids, biologically related from the same womb, raised in the same home with the same values, yet so diametrically different it was like they had been switched at birth. Lianne undoubtedly was far more comfortable with Kasey, an obedient and docile kid with whom she knew what to expect. Jess was in every sense her polar opposite, a "wild child," blazing with emotions and complexities and anything but predictable. Jess was work, and Lianne wanted nothing to do with her. Jess was just something that she had to live with. Tom was left to be the kid's champion, her protector, desperately searching for reasons and excuses.

"Yeah, sure. No problem," I said as the door closed in front of me.

Tom kept talking.

"It's great that I have all this money now, but what am I going to do? What's going to happen to that kid if I die like my dad did?" Tom looked at me.

His eyes caught mine. I looked away. I didn't know what to say. I couldn't tell him that his wife would ever fuck him or love him, that his daughter wouldn't go down a worse path. So, like a guy hawking a weekly Mega Millions scratch-off game, I went for the easy platitudes. "You're not going to die. You're a young guy. You're a runner. You've got plenty of money. You'll probably outlive the rest of us."

"I don't think so," he said, standing up and heading back inside, staring at his jumbled reflection in the sliding glass door.

As it turned out, Tom was right.

# THIRTY-SEVEN

About twenty minutes and a few more speakers later, the service seemed to be winding down. I still wasn't up to walking up there and sharing stories about Tom. Somehow it just didn't feel right to me. I sat back and said nothing, just as I had when he was alive.

The rabbi stepped back up to the podium, said a few more forgettable things, and asked everyone to stand.

"*Yit'gadal v'yit'kadash sh'mei raba...*" So began the Mourner's Kaddish, the Hebrew prayer for the dead. Everyone bowed their heads; some of us mumbled the words in Hebrew, or at least the ones we knew.

Something struck me as off pitch, though. Tom was raised Catholic. His dad was an amateur carpenter who devoted an enormous amount of his life to the church. Wasn't Jesus a carpenter, too? My mind was racing, thinking of my Catholic friend whose best friends, his wife, his kids are all Jews, along with, obviously, the guy who was directing his last ride to the great beyond, Rabbi what's-his-name. I suddenly had a hard time focusing on much other than the whole religious irony of things.

MKat snapped me back into the present with a tap on the shoulder. "Bro, come on, man," he said. "We need to go up. They asked for the pallbearers."

With my head still bowed, MKat thought I was crying. When I lifted up my head, he raised his eyebrows.

"Not sure what's so funny," he told me, "but we got a job to do. Everyone's waiting, brother."

I buttoned my jacket, trying to look appropriately serious. I followed the rest of the guys up front. They were waiting for me to get my ass together.

When we got to the front of the room, the rabbi directed each of us to a spot alongside of Tom's casket. Paul was at the back end; the rest of us found a spot on either side and grabbed the rail. We took a collective deep breath and looked to the rabbi for instructions. Before he could say anything, another song popped on overhead.

Someone had a real sense of humor. It was Southside Johnny, in his best bluesy drawl, leaning into the opening bars of *"We're havin' a Party…"*

"Love it," Don said, bobbing his head. He was impressed.

We all looked at each other. I had no idea what kind of sick fuck came up with the idea of spinning Southside's "Havin' a Party" just as a funeral was ending. Didn't know, but I liked it.

Baldwin started the famous finger snap.

Mark was tapping on the top of the casket.

We looked at each other.

"What the hell? Let's go," MKat said, echoing just what the rest of us were thinking.

It was as if someone had beamed us back to 1979, and we were back in Pop's—hanging out, singing, The Scarf grunting. It wasn't the Doobies playing, but that didn't matter. As if we had been rehearsing for years, all of us started in together: *So listen, Mr. Deejay, keep those records playing...*

After a moment or two of what felt like disbelief, a few others cautiously joined in. Another few seconds and pretty much everyone in the place was singing. The whole thing was straight out of a movie, the kind that tries too hard but, for some reason, still works. A bunch of guys leaning on their dead buddy's casket and a room full of people singing, laughing, and crying all at the same time.

Then, out of nowhere, my friend was back. There was that familiar sideways smile, with his left eye sort of squinty as if someone was shining a flashlight at him. I stared and kept singing. Misted as I was, I couldn't really see all that clearly. It took a second or two for me to snap back and realize who I was looking at. Not Tom, of course. It was his kid, Jess, looking right into me in the same way her dad used to do when he thought he was bluffing at the card table. That's when I knew: Jess was our musical director.

# THIRTY-EIGHT

Since I spent most of my days working with families that were fracturing and pulling apart, it was particularly important to me that my kids maintained and enjoyed some connections with each other as well as with Laurie and me. Something more than the simple act of "being a family." The same dulled, wooden kitchen table that was carved and scratched from serving as a makeshift art studio and used every few months for our card games was converted on Friday nights to a Shabbat table. Neither Laurie nor I made ourselves out to be the best of Jews; we just liked the idea of getting all the kids together, lighting candles, and sitting down to eat, usually splitting up a pizza or dolling out Chinese food onto paper plates. The girls often fought over egg rolls or who would get the last pepperoni, who would sit where, who got to pick the movie we would watch together after dinner, or at least try to anyway.

Those Friday nights were often exasperating and agonizingly stressful. And I loved them. Every one.

At Tom's house, though, the divide between him and Jess in one corner and Lianne and Kasey in the other continued its malignant spread as the girls grew up.

Lianne doted on Kasey, who was always a quiet, sweet, and respectful kid. I don't want to call her boring, but she was generally a bit blank and without much emotion. I can't remember the kid ever really smiling.

Maybe since I didn't have to live with her, I really liked Jess. Quirky and funny, she exuded an unusual charm and had a certain inherent sweetness that made most adults take to her. Unfortunately, "most adults" did not include her mother.

Whenever she went out, Lianne took Kasey with her under the guise that Jess "didn't want to go anyway." When they were all home together, Jess frequently kicked back by picking fights with Kasey, standing in front of the TV when Kasey was watching, or disconnecting the computer when she was using it. Tom told me that the circuitous dynamic almost always ended the same—Kasey, the quiet and manageable one, got to watch her show or play her computer game, while Jess, the straw that stirred the drink, was banished to the solitude of her bedroom.

Having seen this play before, albeit with different actors and story lines, I was infinitely familiar with the aching destruction caused when kids collide and collude with their bickering parents.

One of the roles that helped me spread my lawyer wings and build a practice was the one I played in my frequent court appointments to represent the children in contested custody cases. Formerly designated as a "*guardian ad litem,*" the lawyer appointed to fill this role is now somewhat sadly but creatively captioned the "best interests attorney." When you think about it, the idea that a complete stranger is appointed by a judge to investigate, make recommendations to the court, and even advocate for what is in the best interests of a child he or she doesn't even know is utterly stupefying. Of course, it wouldn't be necessary if the parents themselves could act like adults, set their own bullshit aside, and try to row in the same direction, just for a while, anyway, in order to help the very people they are allegedly so concerned about.

Whenever I have been appointed to be a best interests attorney, I make it clear to both parents from the outset that I didn't ask for the job. I personally wouldn't want some judicially appointed interloper meddling into my relationship with my kids and making decisions that will affect their lives forever.

I once represented a sixteen-year-old girl from a well-to-do family that lived in Chevy Chase, Maryland, a tony and well-heeled part of town on the border of the District of Columbia. The kid attended a fancy private all-girls school, had her own American Express black card, and drove a sharp little BMW convertible that probably cost twice as much as the very un-lawyerlike Wrangler hard top that I tooled around town in. We sat outside a Starbucks one day to talk about what she thought was the best living situation for her and her nine-year-old brother.

"I don't even know why I have to talk to you," she said, eyes hidden behind a very dark pair of Persol sunglasses. "Everything is fine. Whenever my mom yells at me or tries to ground me, I call my dad," she said, tapping her new iPhone wrapped in a hot pink OtterBox case. "I know he'd rather stick a pin in his eye than back up my mom, so it's cool. He tells me he's sorry. That he loves me. Then he buys me something." She looked across the street at the Beemer and smiled, thinking, I am sure, *"See what I mean, fucker?"*

"So how does that solve anything?" I asked. "Don't you need to have some stability, know where you are going to sleep from one night to the next? That your mom or dad will at least be around if you need something?"

"Listen, mister. I don't know why you are here or what you want from me. I can't stand my mom; she doesn't like me much either. My dad always wants to fix everything. So I let him try. It works just fine. Hope that helps. Gotta go." She grabbed what was left of her fat-free Grande Vanilla Latte, got up, and strutted back across the street and into her car.

I put on my best serious concerned lawyer face and tried to talk some sense into both parents about trying to exercise a slight bit of supervision over the airbrushed teenaged Frankenstein they had created. The dad looked at his Rolex, the mom twisted her David Yurman bracelet.

After four days of trial and tens of thousands of dollars in legal bills, the judge simply awarded joint custody. In other words, nothing changed.

After I told Laurie about what was going on with Tom and Lianne, she encouraged me to invite them and the girls over for our Friday night dinners. Lianne was not interested. She liked to go shopping with a couple of other mothers and their daughters, and Kasey naturally went along. Aside from the fact that she was probably not welcome to go with her mom and sister, Jess hated being in the car for more than a few minutes and never would have had the patience to wait or look around while her mother and sister poked through the racks in the Brass Plum department at Nordstrom anyway.

Jess truly seemed to enjoy the nights at our house, and we loved having her around. That's not to say that she was easy. The kid babbled endlessly and, like an amusement ride that doesn't end, she never stopped moving.

"I need to go to the bathroom," she would yelp just as we all sat to eat as if we were across the street and not at the same table. If there was a plate of something Jess didn't recognize, that usually elicited an emphatic and ear-piercing, "That's gross!" She was consistently spilling and dropping food all over and onto the floor, much to Laurie's distress. At the same time, Jess was my dog's favorite guest. He would sit under the table head facing her seat, waiting for the first bite to fall.

"Daddy, the doggie ate my chicken," she whined one night.

"How did he get up to eat your chicken?" Tom asked.

"He jumped up. You weren't looking."

Tom put another piece on her plate.

"I'm not hungry," she said, in one motion hopping out of her chair and shoving her plate into the middle of the table, chicken flopping over the side.

Although appropriately stern, Tom was conspicuously enchanted with Jess, smiling and gentle any time he needed to curb her enthusiasm or redirect her activity level.

"That's not a trampoline, Jess," Tom cautioned her regularly as she jumped on the ottoman in our family room. "You're going to get hurt."

"But it's fun, Daddy," she replied, bouncing, singing, and grinning despite Tom's warnings.

Within a moment, Jess missed a jump, her left leg tripping off the side of the ottoman and causing her to crumple and whack her head on the side of the table. Jess wailed at the top of her lungs as if someone had died. Immediately, Tom ran over and pulled her into his lap, stroking her head with his hand and pulling her head into his chest.

Wiping the tears from her cheek, Jess said, "I love you, Daddy."

"I love you, too, Jessie girl," Tom replied as she pulled away and ran off into another room.

Whenever Tom hosted a card game, he would tell Kasey to say hi, which she did obediently and without hesitation. From there, however, she faded into a book, a television show, or her computer. I usually wouldn't see her again until the next game at Tom's house eight or nine months later when essentially the same pattern repeated itself. From a toddler to a teenager, until her mom started taking her out of the house for card game nights, it was pretty much the same.

"Hi, Kasey."

"Hi."

"How's school?"

"Good."

That was about it.

Unlike her sister, Jess was genuinely excited to see us card game boys. Pulsing with boundless energy, even into her teens, Jess would bounce down the stairs and around the hallway into Tom's kitchen. It was so cool with this kid who always made it seem like her dad's friends were her buddies, too.

At every game, I was met with a "What's up, Uncle Bro?" She had a greeting for the rest of the guys as well. Baldwin would get a "Hi, Baldwin." She especially liked to give a hearty "Yo, Wocky" shout whenever he walked in the door.

Tom told me on at least a few occasions through the years that although Jess had no trouble making friends, she had a mountain of difficulty in keeping them. I suspected that, especially as she got older, kids her age were not all that able or even willing to handle her boisterous and sometimes over-the-top behavior. It may also have been that she was adopted or that she was jealous over the relationship that Lianne had with her sister. I don't really know. What I do know is that whatever the "it" was that brewed silently just under the surface for years ultimately burst and boiled over, nearly drowning Jess and washing her life away.

# THIRTY-NINE
## 2007

It was a Friday night, only around ten or so, when the phone rang and an automated voice said, "Porter, Tho-mas." We had one of those annoying caller ID phones that announce the caller's name or number. Laurie loved the thing because she could decide whether or not to answer the phone. I never answered the phone anyway, so it was just another electronic advancement that maintained little relevance to my day-to-day life.

"Hello. Tom?" Laurie popped the phone onto speaker so the dogs and I could hear whoever was on the other end.

"Hey, Laur," Tom said. "Is Bro around?" Laurie and I were both tired from a long day and were in bed early. I covered my head with the pillow.

"Yeah. Sure. Everything okay?" Laurie asked.

"Uh. Yeah," Tom said. "I guess." He paused. I could hear his breathing, which sounded weird. I tossed the pillow off, leaned across the bed, and sighed in my usual exasperated fashion.

"Hey," I said sleepily. "What's up?"

"It's Jess," he said. "I'm waiting for the ambulance." There was no explanation and, with my usual flair for ineptitude, I was silent.

Listening in, Laurie poked me and arched her eyebrows.

I realized I should really say something. "What happened?" I asked.

No response.

"Okay, Tom," I said finally. "What can I do?"

"I don't know," he said. "I didn't tell Lianne yet. She's on her way home with Kasey. I don't know. I'm just so scared. I mean, I think she's okay. She's breathing. The ambulance is coming."

Laurie poked me again.

"Okay," I said. "Tell me where you are. I'll come over. He gave me the spot, a neighborhood corner about two miles from my house not too far from his place in Brookeville.

Having gotten three of four girls through their teens already, including the one who almost drove me over the south rim of the Grand Canyon à la *Thelma and Louise*, I kept handy what I liked to call my "front door clothes." I grabbed them whenever I got a late-night call from one of my kids—if they'd been drinking, been with someone who'd been drinking, needed a ride home for whatever reason, or even if they needed a simple late-night toothbrush delivery at a sleepover.

The snazzy ensemble consisted of an old pair of green oversized cargo pants, an Asbury Jukes T-shirt from a late-'80s Stone Pony show, and a beat-up pair of Sanuk slip-ons. Nothing if not organized, I also kept a torn zip-up sweatshirt and knit hat handy for the winter months.

By the time Laurie hung up, I was heading down the stairs and out the door. She trailed me to the car, saying, "If Jess is suicidal, you need to make sure they keep her in the hospital. Don't let them release her. Make sure Tom knows to tell them to have her evaluated." Laurie spends her days working with kids experiencing various degrees of emotional difficulties, so this was all in a day's work for her. For me, however, while dealing with the revolving door of clients in crisis was one thing, helping my friend and his daughter who I had held when she was a squirmy, squalling newborn and who was now passed out on the side of the road was something completely different.

Still, I got there, and either I was moving quickly or the local emergency rescue folks were slacking because I arrived before they did.

When I got out of the car, Jess was in a heap on the ground, her head in Tom's lap. She was breathing but not smoothly.

Tom told me that one of Jess's friends had called him an hour earlier and said that she wasn't herself, stumbling around and unable to speak clearly. When Tom asked to talk to Jess, the girl told him that Jess just shook her head and started running down the street. Apparently, the kid hung up, leaving Tom in a panic and unsure what to do. Thankfully, a second phone call came a moment or two later. It was the same girl. Jess was on the ground and not moving. Tom told the girl to wait there for him, but by the time he got to Jess, the other kid was gone.

I sat down next to Tom and tried to think of something caring or insightful to say. Nothing came. Instead, I gave him one of those *Father Knows Best* pats on the back and muttered something inanely stupid along the lines of "she'll be okay." On several levels, I was thankful when the ambulance and fire engine pulled up.

With a blood alcohol content of nearly four times the legal limit, it didn't take long for the folks at the emergency room to figure out that Jess drank about a barrel of what was probably very cheap booze and they had to stick a tube down her throat and add charcoal to clear out her stomach.

After a bit, a nurse pushed through the door into a small waiting area, rolled her eyes, and told me that "the drunk girl's daddy" wanted me to come in. When I walked in I saw a scene inside the hospital room that offered a pretty fair representation of the entire family dynamic. Jess was still out of it, her head propped on a couple of pillows, face stained black around her mouth, and her chin plastered with some of what must have come out when the charcoal went in. Tom was sitting on the bed, holding her hand with one hand and stroking her head with the other. Lianne was sitting in a chair across the room, and from what I could hear, talking to Kasey on her cell phone.

"Oh, she'll be fine," she was saying. "They're doing some tests. You go to sleep and don't worry. What time is your cheerleading picture tomorrow? Be sure to use my curling iron. Oh, never mind. I'm sure I'll be home and we can do your hair together." Ever since she and Tom started dating, I'd barely tolerated Lianne, but right then? I hated her.

I stood in the corner for a while, feeling bad for this kid, this lost and obviously distressed little girl. She may have been fifteen, but as a father four times over, I still saw just that—a little girl.

Tom asked me to stay with Jess while he drove Lianne home. There was no question about her staying or who would be taking her home. Tom just stood up. Lianne nodded her head and picked up her purse, clearly ready to leave. I looked at her, searching for a sign that she was hurting for her daughter, a tear, a sigh even. Nope.

Not one fucking word. Lianne walked out of the room without looking back.

I think I dozed off for a few minutes in Tom's chair when I heard a cough, then a quiet, "Uncle Bro, what are you doing here? Where's my dad?"

"He just left to take your mom home. They've both been sitting with you since you came in here," I lied.

"Both of them, huh?" She knew.

"Yeah. Jesus, you scared the shit out of them. How you doing?"

"I'm okay," she said. "Seems like I've been sleeping for about a week. Plus, my throat is killing me."

"Between the garbage vodka and having charcoal and a tube jammed down your throat, that'll do it to you, I guess." We both smiled just a little.

My cell phone rang. It was Tom. "Is she up?"

"Yeah," I said, "and looking for you. When you going to get back?"

Tom explained that he and Lianne were sitting with Kasey, who was pretty upset about her sister.

"Let me talk to her real quick," he said.

I handed Jess the phone and did my best not to listen. The conversation was short, just a minute or two.

"Okay, Daddy," Jess was saying. "I'm sorry. See you soon." She gave me back the phone just as the nurse came in, threatening to take it away for using it in the ER. I slipped the phone into my pocket.

Jess took a closer look at me and, even in her miserable condition, half giggled. "Nice pants," she said.

"Yeah. Thanks."

The next few minutes were pretty quiet, just the steady beeps of her monitor and breathing. Jess looked at me with watery eyes, the tears eventually smearing the gray stains around her mouth.

"I just don't fit, Uncle Bro," she finally said. "They're all so perfect. Mom, Kasey. Everything is always the way it should be. Everything is so easy. Even for Dad. I know he's sloppy and all that, but everything he does, it seems he just gets it all right." The tears were really running now. Jess was making that noise kids make when they cry and can't catch their breath.

If only Laurie were here instead of me, I thought. She would know just what to say and just how to say it. But Jess was going to have to settle for me. We both would. So I decided to talk to her about someone I knew a lot about. Her dad.

"Jess," I began. "I have no idea what is going on with you or why you feel like this. I can tell you that your father has never been a guy who has things come his way easily. You know what happened to your grandparents."

She nodded.

"Your dad lost both his parents. You're in high school yourself. Imagine how you would feel if both your parents were gone. But he fought. He found a way to survive. He worked to marry your mom, and you would not believe what the two of them went through to have you two girls. Adoption is not easy. It took a lot of time, a lot of luck, and, let me tell you, a lot of goddamn money. Your dad has always worked for everything. Nothing, and I mean nothing, was ever given to him. And listen, I know you have stuff about being adopted. You know I get it."

She was still crying. "I know all that," she said. "But what about him? That doesn't really tell me about him, Uncle Bro. That's the stuff everyone knows. It's the same bullshit I hear from everybody. My parents. My therapist. Now you. It's bullshit. I mean, I know it's true, but really, enough already." She coughed and wiped her mouth on her arm.

Everything I said about her dad was certainly factual, but at the same time, I knew she was right. This girl had just drunk herself to a cocktail short of an early grave, and she was reaching for something more about her parents, something more about who they were.

"Fuck it," I said. "You want to know about your dad? Who he really is? Sure."

I think the "fuck it" got her attention. She stared right into me with those big, brown, bloodshot eyes.

Over the next hour, I told her. I told her how I met her dad, I told her about his taking her mom into the woods to make out when they were in high school. I told her about how Tom would sit in my car and make me listen to Southside Johnny and all his horn players blaring as loud as those tinny speakers would allow and for as long as it took for me to "get it." I told her about Pop's and its pizza, The Scarf, and our well-tuned harmonies. I walked her back through our trips to Atlantic City, the stops at Richman's and Wocky's favorite milkshake, late-night food fests at Tony's, and her Dad's struggles at the blackjack table. She laughed out loud and squeezed my hand tight when I told her about her father's master plan to steal Bob the Big Boy. I did skip over the "Dead Dick Tom" story, though. His daughter didn't need to hear that one.

Talking, really talking. It felt good. Even if it was to somebody else's fifteen-year-old kid.

A good while later, when Tom walked into the room, I was still at it.

"Who you talking to, Bro?" he asked.

I looked up at him, then over to Jess.

She was asleep.

# FORTY

The procession out of the funeral home was ready to start. "Hold on a second," I said, letting the rabbi know to wait.

The rest of the guys took their hands off Tom's casket. "Now what?" Wocky asked. "Bro, this ain't right. We got to get moving."

I walked back toward Jess, her mom, and her sister.

"Come with me," I said, motioning to Jess. Lianne looked at me, not knowing what was going on but too restrained to do anything about it. Jess grabbed my hand and stepped in between Wocky and me.

"Sir, this is not usual," the rabbi informed me. He was not happy about my adding Jess as a pallbearer.

I looked at him and scoffed, respectfully, of course. "Fuck it," I said.

"Yeah, fuck it," Jess agreed.

Jess put her hand on the rail right next to mine and we started to walk her father out of his funeral.

# FORTY-ONE

Intuitive as usual, Laurie knew I should be with at least one of the boys, so she and my kids hopped a ride with Pam while Vinnie got in my car for the twenty-minute trip to the cemetery. "Fuck, Bro," he said. "I still can't believe it. So sad." I could tell he wanted to talk, but I just didn't have it in me.

"I know," I said. What else was there to say anyway? The guy was young, he had kids and died way sooner than he should have. That's it. I flipped on the radio.

"Seriously? What's wrong with you, man?" Vinnie persisted.

"Nothing's wrong," I said. "I just don't feel the need to have to express every goddamn thing that's going on in my head. What I'm 'feeling' and all that shit. I'm not like you."

As he got older, Vinnie had become more and more of a guy who wanted everyone to know how interested he was in their lives. The quality was particularly irritating to me, someone who preferred not to wait for the response to a "how you doing?" greeting, but I never doubted Vinnie's sincerity.

"Okay. Sure. Whatever you say. You've known the guy most of your life. Think of all the shit we've all done together. And you got nothing to say?" Vinnie asked.

"Right. And what part of 'leave me the fuck alone' don't you understand?" I answered.

Vinnie shook his head and cleared his throat in that annoying passive-aggressive way that people do when they want you to know they're exasperated. I ignored him and enjoyed the silence. It didn't last long.

"Listen," Vinnie said. "I know he meant a lot to you, Bro. But, seriously, keeping all this to yourself is not good for you."

I relented just a little. "Okay," I said. "Fine. But that doesn't mean I have to give a big speech, mostly to a room filled with people I couldn't care less about. All right? I mean, seriously, Lianne and the kids—definitely Jess—they know how I feel. I can talk to you guys whenever I want. I don't need to give some pathetic overview of my relationship with the guy. And I certainly don't need you playacting as a therapist. Save that for all those gullible bastards you're trying to sell your magnets or water or vitamins or whatever the fuck it is this month." I knew that it was wrong and felt bad immediately when I said it.

Vinnie used to be a dentist. A talker at heart, I guess it bothered him that when he was with his patients, they couldn't talk back as his hands were usually in their mouths. In a move I questioned at first but later came to admire for its courage, Vinnie ultimately decided that he was not willing to live his life within the bounds of a tedium he couldn't stand. He sold his practice and for the last ten years has been hocking a variety of nontraditional wellness products through different multilevel marketing programs. He was genuinely devoted to each and every product, and when he suggested that one of us try this product or that for whatever symptom may have been ailing our aging card game population, the desire to help was serious and heartfelt. In fairness, we should have respected his work and listened to him once in a while. Of course, listening and respect were not exactly regular traits of ours, so we all did what we did best. We made fun of him without thinking too much about it.

"I get it," Vinnie said. "Drive the car." He got it.

I didn't want to leave things that way, though, and I was mindful of Vinnie's need for constant chatter, so I decided to try to reignite the conversation if for no reason other than to get him to forget my being such an asshole.

"I know what you're saying," I told him. "And I appreciate it, really. You know I do. I just don't feel compelled to talk about it. Tom and me, all of us, we have something that I don't think too many people do. I know what it is. Was. Whatever. He knew. The rest of you know. That's enough for me."

Vinnie was uncharacteristically quiet.

We came to the last stoplight before the turn into the cemetery. Vinnie had his head down, and he started laughing. He was fiddling with something in his hand.

I couldn't help but laugh even though I had no idea what I was laughing about. The guy could never sit still and was always fidgeting.

Vinnie lifted up his head. Having found a tube of Laurie's lipstick in the console, he had smeared a little above his upper lip like one of those "Got milk?" ads.

He didn't have to say a word. I knew the reference to Tom's little extramarital get-together a few years back.

Vinnie said it anyway as only he can. With his big grin and that goofy thing he does when he opens his eyes real wide like a cartoon, he squawked: "Tastes like iron!"

# FORTY-TWO
## 2008

Once we'd all gotten married, Baldwin for a second time, we started going on an annual golf trip each fall, usually to Atlantic City. We did play golf during those trips, but most of us weren't very good. Vinnie and Tom were decent enough, but the rest of us played at varying levels of lousy. Really, though, the golf was just a reason, as if we needed one, to spend a weekend away with the boys.

Every year we went through the same complicated process leading up to the trip. Don shredded sheets of notebook paper, scribbling an "A" or a "B" on each piece and marking one "A" and one "B" with a star. Whoever picked those were team captains. He then folded the sheets into what looked like little spitballs. With the help of a plastic Solo cup, the teams were made. The two captains then met privately and set the first-day matchups (kind of like the Ryder Cup except that none of the participants could actually hit a straight ball more than once or twice a round). Then the two captains let everyone know who would be playing who and the inevitable taunting began. It might sound stupid, and it was. Stupidity, of course, was a recurring theme in our relationship, so we reveled in every minute of it.

For several months leading up to this particular year's trip, Tom had made more than a few passing references at our card games to his frustration with Lianne's lack of interest in sex. Tom's girls were well into their teens by then, and although I had seen for myself the difficulties in his family's dynamics, his persistent grumbling over the last few months had gradually escalated to the point where everyone else was well aware that he and Lianne were having problems. While the rest of us did our best to avoid discussing anything of real importance when the cards were on the table, Tom frequently peppered us with the multitude of daily conflicts that he was experiencing with his wife. She spends too much money, she doesn't treat the kids the same, she isn't respectful of his working in a grocery store. It went on and on. The only topic that was of interest to any of us was the sex thing.

"So, what are you saying?" Mark asked. "How long do you go?" His attention was piqued as Don dealt a hand of five-card stud. One card down, the next three up, last card down.

"I don't know," Tom said. "A long time. I got tired of begging, so pretty much it's just Father's Day and birthdays—mine, not hers."

Mark and I looked at each other. "Jesus," he said, evidently thinking the same thing I was. "More than a week and I start to pull the hairs out of my arms. That's nuts."

Don had a pair of kings up and was getting impatient. "Your bet, Bro. Dollar to you, one raise left." I looked at Don's kings, compared them to my mixed-up mess, and folded.

"Pussy. Won't stay for a buck?" Don asked. Now I knew he had a good hand.

The bet moved to Mark. "I'll see the buck, raise another buck. Now who's the pussy?" The guy with the bigger bankroll was taunting Don. Over a dollar.

Don called and tossed in his buck. Baldwin folded, leaving just Don and Mark to fight over the twelve-dollar pot. Don dealt the two of them their last card each.

I turned back to Tom. Having learned a thing or two from my wife's work in the mental health field, I made a faint and transparent effort at a different approach. "How about marriage therapy or one of those couples' weekend things?"

"She won't go," Tom said. "Says it doesn't matter."

MKat had another idea. "What about that 'horny cream' some women use on their pussies? I hear it makes them want sex like a seventeen-year-old boy."

"Nah. She won't get that either. She's just not interested. We live like roommates, but shit, what am I supposed to do? She's my wife. We have two kids. I made those vows. So, fuck it. It's okay." Tom paused and took a drink of his warm beer. "I guess."

Mark bet another buck. Suddenly, Don was a bit unsure. Not wanting to fold, knowing that there were two raises left, Don raised the bet only a quarter.

"Two and a quarter." Mark didn't hesitate.

"Fuck." Don looked over at Mark, who was raising his eyebrows over and over again, grinning away.

Don gave up. "Shit, I fold." He tossed in two pair, kings and nines. "What'd you have?"

Mark scooped the singles and quarters his way, whistling all the while. "Pair of threes." He stood up, shook his ass a bit, and did a little celebratory dance around his chair.

As for Tom, no one made any meaningful suggestions or expressed sincere concern. It wasn't that we were not interested or worried, but as usual, it was just a lot easier to make fun of Tom's situation than to actually try to help.

"Wouldn't work for me. No fucking way," Mark said.

"Me neither," I had to agree.

"*Nyet*," confirmed Baldwin. The one word he knew how to say in Russian.

"No fucking chance," MKat said.

"Are you nuts?" asked Wocky.

I did it again. Given the chance to keep a rein on the humor and talk seriously, I ignored any helpful impulse. Every day I go into the office and listen to similar tales of sadness from an endless line of strangers. I provide them with support and tell them that things will get better. I offer strategies for dealing with an angry spouse or confused children and hope that some of what I say and do will ultimately land them in a happier and more peaceful place. But with Tom, I sat quietly and nursed my beer, choosing to remain silent and receding within the shuttered laughter of the card game. Most people regret opening their mouths. Me? I regret all the times I didn't.

"Your deal," Baldwin said, sliding the deck to Tom.

# FORTY-THREE
## 2008

Having outgrown the boardinghouse, we were now spending our AC trips in whichever of the casinos would have us for the cheapest. We bounced up and down the Boardwalk, from the Tropicana to Donald Trump's Taj Mahal. All of us had a little extra money in our pockets and a couple of the guys had done really well over the last few years. Mark and Tom sat at the higher-stakes tables that the rest of us couldn't afford, and although we may have felt a bit put off, in return they were able to get us all free rooms.

We still went to Tony's at least once over the weekends, but it was around this time that we started a regular trip to a one-of-a-kind old-time Atlantic City restaurant, Chef Vola's. There are maybe fifty seats in the entire restaurant, which is planted in the basement of a vintage vacation house on South Albion Place, about a block from the ocean. They don't advertise, but I've never once been there when every table wasn't filled. Everyone has to have a reservation, which sounds a lot easier than it is because the place doesn't have a listed phone number. The only way to get a seat at Vola's is to call ahead, usually months in advance, and leave the information on the answering machine. Let them know who you are or, if you are a first-timer, who sent you, along with the day and time you want to have dinner. If they can get you in, you get a call back. If not, you won't hear from them.

As we polished off a few plates of Vola's homemade banana cream pie and warm ricotta cheesecake, the usual "what next" debate ensued. Mark and MKat wanted to do some gambling back at the Borgata. A few financial stresses had me limiting my time at the tables. I preferred to spend my money on a sure thing, like tequila. A few other guys wanted to walk to the Playground, a particularly dumpy shithole of a strip club, and hand a few bucks over to girls who no doubt would fall in love with each of us the minute we walked into the place. And by "love," trust me, I'm not referring to the kind of "everlasting love" that Carl Carlton sang about in the '70s. More like the love that costs twenty dollars for five minutes of a well-shaved leg grinding just under your belt.

Like me, Tom was not one for strip clubs. We didn't have some high horse moral objection to them; it's just that, as Clint Eastwood said in one of his movies, "a man's got to know his limitations." With a shared weakness for naked women that made it much too easy for either of us to start doling out the cash whenever some little pretty flittered her eyes our way, Tom and I both did our best to stay out of the joints.

So, it came as a surprise, to say the least, when Tom said he was all in for the run up to the Playground. After all, in the last quasi-sexual episode he had with someone other than Lianne he'd become "Dead Dick."

"You sure?" I asked him.

We walked a couple of blocks and I wanted to be positive that Tom was coherent, especially after sharing a particularly tasty bottle of Gran Centenario Añejo tequila with Don and me during our Chef Vola's dinner.

"Yeah, Bro," he said. "I'm fine. Only time I see Lianne naked these days is when she gets out of the shower. And I don't think I have had my dick touched in like two hundred years. Other than by me, anyway. Let's go, look around, maybe grab a lapper or two."

Although we were all big talkers, no one, to my knowledge, ever actually strayed and broke the fidelity line. A lap dance with a breathy and perfumed twentysomething stripper was about as far as any of us would go, and that was just fine.

One of the things you rarely see in a strip club, though, at least in the ones that I have been in, are women who are not actually stripping. Once in a while, a couple guys walk in with their dates that, for some reason (assuming they're heterosexual), want to get a sense of what it's like to leer at a young girl riding a steel pole.

With that in mind, I found it a little odd when we noticed a group of about six women sitting at a table, drinking, and taking turns handing dollar bills to a couple of girls in G-strings. But the idea of watching girls watch girls was pretty compelling stuff to all of us slightly graying guys, especially Tom.

We all grabbed a table with a clear view of the women and ordered a round of Budweisers that cost about twelve bucks a bottle. Within moments, the usual attempts at misdemeanor larceny began. Girl after girl came to our table, got down on their knees like a major league catcher, heads at perfect crotch height, and started what was undoubtedly an honest attempt at interesting conversation. They all had very pretty names like Candy, Jasmine, and Magic.

"Hey, baby," Candy breathed. "What's your name?"

"Vinnie," I said. I always used one of the other boys' names in strip clubs.

"Where're you from, Vinnie?" Candy put her hand on the inside of my thigh.

"Southern California," I said. "LA." Sounded good, and I always wanted to live in California.

"You're cute," Candy said. The hand moved up my thigh. "Want a private dance?"

Bad, bad, bad idea. It was time to nip this friendship in the bud.

"Thanks, Candy," I said. "But I think I'm a little sick. My stomach is killing me." I groaned a bit. "Maybe talk to one of the other guys."

Candy swiftly moved her hand of my leg and whisked away without as much as a smile or a "nice to meet you." She left that unmistakable stripper smell on my jeans, a combination of off-price drugstore perfume, sweat, and cherry-flavored jellybeans.

After Candy took off, I noticed Tom was across the way talking to one of the women at the table. He waved, plainly asking me to come over. Not willing to go it alone, I grabbed Vinnie and we headed toward the group of girls.

"Hey, what's going on?" I reached out and, I'm not sure why, awkwardly shook Tom's hand.

Tom looked a little confused at the gesture. "Okay. Sure," he said. "Bro, Vin, this is Jane. She's on a bachelorette weekend with her friends." Jane was all legs and they were stretched out in front of her, crossed at the ankles. She wore strappy leather pumps that allowed a peek at the pink polished toes poking through just so. At first, I couldn't see much of her face through the Jennifer Aniston-style hairdo splashing down onto her shoulders. When she looked up and extended a hand to say hello, I immediately noticed her eyes, which, while maybe a bit too big for her long and narrow face, were almost bright black, if there is such a color. I couldn't look away.

As soon as I was able to snap out of my little trance, I saw that Jane was drinking a heavily iced cocktail out of a plastic penis-shaped straw. There are those times in life when I'm sure every male wishes he didn't have an uncontrollable appendage strapped between his legs. This was just such a time for me. I immediately got hard staring at Jane, and I couldn't help but wish she was drinking from my straw, which was certainly a lot bigger than the one that she had pinched between her lips.

"I think we're going to head out. You coming?" Vinnie asked me. With the rest of the guys already out the door and waiting for us out front, he was ready to roll.

Tom got up. As he did so, I noticed that Jane was holding his hand. He nodded at us and leaned in, something clearly on his mind. "I think I'm going to hang out with her a little," he said. "Can you guys stay around?"

"You're kidding, right?" Vinnie said. He was not interested.

Neither was I, but at the same time, I was impressed. I was also a little bit proud and maybe just a tinge jealous that my friend had been able to excite some interest from an attractive girl, especially one who appeared to be looking for one last fling before she tied the knot.

Tom dug deep. "I'll buy," he offered.

We sat down at the table.

During the next hour, things got a little nutty. Here was Tom, a married guy who I don't believe ever cheated on the only girl he'd ever had intercourse with, making out with a woman he just met. In a strip club. It was too much for us. Every time I glanced over at Vinnie, we just shook our heads or cracked up.

After a while, Tom told us that he wanted to head back to the hotel with Jane. I decided not to say anything. Whatever Tom wanted to do with this girl, that was his business, not ours. Vinnie agreed, and the four of us grabbed a cab back to the Borgata.

Since Wocky couldn't make the trip this time, we were left with an odd number so the three of us were sharing a room. By the time we got to the hotel, it was about 2:00 a.m., and with a tee time just a few hours away, I was ready to hit the sack. Not wanting to crimp our newfound playboy's style, however, we cut Tom some slack and told him that we would be up to the room at 3:30.

Tom wasn't concerned about the time limit. "No problem," he said. "We'll be done by then."

As we turned toward the casino and away from Tom, who was already heading toward the elevators, Vinnie gave his assessment: "Done by then? He'll be done in four minutes."

As promised, we got back to the room at 3:30. All was dark. Tom was in the cot. One bed was pretty rumpled, the other made and untouched. I figured things out before Vinnie and immediately dropped onto the made bed.

"Tom, what the fuck?" Vinnie yelled. "Switch beds." He shook Tom's shoulders. "You fucked her and I have to sleep in your jiz?"

Tom rolled over. I wasn't sure if it was the light, but it looked like he had something on his face.

"I didn't fuck her," Tom said. "I just went down on her."

"Are you seriously nuts?" Vinnie said. "You went down on a girl you met in a strip club a couple of hours ago? And you didn't even get anything back?"

I looked a little closer. What was that on his face?

Tom sat up. "I got a weird taste in my mouth. Tastes like iron." Now I knew. The proof was on Tom's lips and around his mouth like a four-year-old with an ice cream cone. Only Tom, a guy who had slept with one woman his entire life, could lick away at a woman's vagina without having even the slightest idea he was lapping up menstrual blood in the process.

I was speechless, not to mention grossed out, looking at my friend naked in the dim sandy light of a bedside hotel lamp.

"Oh, Jesus," Vinnie said, falling back onto the bed.

Not sure of what the fuss was about, Tom got up and stepped over to the dresser. He stared into the mirror, then back at the two of us. A still slightly drunk smile spread across his face. "Hey!" he exclaimed. "I could have had a V8!"

# FORTY-FOUR

There wasn't any music playing at the cemetery. The rabbi, standing next to Tom's grave, said a few prayers. I think they were prayers. I didn't really listen and, if I had, I wouldn't have understood them.

After the short graveside service, the rabbi said his goodbyes while many of us waited in line to dump a little dirt on top of Tom. He'd been lowered into the ground by some weird and creaky mechanized contraption, and I again started to drift, probably from some sort of subconscious avoidance response. I wondered about the guy who invented the casket-lowering machine. Whoever he was, it was brilliant. No more ropes and people bending over breaking their backs helping to drop a wooden box into a six-foot hole.

The whole business of helping to bury a dead person was another of those odd traditions that I, of little faith and even less knowledge, never really understood. In the Jewish religion, helping the body of the deceased to be honorably and properly buried is supposed to be a kindness. Burial, for Jews, is a both a commandment and another "gift" to the guy in the box. I rubbed my forehead and sighed, laughing a little to myself thinking of Tom looking up and thanking all of us for dropping a shovel of dirt on his noggin.

*"Hey, thanks for that but, uh, Bro, you missed a spot."*

*"Cripes, that hurts! No more rocks, huh?"*

By the time it was my turn, most everyone had already given Tom the gift of dirt and were on their way back out of the cemetery. Lianne and the girls were still there, looking down at the mostly filled hole in the ground. Laurie, Pam, and the other wives were also segregated and gathered closely together just a few feet away.

All of us seemed there, just there. None of us was talking. We weren't doing much of anything, just standing and looking off somewhere. I had the shovel in my hand, a little water running down my cheek. Sweat maybe. Or not.

I looked around and caught Don's eye first. "Go ahead, Bro," he said. "Say whatever it is you want. It's just us."

I sighed and gave it my best shot.

"If it's okay, I just want to take a minute and say a couple things, mostly about Tom. Also to him, I guess. Not only Tom, though. Really I kind of feel like it's just as much to all you guys. I'm just sorry it took one of us to die for me to say a few things that have needed to be said for a long time."

I stuck the shovel back in the ground, plunked myself down onto the grass, and leaned back, inadvertently hanging my feet over Tom's head.

MKat made a weird face and lowered his sunglasses. "Uh, Bro. Easy now. Say what you want, but how about you slide back a bit? Unless you're planning on getting in there with him."

"Huh?" I turned my head toward MKat, not quite getting it, then looked down into the hole. "Shit. Sorry."

"It's all right, Uncle Bro," Jess said. She sat down and hung her feet next to mine. "He wouldn't care." That smile again. Tom's smile.

"Here's the thing," I continued. "I sat through that service and, to be honest, couldn't wait to get the hell out of there. Not because I was trying to be disrespectful. It's just that I couldn't believe the guy is dead. Still can't. The whole thing is just beyond comprehension. I mean, just last month at Baldwin's house, Tom was high-fiving everyone after raking in what—thirty bucks in a hand of showdown? First time he ever won, I know, but really?"

"Thirty-five, actually," Baldwin put in. We could always trust him to keep an accurate count of who won or lost and how much.

"Whatever," I said. "Christ, Baldwin. Who cares?"

"I don't know, I thought it might be important to your story." He rubbed his chin.

A tick behind as usual, it took me a quick second to grasp the sarcasm. A couple of the guys laughed.

"Let the man talk," Don said. At least he understood the seriousness of the moment. "But hurry it up, would you, Bro? I'm hungry."

"All right. All right. I'll be quick." I took a breath and wiped my forehead with my now-wilted and wrinkled shirtsleeve.

"A lot of things can happen to a person to affect his life. We've all been married and we all have kids. Obviously, our families are always going to be what's most important to us. Our wives. Our children. We all know that and that probably doesn't make us any different from everybody else we know."

I was doing it again, just like when I was in the hospital with Jess—spouting that prepackaged crap that everyone probably says when a friend dies. He was a great father. He was a good husband. He loved his family. Christ. I was making myself sick. I took a breath and tried a different, more honest tack.

"I can't speak for you guys, but when I got the chance to come to that first card game at Tom's house when we were at Sherbrook, well, that night changed my life. And you guys have changed my life. Tom changed my life. Think of the laughs we have had over the years. The golf trips in the last twenty years. I've thought about this shit a lot over the last couple days. But, really, it's more than that. It's not the trips or whatever it is we do together. It's those moments we'll never forget. It doesn't matter where they happened, it's just that they did happen and every time I got to share them with you guys. I wouldn't give any of it up. Seriously. Not for anything. Not even for Mark's farm. Well, maybe for the farm."

MKat jumped in. "Not me. I'd dump all you fuckers in a second for that farm."

Ah, yes, we all loved the farmhouse that Mark had bought for his family a couple of years ago down in Virginia somewhere. I say somewhere because even with GPS in all of our cars, we still needed a trail of bread crumbs to find the place.

"Anyway, I guess what I'm trying to say is that while I know he's gone, that's not the only thing I've been thinking about. I mean, is this it? Are we done? How can things be the same without him? I know it sounds crazy, and really, I'm sorry..." I looked over at Jess and put my arm on her shoulder. "I know you guys lost your dad and I know it's selfish. I just wonder if his being gone means we've lost more than just him. As if that wasn't bad enough. But really, is that it? Are we... done?"

Finished with my stammering, I rubbed my eyes and flinched. As a guy who last cried when my old golden retriever died about ten years ago, I hoped it was just my contact lenses. I know my voice was a little shaky. I'd always preferred to keep this kind of emotional stuff pretty well buttoned up, and this whole situation was making me all different kinds of uncomfortable.

The rest of the guys just looked at me from across the other side of Tom's grave.

A moment of silence passed, then Baldwin clarified things for everyone. "Bro," he said. "You've got the game next month, right?"

They all looked over at me. A couple of smiles.

"Yeah, yeah. I got it."

I grabbed the shovel, scooped up some dirt, and tossed it in. Then I stuck the shovel in the ground. "Let's get the fuck out of here," I said.

Walking back to the car, I took a breath and looked up. A plane shimmered in the blue sky, reflecting a sharp light into my eye. I squinted a bit and remembered.

# FORTY-FIVE
## 2011

It was my first time on a private plane.

About ten years ago, Mark made a promise that if he did well after his company went public, he would take all of us on a trip for our fiftieth birthdays. Damned if he didn't do exactly what he said he would.

In the year leading up to that trip, we had a lot of discussions about where we should go. We tossed around Florida, Arizona, and Oregon, and even considered going to Ireland. If it was on a map, we talked about it, and after interrupting several hands over a few months of card games, it was settled. We'd spend our trip in two places—Northern California and Las Vegas. Northern California won because it was home to Pebble Beach, the most famous of all golf courses in the United States. And Las Vegas made the cut, because, well, it was Vegas.

One Saturday morning, a few weeks before the trip, a Federal

Express package was dropped onto each of our front doorsteps. Inside each were shirts, golf balls, and tees from Pebble Beach, along with a sharp-looking Zippo lighter. Everything had a logo, and our boy Mark had created them especially to commemorate the adventure.

I gave Tom a call as soon as I got my package.

"You get yours, yet?" I thought it was all very cool, but Tom didn't sound all that hyped.

"What am I going to do with a Zippo lighter?" he said. "I don't smoke. Lianne thinks I don't, anyway. And the shirt, Jesus, that big logo is going to drive me nuts. I won't be able to focus."

"Focus on what?"

"It's going to scratch me all the time. I won't be able to swing the club."

"You can't swing it anyway," I reminded him.

"I know. I'm just saying."

"Saying what? That you're pissed the guy is spending a small fortune flying us to Pebble and Vegas? That you are unhappy with the shirt he bought you? Really?"

"I'm just not going to wear it," Tom said.

"Okay with me. You want to skip the trip, too?"

"Come on. I didn't say that. I just don't like the shirt. Or the lighter."

I took the phone away from my ear and gave it a double take. I wanted to make sure I wasn't really dreaming and that this moronic conversation was really taking place. Sadly, I wasn't and it was. I couldn't listen anymore.

"Okay," I said. "Go burn your shirt. Use the lighter. I'll see you on the plane."

I was used to flying Southwest. Same drill every time. Book the flight months in advance when the lowest fares come out, then go on the airline's website the day before the trip and try to get a boarding pass marked "A" with a low number. Then you get in line with other "A" boarders, shoving and squeezing into numerical order. God forbid your pass is marked "A-21" and you accidentally find yourself in front of some guy who has "A-19." Hell hath no fury like the victim of a boarding line cutter.

The real wretches are those bottom feeders with "C" passes. These are the folks who didn't pay attention to the twenty-four-hour rule and checked in online whenever they felt like it. Their punishment is clear and unforgiving. They are destined to sit in the back of the plane, usually next to the bathroom and in a middle seat between some fat guy with a bag of Cheetos who should have been made to buy two seats and an old lady with a peanut allergy.

This was nothing like Southwest. Our limo dropped us off in front of a small terminal building and our bags and clubs were unloaded right from the limo, delivered to the small plane waiting about a hundred yards away. From the terminal, we walked directly onto the plane. No lines, no security, and we all kept our shoes on.

After standing outside the plane for what felt like no time at all, I was the last to step up. I really wanted to take in the moment, knowing that the next time I was at the airport, I would be back with the rest of the world, pushing and squeezing, hoping for an aisle seat.

Mark stuck his head around the entry door. "Hey, Bro," he said. "You coming? We got bagels."

"Yep. Be right there." I knew this might be a once-in-a-lifetime opportunity, so I stopped at the top of the stairs, turned around, and did the best Richard Nixon imitation I could muster, waving two peace signs and making a squished-up Nixon face. Of course, with everyone already in the plane, I figured no one would actually see it.

"Twenty bucks. Pay up," called Mark.

"How'd you know he would do it?" Tom asked.

"He's been talking about it since we knew about the plane. Those dopey multiple choice tests he gives us all the time. Guy's a fucking idiot with the history shit. Twenty bucks. Pay up," Mark repeated.

"Goddamn it," Tom said. "I knew that."

Mark squealed like a stuck pig. "Twenty bucks."

I ducked my head into the plane just as Tom was shelling out for another lost bet.

# FORTY-SIX
## 2011

At a card game a couple of years earlier, Tom, Mark, Baldwin, and I decided that we would learn to ride motorcycles. We'd buy bikes, get matching leather jackets with some monster design on the back, and ride together in a sort of mini-motorcycle gang like John Travolta and his buddies in *Wild Hogs*.

The fact that the rest of the fellows thought we had lost our collective minds did not deter us, and unlike some other boneheaded ideas that we frequently referred to as "drunken plans," we actually went through with this one. The four of us signed up for the motorcycle safety class, took it over a weekend at a local community college, and even went to the Motor Vehicle office together for our licenses. Before taking the class, neither Tom nor I had ever been on a motorcycle, but both Mark and Baldwin had some experience. Mark had done some riding in the Air Force, and Baldwin learned by borrowing a neighbor's bike for beer runs after school back in the '70s.

Mark had informed us that he was going to rent motorcycles for the trip. It was no surprise then when a truck pulled into the parking lot at Pebble Beach with four, sparkling Harleys ready for the Pacific Coast Highway. Knowing that the bikes were coming did nothing to dampen our anticipation. We were like kids in a candy store, or, more recently, like Tom in an Atlantic City strip club. Behind the trailer of motorcycles, two convertibles waited for the rest of the pussies who obviously lacked the guts to spend their cliché midlife crises in leather and boots on two wheels.

Once on the bike, it took every ounce of my self-control to keep my eyes on the road and off the amazing views along the way. We swung past the Lone Cypress, sitting on a stony ledge overlooking the Pacific Ocean, and zoomed past Fanshell Overlook where hundreds of seals grabbed some rays on the rocks.

Point Jack was our last stop on the way to Monterey. Tom, who shared my interest in mundane historical facts, walked with me to look at a sign near the parking lot. Point Jack is the rocky southwestern end of Spanish Bay, so named because the explorer Gaspar de Portolà landed there in 1769. It's been the site of several shipwrecks, but that sign had nothing to do with lost boats. It read:

*Who was Jack?*

*Jack was a Chinese man who lived alone*
*in a driftwood home near this point in*
*the early 1900s. He made a living*
*selling trinkets to tourists and tending*
*goats. No one knows for sure if the*
*point was named after Jack or if he was*
*named after the point.*

Except for the goats, Jack the Chinese Man seemed like a guy who would have fit in well with this bunch.

We hounded a few other tourists to take way too many pictures of us, and then we were ready to finish the ride up to Monterey and grab some breakfast. The guys in the cars got in and zipped off while the four of us hopped on the bikes and zipped up. Just as I was ready to pull out behind Baldwin and in front of the other two, I looked in my rearview mirror to see Mark waving me back. Evidently, Tom's bike wouldn't kick over and start. I didn't know what Mark paid to rent the things, but he didn't seem too upset.

"Don't worry about it, man. Leave it here and jump on with me. I'll call the company and they'll come pick it up. No big Cecil." (We all knew a guy in high school named Cecil Diehl, so whenever anyone meant "deal," we said "Cecil.")

Tom felt bad. "Seriously, Mark, I didn't do anything," he said. "Shit. I'm sorry. Plus, I really wanted to ride."

"Jesus," Mark said. "Don't worry about it. We'll stop on the way back and call the company. Leave it here."

Tom looked at Mark, who was still showing not one iota of concern. He hopped on the back of Mark's bike.

After breakfast on the patio of a little oceanside restaurant in Monterey, we all headed back toward Pebble to tend to Tom's broken-down bike. Everything looked just as we left it when we pulled back in. A few parked cars, several bicycles tied up, and lots of tourists roaming around. The waves were still beating like a hurricane on the rocks below. One thing was missing, though—Tom's bike.

"Hey, Mark, did you already call the company?" Tom asked. "They must have come to pick it up." He was relieved.

"No, I didn't call yet," Mark said. "Where's the bike?"

"What do you mean? I left it right there."

"Well, it's not there and unless some fucking guy came along and hot-wired the thing, it can't be too far. Throw me the keys."

Mark's demeanor had noticeably changed, not without reason.

Tom made a weird smile. It reminded me of a little kid who was learning to toilet train but forgot about it and had an accident in his pants.

"I don't have the keys," he said. "Just left them in the bike."

"Really? Are you kidding?" Mark was astounded.

By this time, the rest of us had things figured out, so we slowly backed away, pretending to gaze out into the ocean.

"You left the keys in the bike?" Getting more agitated by the moment, Mark was looking at Tom like, well, like he was a moron.

"Yep."

Not normally a man of few words, Tom's lips were pursed and he was staring at the pavement.

"Man," he said. "I am so sorry. But at least you got the insurance, right?" He looked at Mark, grasping for redemption.

We all looked back at Mark. "Didn't think I needed it," Mark said. Now he was the one who looked like he had a doody in his pants.

Mark used his cell and made a call to someone.

Assuming Mark had it handled, we all took off, shaking our heads. To be safe, Tom got on the back of my bike this time.

With the ride done, it was on to a more sophisticated and less dangerous activity. It was time to play a little golf at Pebble Beach.

Tom's ball was under a tree.

I was playing with Tom, Mark, and MKat. We had two caddies

carrying our clubs. At first, that embarrassed me a bit. But two and a half hours later, I came to really like the idea of a guy lugging my golf bag around while I moseyed along, enjoying the endless views that made up Pebble Beach.

We were on the twelfth hole, a par three with a green surrounded by trees. One of our caddies was a heavyset guy named Monk whose puckered and sunbaked, raisin-sized noggin did not match his city-block-like frame. Tucked under a faded, grass-stained hat with "Pebble Beach" scripted across the front, Monk reminded me of the old joke where the guy in the bar asks the naked genie for "a little head."

Monk was bent behind Tom, his giant paw on Tom's shoulder. He looked to be helping Tom with his second shot. They were yakking, something about which club Tom should hit. I stood in the fairway with MKat and Mark.

"What's he worried about?" MKat said. "Doesn't matter what club he uses. The guy's going to whack it right into the tree."

"Probably bounce back and crack him in the head," Mark added, lighting up his cigar.

"Come on, Tom," MKat called. "Hit the fucking ball already." Patience wasn't one of MKat's strong suits to begin with and his was wearing thin.

I exhaled with one of my standard-issue sighs.

The three of us walked a little closer.

Tom had his plan set. "I can't get it out of here," he said. "I'll just punch it into the fairway, then try to get on with my next shot."

Monk would have none of that. "Look here, Tom," he said and smiled, pausing no doubt for dramatic effect. "Buddy. You are at Pebble Beach, the greatest golf course on the planet. Let me ask you a question."

"Sure. What's the question?" Tom replied, seeming a little annoyed that the career caddie was talking him up while he was trying to figure a way to get out of a weekend hackers' jail.

"You here to play some golf or be a pussy?" Monk asked him.

"He's here to be a pussy," MKat answered from midway across the fairway.

"Same as he is everywhere else," Mark chimed in.

"Just hit the ball already," I said, ready to move on.

"Fuck you guys," Tom said, taking the challenge. "I'm here to play some golf. Hand me the wedge, Monk. I'll take it over right onto the fucking green."

"There you go, motherfucker," Monk said, handing Tom his wedge. "You the fucking man."

Clearly knowing what would come next, Monk shook his head, a pleased smirk on his face. While Tom was looking the other way, lining up his shot, Monk ducked behind a tree and stuck a half-smoked cigarette butt into his mouth.

Tom took his swing and actually made good contact with the ball. Unfortunately, the ball made even better contact with the tree and careened back at Tom, who had to lunge into a bush in order to avoid getting whacked in the head by his own ball.

"At least you tried, man," Monk said. "Good effort." He was having himself quite a good time.

"Told you," Mark exhaled, blowing a nice-looking cigar smoke ring across the fairway.

# FORTY-SEVEN
## 2011

I could have spent the whole week in California. I loved it there. Everything was so laid-back except for the lost motorcycle adding another ten grand to Mark's tab. But we all hung out together, ate together, and drank together. I knew it would be different in Vegas, the fellows splintering into alternate directions to wander about, shoot craps, and watch young girls flirt with guys about half our age. What I didn't know was that we'd be spending our Vegas nights perched atop the Palms Hotel. Crazy, over-the-top, and actually a little intimidating, the two-story, nine-thousand-square-foot Hugh Hefner Sky Villa was we where hung our hats.

Inside the Villa was a glass elevator, a full kitchen, and bar. The bathtub was big enough for all of us to all get in and play a few hands if we were so inclined. Flat-screen TVs lined half the walls. The rest of the walls were plastered with photos, both black-and-white and color, of decades' worth of Playmates.

Along the back edge of the suite were a glass wall, a Jacuzzi, and pool with a Playboy bunny painted on the bottom. The pool jutted out and extended over the hotel, providing a pretty terrific view of the Vegas strip.

One of the large bedrooms contained the requisite Hefner bed: round, rotating, and directly underneath a ceiling of mirrors. Since none of us had any plans to stray from our marriage vows, nobody wanted the Hefner bedroom. We had to make a decision in our usual way: Baldwin pulled out a deck of cards and each one of us picked one. I drew a three of diamonds—good enough, unfortunately, to drop me in the round bed under the mirrors for two nights. A cool and sexy spot for a couple exploring each other for the weekend, but a lot less desirable for a fifty-year-old guy all alone in his Dick Tracy boxer shorts just trying to get some sleep.

The first night in Vegas we ate together at a paint-by-the-numbers kind of restaurant in one of the hotels on the strip. After dinner, everyone went back to the Palms to gamble, drink, and, as predicted, ogle younger women. Knowing we would split up, we agreed to meet outside the entrance of the Ghostbar, which is located on the rooftop of the second tower at the Palms.

Having read about it online, I already knew that the Ghostbar wasn't going to be my kind of joint. I was never into the disco club scene, unlike Vinnie and MKat, who always enjoyed it. Even when we were younger, I dreaded the nights those guys would drag me into DC for hours of loud, throbbing techno-pop music at the Pier or to the Chez Paris in AC. I'm not much of a dancer, so I've always preferred to find a spot at a long oak bar and sip something dark from a short glass with ice, enjoying rock and roll with my drink.

At those clubs, though, it was always the same. MKat and Vinnie would spend the night dancing, drinking, and meeting gobs of girls while I sat fading into the background of an out-of-the-way bar section somewhere, trying to look interested.

I had an idea what to expect, then, when we all met up at Ghostbar around 12:30 that night. Continuing the weekend's over-the-top generosity, Mark had sprung for a private table overlooking the dance floor. When we got there, he ordered a couple bottles of liquor, including one of my favorite tequilas, Dos Lunas. After a few toasts that no one could hear, most everyone took off to fan the bar and take in the views from the patio outside. Tom and I stayed behind to hold down the table. The pounding music, blaring lights, half-crazed dancers, and overall sensory overload reminded me of all the reasons why I typically tried to avoid places like this. But I did have a best buddy sharing what was "better than mother's milk" tequila, so really, things weren't so bad.

Tom was unusually quiet. We drank our tequila and looked around.

After a little time and several glasses of Dos Lunas, both Tom and I noticed a few young women on the dance floor together. Tom and I shared the lesbian fantasies of most men, so we both got a bit more animated. He pulled his chair closer to the table and leaned in just as Vinnie flopped back down next to us.

"Jesus," Tom said, "look at them. Did girls look like that when we were in college?"

Vinnie laughed. "You mean at some point during the decade you spent in college?"

Tom didn't notice. His eyes were affixed to a particularly sparkly redheaded twentysomething in a mighty short sequined skirt.

"Very sparkly. She's very sparkly," Vinnie said, impersonating Dustin Hoffman in *Rain Man*.

I had to look. Pretty girls were dancing together. Not much more was necessary to keep my interest.

Vinnie then went into some sort of trance, humming "mmm" over and over again.

After a few minutes, I was making myself uncomfortable with all the staring. I could only imagine what those girls would think if they noticed the three members of the "over-the-hill gang" gawking from across the room.

Tom and Vinnie were still glued, sipping cocktails and nodding their heads in an odd attempt to meet the beat to the music.

"Come on, fellas," I finally said. "This is embarrassing. Any chance you two can be a little discreet?"

Vinnie looked at me. His English was broken. "Huh? Oh. Yeah. You're right, Bro. But, Jesus, look at them."

Vinnie turned away and pulled his chair back in toward the table. He noticed that Tom hadn't moved.

"Tom, man, Bro's right. Let's have a drink. Those girls could be your daughters, for Chrissakes." We both laughed, knowing that Vin didn't care much how old they were as long as they had breasts.

But the statement seemed to get Tom's attention. He turned toward us immediately. He actually stared at us for a moment. I nuzzled my tequila and watched him. I could tell he was thinking of someone else. He looked at his watch, then back up at us.

"Got to take a walk," he said. He shoved his chair in, kicking the leg a bit as he did so, and then took off and left without turning back.

Tom stomped off, looking equal parts stern and exasperated as we watched him cut a wide path around the dance floor. I scanned the room for another couple of minutes, wondering how in a few minutes things could get so fucked up. But, of course, I knew. In cards, you can fold and leave your money on the table. In life, you have to play whatever shitty hand you get dealt.

The week before we had all gotten on Mark's jazzed-up private plane, I had once again drawn one of my least favorite judges in the entire Montgomery County courthouse. Most judges I know have the same temperament as when they were in the trenches practicing law. Good, bad, or anything in between, you got what you got whether the guy was calling you about his client or if he was sitting on the bench making a ruling in your case. A funny thing happens to some of those folks when they put on a robe. They get to sit higher than the rest of us, peering down at the nattering litigants below, having convinced themselves that their level of intellect has been raised along with the height of their chair. One such jurist, Charles McAuliffe, was a middling and mildly disheveled member of a dying branch of the bar, a "general practitioner." Charlie had an office in a shabby circa-1960s townhouse near the courthouse with a secretary who worked for him for a couple of decades. He dabbled in many areas of the law, from family to bankruptcy to criminal and personal injury, doing none of them particularly well but presumably just well enough to keep paying the bills, one of which included golf dues to a local country club where he became close friends with a friend of a friend kind of guy who knew the recently elected Maryland governor. When a local judge retired, that was enough to get Charlie on the list of possible replacements, and he ultimately got the appointment to the circuit court bench. Almost immediately, Charles—no longer Charlie—transformed into an imperious and, how should I say it, douchebag. If you spoke out of turn in his courtroom, you were admonished; if a male lawyer wore anything other than a white shirt with a dark suit and tie, Judge McAuliffe would call him to the bench and give him a stern reminder of what was appropriate protocol in "my courtroom," all the while leaning forward and wagging a long and curly index finger inches from the lawyer's face.

Judge McAuliffe hated family cases and did all he could to avoid them. He would have his clerk look at the next day's docket, and if a family case appeared on the list, the clerk would be sent scurrying about the courthouse, trying to find another judge to step in and take the case. If he was unsuccessful in dumping the case onto one of his brethren on the bench and you were the lawyer unfortunate enough to end up with Judge McAuliffe hearing your custody case, it was the same mind-numbing speech, over and over again. I heard it so many times, I could have given it myself, probably with better results.

"Good morning, Mr. and Mrs. ... uh," Judge McAuliffe said to begin my case a few weeks earlier, looking at a stack of file jackets piled in front of him and trying to figure out which poor family was entrusting their future with him on this particular morning.

"Sandberg. Good morning, Mr. and Mrs. Sandberg," he said, having received some guidance from the courtroom clerk.

After curtly acknowledging myself and the other lawyer, he asked the parties to stand. "Because I have something important to say and I want to be sure I have your attention."

"My name is Judge Charles McAuliffe. I was appointed to the circuit court bench by our great governor," he said. "The state of Maryland pays me one hundred and eighty-seven thousand dollars per year to hear cases just like yours each and every day."

I assumed that was a lot more than he made in his law practice, but I couldn't be sure.

"Over the next few days, my job will be to decide what is in the best interests of your two children. I did not bring them into the world—you did. But since you are unable to do right by your kids, although I don't like it, I will make that decision," he said, trying a little too hard to make eye contact with my client and his wife across the way at the other table.

"Before today, I did not even know your names."

*Probably forgot already*, I thought.

"Over the next three days, we will meet in this courtroom and begin taking testimony at nine o'clock in the morning. We will break for lunch from 12:30 to 1:30 and then I will hear more of your case until 4:30, at which time I will break for the day. Each of you will call witnesses, testify yourselves, and present whatever evidence your lawyers think is appropriate to support your case. At the end of the three days, the lawyers will make closing argument, not exceeding fifteen minutes, and I do mean fifteen minutes, each."

Although many other lawyers railed at having their soaring oratorical skills reined in to fifteen minutes, it was perfectly fine with me, knowing that Charlie's attention span was maybe half that long, at best.

The judge paused, for dramatic effect, no doubt.

"When the lawyers are done with their arguments, I will retire to my chambers for another fifteen minutes and then I will return to the bench and announce my decision. That decision will affect you and your children, your entire family, for the rest of your lives. And when I am done, I will say goodbye, go out, hit a bucket of golf balls, and never think of you people again."

He got up, clearly impressed with himself, and said, "I will now take a fifteen-minute recess."

Everything for this character was done in fifteen minutes. I was sure he fucked and ate in fifteen-minute increments as well.

Finishing the sermon, he said, "If you two want to try to control your own destiny and try to settle things, now would be the time. If not, I will be back in a few moments to do what the governor appointed me to do."

If these people had the capacity to control their own destinies, they would have done so a long time ago. The speech, although clearly well-rehearsed, was a worthless waste of time and effort, given by a guy who had no real desire to actually do the job that he was so up front about being paid to do. When Judge McAuliffe returned to the bench, we were all standing, and he was immediately aware that no progress toward settlement had been made. He sat down in a huff and looked over at me, palpably irritated.

"Opening statements," he said.

After waiting about five minutes longer than Judge McAuliffe, Vinnie and I simultaneously got up to go look for Tom. We were definitely worried, but neither of us said anything. We didn't have to. After so many years, we'd developed this instinctual understanding, a feeling whenever something was wrong for one of us. Nevertheless, knowing that something was wrong didn't get us to actually do anything about it unless ordering some more ice to chill our tequila qualifies as "trying to help."

I remembered a few years back when Tom showed up a little late for a game at Wocky's house. By that time, the rest of us were sitting around Wocky's kitchen table eating some Ledo pizza and belaboring some issue that no one would remember the next day. Tom didn't say or do anything in particular. He dropped the old money bag on the table, grabbed a plate, and sat down with the rest of us. I looked at Vinnie and a couple of the guys glanced up and around. It was there. A sense that something that was not right. By then, we all knew there was trouble at home. But no one wanted to dig deeper.

Baldwin broke the silence with a "let's play." That's exactly what we did. Same as always. We knew. We cared.

We said nothing. We played cards.

At close to three in the morning, we figured Tom wasn't going too far. We did a loop around the casino and headed back up to the suite. Through the front doors and at the pool in the back, we found him lying in a pool lounge chair looking out at the lights below. Don was in the chair next to him, wearing an old newsboy-style hat that looked stolen from an old uncle's attic. He looked up at us and didn't say anything, but he did wave his head, motioning for us to come over.

Vinnie and I sat down on the lounge chair opposite Don with Tom in between us. I tried to be sensitive and leaned over to slap him on the knee. "Okay," I said. "What's up? Why'd you leave?"

"You guys were right," he told us. "They could have been my daughter."

"Who?" Vinnie asked.

Vinnie must have had one tequila too many, so I filled in his blank. "He means the girls in the bar."

Vinnie nodded. "Okay. So? We all looked at them. So what? Still don't get why you left. It's not like that's the first time we were looking at girls way too young for us. I mean, I got a daughter, Bro's got four. What's the big issue?"

Tom stared ahead into the lights of Las Vegas. "Not Kasey or Jess. My other one. Thirty-three years ago this month."

"What are you talking about? What other one?" Vinnie asked.

I looked over at Don. He got it. I got it. I just didn't know what to say. I looked out over the pool and off at the lights of Vegas.

Don filled my discomfort gap. "Wow," he said. "It's hard to believe it's been that long. You still think about it?"

"Yeah. I do. It was a girl. I guess it just hit me right there. She would be thirty-two now."

Sex on the golf course. Lianne getting pregnant. Vinnie finally figured it out. "Jeez," he said. "Sorry. We didn't talk much about it. I kind of forgot."

Tom looked at him. "Much? Funny. We *never* talked about it."

"What were we supposed to say?" I said. "I know we all figured you took care of it. If you needed something, you would have asked. At least that's what I thought."

Tom's neck snapped slightly, but he didn't look at any of us. "You could have asked if I needed help," he said. "Shit, man, she was pregnant. You knew how her parents felt about her hanging out with me. And how about after? No one ever asked what happened. What we did. Nothing. Ever. Thirty-some fucking years and not a word from any of you guys."

He was right, of course. But I still didn't feel like it was all on us. At least, I wasn't ready to admit it. Instead of apologizing, like a friend, I argued, like a lawyer.

"Okay, " I said. "So what do you want from us now? We've been together hundreds of times since. You never mentioned it either. Now you want to make us all feel like assholes? Nice."

Tom shook his head but didn't say anything. Neither did Vinnie, who had moved over and was leaning back on his own lounge chair. Ever the diplomat, Don spoke up. "Okay," he said. "We're sorry. How about you tell us now?"

Tom let out a sudden noise, like a laugh. Maybe it was sarcastic, maybe not, but either way, he started talking.

"After we found out Lianne was pregnant, I really didn't know what to do. We couldn't tell her parents. I didn't talk to you guys about it. I don't really know why. And, Bro, you're right, I could have." There it was again, the same crooked half-smile he had when he was seventeen but now tinged with the sadness that time and regret can add to a person.

"I had to do something," he went on. "I asked Paul if he knew anyone or had any ideas. I know, bad move. I thought so too at the time but really didn't know where else to go or who else to ask. Lianne was hysterical. If you guys remember, she stayed out of school for like a week. She told her parents she had a stomach virus and just felt sick. Some virus, puke on schedule each morning. I guess with a teenaged girl, they just decided to leave her be and not push her too much. Anyway, Paul told me about this place near Wheaton, in Kensington, a clinic that would do the abortion. One Friday during lunch while her parents were at work, Paul and I picked Lianne up and took her to this clinic to get it done. Everything seemed fine. She was in and out in a couple of hours. We dropped her off back at the house and took off."

"Jeez," Vinnie interrupted. "Crazy how easy it is to get an abortion."

"Well, yeah," Tom said. "That part wasn't terrible. For me, anyway. Lianne seemed pretty okay with things and more relieved than anything else. It was what happened after that was worse." Tom stopped. "Hey, Bro, can you grab me a beer?"

I went in to the bar, pulled out a cold Rolling Rock long neck, and popped the twist off. I walked back onto the pool deck and handed it to Tom.

"So, what happened?"

Tom took a swig of the beer. "I got a call the next morning. It was Lianne's dad. He said they were at the hospital and I needed to get down there right away. He scared the piss out of me. Before I could even ask what was going on, he hung up. I woke Paul up and told him I needed a ride to Holy Cross Hospital. I have to give him credit. He popped up, didn't ask me much, and off we went. When we got to the hospital, I found Lianne's mom and dad in the lobby. They were definitely waiting for me. Her dad sort of grabbed my arm and pulled me aside. Paul stayed with us. Her dad told me that she had a lot of bleeding. They thought it was her period. Then Lianne told them about the abortion. The bleeding kept getting worse, and they called an ambulance. She apparently got some sort of perforation during the abortion. She lost a lot of blood, and by the time they got her to the hospital, the doctors told her parents that they had no choice but to operate. She wasn't going to be able to have kids."

"Oh, man. That's awful," Don said. "I'm so sorry, Tom." He sat up on his lounge chair, reached over, and put his arm on Tom's shoulder.

Vinnie and I were quiet.

"At first, I thought her dad was going to kill me, but I guess he only hated me."

Vinnie piped in, the first sound from him in some time. "That's why you adopted kids?"

"Yeah," Tom said. "Actually I was the one who wanted kids. Lianne was the one who didn't. But after Bro and Laurie adopted Whitney, I convinced her that we needed to have kids. That it would be good for us to have a family."

It was hard for me to believe that after they visited us that afternoon, Lianne changed her mind about wanting children. If anything, I remembered that she looked at the baby like she had three heads. I wondered what it was that Tom had to do exactly to "convince her" they should adopt a baby, much less two of them. Although, after tonight, it was clear that Tom, our Catholic boy, counted himself as a father of three.

Tom put his beer down, the story obviously finished.

We all sat back into our lounge chairs. I looked out onto the lights of Las Vegas. This was one time that our not saying anything was exactly the right thing. Tom needed us to sit and listen, which is exactly what we did. Somehow, I knew that was good enough.

I woke up the next morning and walked downstairs from the Hefner bed. Tom, Don, and Vinnie were still in their lounge chairs.

Across the pool, Mark, MKat, and Wocky were also asleep. Wocky was covered in towels, using them for blankets. Baldwin, ever the early riser, was in the pool. "What happened to you guys? We met these amazing girls. Let me tell you. You'll be sorry you missed it."

I looked over at Tom. He was still sound asleep under a beach towel monogrammed with the Playboy bunny.

No, Baldwin, I wasn't going to be sorry.

# FORTY-EIGHT

It was a sunny Friday morning in June.

I was walking back to my office from the courthouse after allowing yet another five or six hours of my life to tick by while doing all I could to save a client from a shit storm of epic proportions. More than a year earlier, the woman had left her husband and children to "find myself and make some sense of my life," as she put it. During that year, she made little to no effort to contact her kids. She sent a couple of texts and a maybe made a phone call here and there but not much else. The kids mostly learned of their mom's whereabouts by following her narcissistic travelogue on Facebook. The lady couldn't find a way to have a five-minute conversation with either of her children, but she sure knew how to post pictures on the Internet. There were pictures with men, pictures with women, pictures in bikinis, pictures in little black dresses. From New York to LA and all parts in between, she certainly had plenty of time and opportunity to find *something*.

For some reason, after spending a year away from her family searching for herself and trying to makes sense of things, she sincerely believed it to be in the best interests of her teenaged children that they leave their father to come live with her. She filed a custody case and went through two other lawyers during the course of the litigation. Her prior lawyers must have given her some advice that she didn't like since she hired and fired them both, one after the other, and somehow found her way to my doorstep.

It always gives me pause when a potential client has gone through more than a lawyer or two before coming my way. While there are certainly more than a fair share of dickheads in my line of work, most of them are decent, hardworking, and pretty honorable folks. So when this lady sat in my office with a mountain full of paperwork and a file stuffed into a couple of Nordstrom's shopping bags, I should have known better. I'd like to say that I sincerely thought I could right this ship, get her what she wanted, maybe even convert the woman into a well-meaning parent. But that's bullshit. The fact is that I have a family to support and a business to run. This lady had money and needed a good lawyer. I like to think I am a pretty good lawyer, and I'm in business to make money. I took hers and signed her up.

Unlike other areas of the law, a divorce lawyer needs to wear different hats, from litigator to therapist, sometimes even serving as a friend or a surrogate parent. It's kind of like a Rubik's Cube, different colored parts, all separate yet connected and interchangeable.

During my few months working with this woman, I listened, I advised, I argued, and I cajoled. As the trial approached, it was clear that things were not going to go well. The kids wanted to stay with their dad, the court-appointed best interests attorney thought they should stay with their dad, and the mental health professionals providing expert testimony were all lining up with dad. As a lawyer who prides himself on not losing, primarily because I have a relatively good sense of when to cut and settle, I tried to convince my lady to pivot, resolve the case, and get as much time with her kids as she could. In the weeks leading up to trial, however, she would have none of it. Ignoring the very clear writing on the wall, not to mention my almost five-hundred-dollar-an-hour advice, she instructed me to prepare for trial, so I did.

On the morning of trial, the judge called all of the lawyers into his chambers, discussed the case, and essentially told us how things were going to end up. He asked about the parties' respective positions and let us know that he had read through the file and reviewed all of the expert reports. He was respectful and polite. He also made it quite clear that my client was going to get her cute little ass handed to her. He suggested we take a few minutes before starting the trial in the hope that we could resolve things ourselves without having to spend a few days of court time simply delaying the inevitable.

Once advised of the judge's perspective, my client grudgingly allowed me to have some discussions with her husband's lawyers. Many trial attorneys like to have a second, usually younger lawyer sit with them at the trial table to assist or at least look like that is what they are doing. I have always preferred to try cases myself. For some reason, it makes me feel like the odds are stacked against me—two people over on the other side with books and piles of paper, passing notes about strategy and cross-examination, me by myself, looking like I am just trying to keep up. I think that judges get that feel on occasion, too, and looking like I am the underdog sometimes buys me a break.

I went back and forth with the two lawyers on the other side for several hours after meeting with the judge. Through lunch and into the late afternoon, we quibbled over times that the kids would be picked up and dropped off, how late they could watch TV at the other parent's house, what activities they could participate in, and who would pay for how much of each. About four o'clock or so we reached a deal and settled in a way that I was confident was more beneficial to my client than the judge's decision ever would have been.

We all walked into the courtroom where the judge put our agreement on the record. I shook hands with other lawyers and headed to the elevators, feeling pretty good.

Unfortunately, my lady didn't see our results exactly the way I did. As we left through the front doors of the courthouse, she made it clear that "we lost" and, like her other lawyers before me, I was a "blood-sucking moron." I stared as she walked away. I sighed and shook my head. A quick scan of my phone revealed a dozen or so emails from other clients. Pterrance@gmail.com hadn't received her alimony check that was due today, and it was already late in the afternoon. Mykidsnme@verizon.net had her tit in a ringer because her husband took their son for a haircut without telling her. Jbradford@comcast.net reminded me of my hourly rate and expected a call "immediately." Each and every one was agitated, miserable, angry, or some combination.

When had I signed up for this life of bullshit?

I slipped on my Ray-Bans for the walk across the parking lot back to my office.

# FORTY-NINE

**M**y phone rang again. I had to juggle the file I was carrying and grab the phone with my left hand. I looked at the display. It was Lianne's number, but since she never called me and her husband had an annoying habit of misplacing his phone, I assumed it was Tom.

"Hey, Tom," I answered. "What's up?"

There was some static on the other end.

"Tom?"

"Um. No. Sorry, Bro. It's me. Lianne. Tom is sick. I mean he's in trouble. I ... God, I don't know what I mean."

Lianne had always been prone to exaggeration, but this sounded sincere.

"Lianne," I said. "What's going on? What are you talking about?"

"Shit. I'm sorry. Tom. He fell or collapsed or something. I tried talking to him, but he wouldn't get up. I called the ambulance. He's at the hospital. They say he is bleeding internally. Some sort of aneurysm. Something like that. I just can't understand it. The doctors—well, it doesn't sound good. I'm so upset. The girls…" Her voice trailed off. She was silent.

"Lianne. You there?"

"Yes," she whispered, crying a bit.

"Okay, where are you? Where are the girls?"

"We're at Montgomery General. The girls? Shit. I don't know. I tried to call them both. I think Kasey's working. And Jess. Who the fuck knows where she is." This was more a statement rather than a question. "Bro, can you try to find them? And call the rest of the guys. Paul, too. It doesn't sound good."

It was the second time she mentioned that. "Don't worry, Lianne. I'll call Laurie. She'll track your kids down. I'll get a hold of everyone and be over as soon as I can." I swallowed. "Paul, too. I'll call him. Tom's going to be fine."

"No, he's not." She hung up.

# FIFTY

I got to the hospital and found Lianne and Jess talking to Baldwin's oldest brother, Jimmy, a vascular surgeon who was doing rounds in the hospital when Tom was admitted. Kasey was sitting in a chair a few feet away, characteristically silent and looking out the window.

Jimmy and I were friends, and I also had represented him in a thorny divorce a few years earlier. I walked over to the three of them. "How we doing?"

"Hi, Uncle Bro," Jess said. She had her arm around her mom's shoulder. Lianne was staring down at the tiled floor. It was immediately apparent that Jess was the one holding things together.

"Hey, JB," Jimmy said. "Lianne, you okay with my filling him in?" Lianne nodded, still looking down.

"Okay. Here's the deal. Tom passed out because he was hypotensive."

"Jimmy, do me a favor, keep it simple. In layman's terms, if you can." I felt that medical phobia thing starting to kick in. Too many details and I would pass out.

"Sure. What I mean is his blood pressure was very low, so he fainted. When he got to the hospital, I could palpate, I mean, I could feel a mass in his belly. It was kind of expanding and contracting. Pulsing. We sent him for a CT scan and that confirmed that he has what I thought. It's called an abdominal aortic aneurysm. Basically, it's leaking blood into his system and we need to operate before he bleeds to death."

Lianne had been right. It didn't sound good. I was getting light-headed and sat down.

Jess was the one asking the questions. "Dr. Baldwin, what is it you have to do to help my dad?"

Jimmy looked at her, pretty impressed with the kid I'm sure. "What we do," he said, "is go in, basically repair the tear with a graft, and sew it shut. We have to stop the bleeding. Now, I'll tell you both, one of the things we worry about is how the bleeding has affected his intestines. If it's bad, the intestines could shut down and, well, he could be in trouble. Hopefully, that's not the case, and he'll be just fine."

I felt sick. Lianne was crying softly.

"Mom," Jess said. "We need to tell him that they can do the surgery."

Lianne didn't move.

Jess looked at Jimmy. "Is there something we have to sign?"

"Yes. Lianne, I just need your signature here on this form and we will get him ready."

Jimmy handed Lianne a clipboard. She finally looked up, signed the paper, and handed it back to him without reading a word.

"Great. We'll get him prepped. You can sit with him while you wait. He's awake and knows what's going on." Jimmy tucked the clipboard under his arm and walked down the hall.

# FIFTY-ONE

It didn't go well.

After the procedure, Jimmy talked privately to Lianne and the girls, then worked his way out to the waiting room. By this time, the rest of the guys had made it over. We all sat around waiting to hear that everything was going to be fine.

Even in this place, at this time, we maintained our ability to get back in our own card game bubble. Baldwin was dealing blackjack to whoever wanted to play. MKat and Mark were playing some annoying dollar bill bluffing game called liar's poker where each one calls out a series of numbers from the front of the bill, either repeating the numbers accurately or bluffing. The other guy than has to call his series, which is higher than the other's call, or ask the other guy to show the bill. If the other guy is bluffing, he loses the dollar, if not, he gets yours.

"Three sevens," said MKat.

"Four fours," answered Mark.

"Four sevens," MKat said.

"Let's see 'em."

"Dick." Having been called on the bluff, MKat tossed the dollar bill at Mark.

"What's the deal with the rooms this year?" Vinnie asked. He skipped a card game here and there but did make sure not to miss any of our annual trips. It had been a year since our fiftieth birthday tour, and we'd be back to AC this year.

Wocky's ears perked up. "Borgata? I love that place."

"I like the Trop," Don said. "We've been there so many times." He was always the one for tradition.

"Trop's a dump," MKat put in, calling it accurately.

"Maybe that new place up at the end," Baldwin suggested. What's it called? Revel. Plus, it's on the boardwalk." He and I were the early risers in the bunch, and both of us liked to run on the boardwalk in the morning, getting a little exercise.

We saw Jimmy and the travel plans came to a halt.

I jumped up and walked right over, and I'm sure a few not-too-complimentary but accurate remarks were made about my stepping in front of Jimmy as though I was more important than the rest of the guys.

Before he could get too far into the waiting room, I was right there. "Everything good?"

"Hey, JB," he said. "No, not really. Let me tell all you guys at once so I don't have to do it again." He squeezed past me so the others could circle around. Jimmy wasn't friends with most of us, but because of his brother, he knew everyone in the group. The grief seeped through him. He took off the surgeon's cap and rubbed his forehead, blinking the water from his eyes. Then he spoke.

"When Tom had the aneurysm, what basically happened is what I was worried about. The blood supply to his intestines was cut off. Without blood for that length of time, his intestines, his insides, well, they basically died. There is nothing we could do."

I heard myself say the words, but it was like someone else was talking, not me, and I was watching the whole thing from my couch.

"You're telling me he's dead?" I couldn't fathom this.

Don put his hand on my shoulder.

I don't think anyone else moved.

"No, he's not dead. But he doesn't have long. We're giving him some medicine to make him comfortable. That's about it."

"Where are the girls?" I didn't know what else to say.

"They're all back with Tom. He's awake. Lianne and one of the daughters are in the hallway outside his room."

"Which kid?" I asked.

"Oh, sorry. The one that looks like him. Jess? She's in there with Tom. I don't know the other daughter's name. They're twins, right?"

The blur continued for me. I think it was Don who asked Jimmy if Tom knew what was going on.

"Yeah," Jimmy said. "He knows. I told Lianne that some folks don't want the patient to know that he's not going to make it. They just want us to make him comfortable and let him go. That way there's no fear, the patient just goes to sleep, and that's it."

Jimmy paused. "Actually," he said, "it was Jess who told me that her father would want to know. I asked Lianne about it, and she seemed to agree. So, Jess and I went in and I told him. She's been in there with him since then."

"Can we see him?" Baldwin asked his brother.

"Oh, yeah. Absolutely. Jess told me that he would want to see you guys."

Vinnie asked if Lianne was okay with all of us horning in.

"I told her that Jess thought he would want to see you guys," Jimmy told him. "She didn't say no. She didn't say anything, so I took that as a yes. Come on back."

# FIFTY-TWO

Lianne stopped me as we all filed past her to Tom's bed. "Did you call Paul?"

I thought for a second and couldn't remember. The whole afternoon was washing by like a late summer thunderstorm. "I think so," I said. "Yes. Let me look to be sure."

I pulled out my phone and looked through my outgoing calls. "Paul Porter" came up. "Yes," I remembered. "I did. Left him a message first. Told him to get down here. I called him before the other guys. He's not here. Shocking," I muttered.

"Lay off him, Bro," Lianne said. "You guys always shit all over him. He's a decent guy."

"That's fine," I told her, in no mood to argue. "But I tried to reach him. You call him. Do what you want. I need to see Tom." I walked past her and into Tom's room. It didn't surprise me at all that Lianne stayed put in her chair in the hallway while the rest of the guys filed past.

We were standing around Tom, who had a bunch of wires connected to him, a few lines sticking into his arm and God only knows where else. I tried to look away and beyond the bed.

Jess was sitting on the back of a chair next to her dad, with his royal blue Asbury Jukes' knit hat pulled down over her forehead. A sprig of bangs swept gently across her eyes. She had her iPhone playing with the speaker on. Southside's "All the Way Home." She was singing along, softly. Her head was bobbing back and forth to the music. She mouthed how it was late and *"if you don't feel like leavin' alone…"* as Southside went on to promise that he would walk her all the way home.

She gave me a "glad you guys are here" look. "The nurse told me I had to turn off the music."

"Yeah, they don't like electronics on in here," Baldwin explained.

"I told her to fuck off," Jess said.

Tom limply lifted his hand from under the sheet and turned his thumb up.

# FIFTY-THREE

Like me, no one really knew what to say. What does a group of fifty-year-old guys say to an old friend who has a few hours, maybe minutes, to live? Something retrospective, maybe. Possibly a few words about what a great guy Tom was, how he had a good life, raised terrific kids. Not exactly.

Along with the others, I sat there, just listening to Jess's music. With all of us squeezed in around our dying friend, it was quiet, yes, but, crazy as it sounds, there was nothing awkward. Nothing uncomfortable. Of all the emotions, the things to feel right then in that moment, I felt peace. With these people, friends I had known since high school, there was, I finally had figured out, no need to say or do anything. We never really did. We were that unmade bed from the night before. Not lavish or complicated or fancy. Just warm. Just there. Right.

Baldwin grabbed the other wood-framed chair, and Mark broke the silence. "Shot of the day?"

Mark was always big on everyone reenacting his best shot after a round of golf. A few of us had played last weekend, and Mark wanted to hear the highlights. "You first, Wocky."

"That tee shot on twelve. Thought I pulled it a little right, but it skipped past those trees and rolled right onto the green." Wocky's face was lit up, like he was watching his ball roll right onto the green from here in Tom's hospital room. "Lying one and putting for eagle, baby."

MKat filled in the rest of the story. "Yeah, that was great. He four putted and made a bogey."

"Such a dick," Wocky said. "He just asked for shot of the day. It doesn't matter that I made a five."

MKat wouldn't leave him alone. "It mattered when you paid me the ten bucks for losing the bet though, didn't it?"

Sensing another standoff, Mark jumped back in. "Baldwin?"

Baldwin was slumped in the chair but perked up a bit to relate his moment in the sun. "I made that long putt on fifteen. Sort of weaved down the green and to the right. If it hadn't gone in, it would have been twenty feet past."

Mark was clearly waiting for his turn. "Okay, okay. Remember that approach I had on eighteen?"

"No," Vinnie said. "Not really."

"Come on, man. I took all those extra clubs with me and walked under the trees right of the bunker. I called you over to give me a line, remember?"

Vinnie wasn't giving in. "Nope," he said. "Sorry. Don't remember a thing."

Unperturbed, Mark went into a lengthy overview of his walk down the fairway and the complicated club selection process. He spared us no detail of how he decided which was the best club to use to get through the trees and past the bunker, given the difficult lie in some dirt next to a tree root.

"I shortened my swing to one quarter, choked down on the club, and ..."

Now I was getting a little antsy. I put my hand on Tom's arm. "What the fuck, Mark?" I said, pulling back on my lips and shaking my head in a kind of disbelief. "The guy's about to die and he's listening to you drone on about your shot of the day. Those are the last words you want your buddy to hear? How your ball nicked the bottom of the tree and somehow miraculously made its way to the green like some sort of magic bullet?"

"Jesus, Bro," Don said. "How about some sensitivity?"

Tom coughed. In a dry-throated whisper, he said, "It's okay. Did he make it?"

"Make what?" I had forgotten all about Mark's story.

"Nah," Vinnie finished. "You know this guy can't putt for shit."

We all laughed. Jess laughed. Tom tried to laugh. He blinked hard and pointed at no one in particular, maybe at all of us, and wheezed two words that somehow captured our lives together. "You guys."

Then he died.

# FIFTY-FOUR

Jess turned off the music and left, the rest of us trailing behind her. She leaned over and spoke to her mom. Lianne looked up at her daughter, listened, and went into Tom's room. All of us just leaned against the wall, drawing dirty looks from some of the hospital staff that had to squeeze by. After a few minutes, Lianne came back out and sat down on the bench.

I sat down next to Lianne and put my hand on top of hers, simultaneously choking back tears for Tom and trying to mask my long-standing dislike for his widow. "Anything I can do to help?" I asked.

Before she could respond, Paul walked up to us. He wore a gray suit that hung off his shoulders just enough to tell that he was probably a size forty jacket wearing a size forty-four. His tie was a bit dislodged from his collar, one side of which was poking up into his chin.

"Where is he?"

I didn't say anything. I just gestured with my head toward Tom's room.

After about ten minutes, Paul came back out of the room, carrying his suit jacket. We were all still in the hallway, not saying much.

"Hey, Lianne," Paul said. "He just doesn't look too good. He's not talking or even moving. What's the prognosis?"

Dumbfounded, no doubt, Lianne looked at me, then up at Paul, but she didn't respond. I thought she had told Paul about his brother before he went into the room. I realized then that Lianne thought I'd told him.

"Un-fucking-believable," MKat said. "The prognosis is that he's dead."

# FIFTY-FIVE

I had never been a guy with big ups or downs. Not too many mood swings. When things were good, I coasted and enjoyed the ride, but stayed pragmatic and mindful that it would not last. When work was difficult or I was in one of those periodic downturns with Laurie that every relationship has, I tried to be patient and wait it out as best I could. "My Way," just like the old Sinatra song. But this? Shit. I was just so goddamned sad. How was I supposed to feel? What was I supposed to do? Did life really just go on even if Tom was gone? A guy whose life was braided with mine for almost as long as I could remember? In the first few days after he died, I thought more about me than about him. What I should say at his funeral, to his kids, to Lianne. What it was that *I* should do to make things better. Now that I had said what I said, did what I did, what's the difference? He's in a box, underground.

I finally got it. It didn't matter what I said at that funeral. It just didn't. It's not about me. Tom's dead. I was miserable. That's it.

Although I complain about my work without pause, I have learned two very important life lessons from listening to the queue of dreary and depressed folks who have made their way to my office over the years. First of all, it is highly unlikely that there is someone better out there. The overweight fellow who ignores his wife, falls asleep watching reruns of *Two and Half Men*, and heads off to the office in different colored oxfords is not particularly likely to find a leggy, high-society blonde waiting for him on the other side. "Ones don't marry tens," another divorce lawyer once told me a long time ago, and she was right.

The other common "miss" for married couples is that they don't spend enough time together. I'm not talking about trips to the pumpkin patch or going to their kids' soccer games. I mean just the two of them, getting dressed as if they were still dating, heading out for a beer, dinner, a movie, whatever. Relighting that spark that sent them together down the aisle in the first place.

I love my kids and have relished the times I have spent with all of them. As they have grown into young women, each in their own way, I still look back and miss all the family time that we had when we lived together, under the same roof. Still, one thing I have looked forward to since Laurie and I started having children is our Saturday "date night." Laurie takes a long bath and does the "big shave." If it's summertime, she will throw a slinky dress or tight T-shirt and jeans on over some heels and out we will go. Of course, I dress the same, regardless of the time of year or how old I am. I'm always in my wheelhouse in jeans, boots, T-shirt, and a distressed leather jacket from my ever-growing collection.

Although Laurie has tried over the years to get me to modify my pick of clothing, sometimes bringing home linen pants or, to my horror, loafers for me to try on, by now she just rolls with it, knowing I am who I am and I like what I like. Lucky for me, that seems to be fine.

The Saturday night after the funeral, Laurie and I were getting ready for our date night. The plan was to head out to a local restaurant that opened nearby a year or so ago and was owned by a nice couple in our neighborhood. We were going to just drop in, have a few cocktails and a little dinner, talk to whomever we might see, and come back home for some "sexy time" and the satisfied deep sleep that comes after.

On the way out, I had another thought. "You mind if we skip the bar tonight? I kind of want to take a ride around some of the old spots," I said.

"Sure," Laurie answered. "But if you're driving, can you make me a roadie in a to-go cup? One of us should be able to have a drink or two, anyway."

I mixed her a very dirty martini, dumped in a few extra olives and a lot of ice, and off we went.

"This is about Tom, right?" Laurie asked, perceptive as always.

"Yeah, I just felt like roaming around, showing some of the places to you," I said as if I had never taken her to any of those spots before.

"That's fine," she said as she clicked on the radio to the E Street station on Sirius. She always put up with my lifelong love of all things Bruce even though her musical tastes bent more toward Elton John and "easy listening."

Our first stop was Pop's—what used to be Pop's. The neighborhood having become much more ethnic over the years, Pop's was long gone, replaced by a brightly painted Latin café called Picante.

I stared at the sign as several people walked in.

"Want to go in?" Laurie asked.

Preferring to remember Pop's as Pop's and not its present iteration, I put the car back in drive.

We swung by where Big Boy used to be, a small office building now sitting in its place, and also to Sherbrook, which still looked remarkably the same more than three decades later.

"I ever show you Tom's old house?" I asked Laurie.

"Actually, I think that's the one stop on this tour I haven't seen," she said, rattling the half-melted ice cubes in her cup to make sure I knew it was time to wrap things up and grab a second round somewhere.

After a quick U-turn in front of Sherbrook, I found Lima Drive and made my way up the hill toward Tom's old house. The street was still dark. In all these years, I supposed that people must have preferred it that way or they would have had a streetlamp or two put in. Like our high school, the house was as I remembered it, prim walkway in front, the yard consummately landscaped and strangely idyllic, just like Tom's dad kept it all those years ago, like a TV show from the '50s. The beaming light from the church still engulfed the place yet somehow seemed softer, an incandescent big brother. Just like the night I first walked up to that screen door.

"Jesus, how did anyone ever sleep in that place?" Laurie asked.

"Good fucking question," I said. "One more stop. We have to get out of the car but it will be quick. Promise."

We drove back across New Hampshire Avenue and parked on a side street where we could see the front of the church. I took Laurie to the same spot Tom had sat, a guy whose parents by then were both dead, whose girlfriend had gotten pregnant the same night they both lost their virginity, a guy who didn't quit on me when I was feeling around for a rubber band on a frat room door knob. The same spot where we stared at the eternally youthful Bob the Big Boy hoisted up high, and I told her the story, probably for about the fifteenth time.

Before I could get out Tom's "that's what I'm talking about" I was crying again, now for the second time in less than a week.

Laurie put her arm around me and pulled my head into her shoulder. "Want to go home and fuck me?" she asked.

# FIFTY-SIX

The month after Tom died, it looked like we were going to skip the game. In the days before technology took over, that month's host actually called everyone a week before, both as a reminder and to find out if anyone was going to miss. Now it was a short email to the group, looking for a quick reply. No one ever expected a lengthy or witty answer.

Usually, within a few minutes after shooting out the email, there came eight or nine quick responses of "in." The only one who usually added anything to his reply was Baldwin, who was always interested in the meal being served, as if he had something else to do if the dinner didn't sound up to snuff. So when I got several "can't make it" responses mentioning work, kids' activities, and other seemingly benign conflicts, I knew something was up. I wasn't sure whether to email with a "what the fuck?" kind of response, call everyone and bitch, or just let it go and skip the game. Despite being particularly buried at work and trying my best to comprehend and manage the latest drama that went hand in hand with being the father of four girls, it was the card game that I couldn't stop thinking about.

I called Baldwin. The keeper of the rules, planner of the trips, our own "sergeant at arms," Baldwin would have spoken with most of the guys and would be able to give me some sense of how to handle it.

"Here's the thing, Bro," he said. "We all want come. Everyone wants to play. It's just no one's sure how it will go without Tom around. I'm in, but these other guys, I think they want to skip. Maybe just this month."

It didn't seem right to me. "We skip one month, it makes it easier to skip next month, too," I told him. "You know that's true."

Some silence passed, enough of a moment for me to wonder if he'd hung up. Then Baldwin spoke up. "Yeah. I know. I miss him but don't want to have to miss all you guys, too. I'll make the calls. We'll get everyone there. Vinnie, too."

The man knew how to get things done. Within a few hours, I got eight emails that all said the same thing: "IN."

# FIFTY-SEVEN

"**D**inner was great, Bro," Baldwin said happily. He leaned back in his chair, his arm stretched behind Wocky. "Delicious."

It hadn't actually been anything special. I had cooked some burgers and dogs and Laurie did what she always does when I host the game—she made everything else.

"So," Wocky said, "Are we leaving the chair there during the game, too?" His voice was curious. "Sorry, Bro, but it's creepy."

I thought maybe the fellows would like the idea. This was the first game since Tom died, and I thought it might be a cool way to keep him with us. After all, we weren't much for the sappy "Auld Lang Syne" sort of thing, so I thought this was a good way to remember him, kind of like holding his spot. We could pour the guy a drink. Maybe make a toast to the chair, as if Tom was there somehow. Sing a little of Springsteen's "Blood Brothers." I just thought we should do something in his honor, and the idea of the chair seemed like a good idea earlier in the day when I was setting everything up for the game. Now that seven of us were sitting around my table, Vinnie having showed up after all, and staring at the thing, it was obvious that the empty chair idea wasn't exactly winning everyone's hearts.

"I don't know, Bro," MKat said. "I agree with Wock. It's fucked up. Let's lose the chair."

It was one of the only times in four decades that I can remember MKat and Wocky being on the same page.

Mark, sitting next to the chair, put his arm over the back and shook his head. "If his ghost loses like he did, then fine with me, keep the chair."

I looked over at Laurie, who was at the sink, moving the dirty plates into the dishwasher. She turned over to me and nodded, with the "told you so" look I've seen many times before, reminding me how she'd mentioned a few hours ago that the chair was a bad idea.

"All right," I said. "I'll get it out of here."

I got up to get rid of the chair just when the doorbell rang. As usual, my two dogs barked and raced to the front door.

"I'll get it," Laurie said, always the one to answer the phone when someone called and get the door if the bell rang.

"JB, someone is here to see you."

"Really? Now? Just have him come in."

There was a pause before she responded. "No, you need to come. She doesn't want to come in. She has something for you."

I shook my head, a little annoyed. She?

Of course, no one else at the table noticed much. MKat was already dealing the second hand of the night while Baldwin was shuffling the extra deck for the next hand.

"Deal me out of this one," I said, walking through the kitchen toward the half-open door. I could hear Laurie talking as I pulled it toward me.

She looked pretty. The pink and green hair tones were gone, replaced by her dad's light brown color. She brushed the bangs back and half smiled, maybe a little nervously. I couldn't really tell.

"Hi, Uncle Bro."

"Hi, Jess."

# FIFTY-EIGHT

"I knew you guys had the game tonight," she said. "Third Monday, right? I called Auntie Laurie and she told me the game was here this month. I wanted to stop by and see you."

I wondered if any of our other kids knew when we all got together to play cards. Tom's kid still had a disarming way about her and an air of maturity that most twentysomethings can't grasp.

I wasn't sure what to say. "Sure is, Jess. What's up?"

She looked down at her shoes, some worn-through flip-flops. "I felt like I should stop by," she said. "I've been missing him, and I knew you guys would too."

"Want to come in? Say hey to everyone? They'll be happy to see you."

"No, but thanks. I'm supposed to meet my mom and sister for some dinner at the mall. We're going to do some shopping."

"Nice. Good for you." I didn't want to say it but I knew her dad would be happy to see the three of them together, with Jess no longer an outlier.

She looked away, breaking eye contact. "Yeah, I'm on some meds," she said. "I'm doing okay. I'm trying. We'll see."

I started in with an "it's going to be fine" platitude when she cut me off.

"Anyway, Uncle Bro, I thought you guys might need this." It was Tom's old green money bag, secured with rubber bands, the same way her dad brought it to every game for years.

I looked at the old money bag, then up at Jess. She handed it to me, the both of us looking at each other, knowing we felt connected somehow.

Jess reached across with her other hand and patted my shoulder. "You're good, Uncle Bro. Win some money." And she left.

# FIFTY-NINE

"You here to yak with some neighbor or play cards?" Baldwin said, irritated. The usual maelstrom of conversations volleyed back and forth across the table. Wocky was arguing with MKat. Mark and Vinnie talked business. Baldwin had his hand on Don's shoulder and was watching Laurie bend over, as he no doubt whispered to Don what kind of deviant sexual act he would like to subject her to.

"It was Jess," I said. The room went silent for a moment. "She brought over Tom's money bag. Figured we would be short on change."

Baldwin made a face. "Jesus, that thing is old as dirt."

MKat went a little further. "I'd stick my finger up Bryna's pussy before I stuck my hand into that thing."

"Stop talking about my mom!" Wocky said. "Why do you always have to do that shit?"

"Lighten up, Wock," MKat said. "It's not like I said that I wanted to fuck her in the asshole."

"Dick." Wocky slurped his beer, belched, and pursed his lips, blowing the burp smell into the side of MKat's face.

"That was so nice," Don cut in, clearly attempting to move things forward. "Why didn't you invite her in?"

"I did, but she wanted to roll," I told him. Then I unzipped the bag and reached in, but not before looking at MKat in a "here goes" kind of way. I pulled out a wad of crisp singles and a couple of rolls of quarters and dropped them next to a shuffled deck of cards. "Deal 'em up, Baldwin."

Before closing the bag, I noticed there was something else inside and yanked out a Ziploc. Inside were two photographs, both facing each other so only the white backside was showing.

While Baldwin dealt a hand of seven-card stud, I looked at the pictures. The first was with all of us in front of Tony's in Atlantic City, taken one night in the late '90s; Tom was in the middle, his left hand sweeping some hair across his forehead. As usual, he wasn't quite ready as the picture was snapped. Vinnie and I flanked him on either side, arms over his shoulders. Everyone else—MKat, Don, Mark, Baldwin, and Wock—were fanned out along Atlantic Avenue, tucked in tightly so we could all fit in the shot. From one side to the other, our smiles were so wide, they could have touched. We looked older, sure. We also looked like we usually did every time we were together. Happy.

The second shot was more recent, maybe from a few months ago during a game at Tom's house, shot on the sly, probably from a phone. Cards and some money on the table, along with whatever was left of dinner on a plate or two shoved to the side. Unlike the other picture, there was nothing particularly special or even memorable about this one.

Yet something about this one caught my eye, and, while I scanned it for a bit, Wocky and MKat were once again arguing. What about, I had no idea. But it didn't really matter. We were all where we should be on this, the third Monday of the month. I looked around, taking it all in.

I must have been lost for a couple of seconds, maybe more, when the bet came my way.

"Your bet, Bro, or you want us to get out the glue sticks and do some scrapbooking?" Still obviously impatient when he had a good hand, Baldwin was tapping his finger incessantly on the table in front of him, hoping I wouldn't notice the two queens staring across the table at me.

"Out," I said, and folded my cards. Before I tossed the picture back in the bag, I looked again.

There was one thing about this one that was different.

Tom wasn't in it.

David Bulitt was born and raised in Silver Spring, Maryland. A father of four and a divorce lawyer for more than twenty-five years, he lives in Olney, Maryland, with his wife, Julie, their youngest daughter, and two dogs. He still plays cards with his buddies every month.

To read more about David Bulitt, upcoming appearances and his next book, *Because I Had To*, visit www.davidbulitt.com.

He is available for select readings and discussions. To inquire about a possible appearance or contact him directly, send and email to db@davidbulitt.com.

CPSIA information can be obtained
at www.ICGtesting.com
Printed in the USA
FFOW04n0756110515
13280FF